Should an Eagle Fall

SHOULD AN EAGLE FALL

KEN HODGSON

FIVE STAR
A part of Gale, Cengage Learning

Detroit • New York • San Francisco • New Haven, Conn • Waterville, Maine • London

All Scripture quotations are taken from the King James Version of the Bible.
Five Star Publishing, a part of Gale, Cengage Learning.

Set in 11 pt. Plantin.

LIBRARY OF CONGRESS CATALOGING-IN-PUBLICATION DATA

Hodgson, Ken.
Should an eagle fall / Ken Hodgson. — 1st ed.
p. cm.
ISBN-13: 978-1-59414-865-1 (alk. paper)
ISBN-10: 1-59414-865-1 (alk. paper)
1. Ranchers—Fiction. 2. Texas—Fiction. I. Title.
PS3558.O34346S56 2010
813′.54—dc22 2010003989

First Edition. First Printing: May 2010.
Published in 2010 in conjunction with Tekno Books and Ed Gorman.

Printed in the United States of America
1 2 3 4 5 6 7 14 13 12 11 10

Among the natural rights of the colonists are these: First a right to life, secondly to liberty, thirdly to property; together with the right to defend them in the best manner they can.

Samuel Adams

Who made thee a prince and a judge over us?

Exodus. II. 14

Prelude

The sharp eyes of a natural killer scoured the rolling and rugged west Texas landscape. It glided easily, kept aloft by rising currents of warm air. Nothing could move among the mesquite- and cactus-covered country below and escape its keen gaze.

Most of the creatures it had encountered were far too large to be successfully attacked. Several small, spotted ground squirrels had attracted its attention, but the agile little rodents quickly dove into their underground burrows to safety. Swift cottontail rabbits managed to dash into a thick shield of thorny bushes before the hunter's rapier-like talons could sink into their flesh.

As the day drew long, the raptor became ravenous. It also grew confused. In all its memory, nothing like this had ever occurred. Food had always been provided.

No longer. For some unknown reason it had been cast out into a strange world to fend for itself.

Driven now by instincts that had developed in its species over millennia and been passed on by braided strands of DNA, it knew that killing meant survival. Killing was a natural thing. Anger, greed or malevolence held no part. When it found prey and struck, it would eat.

And eat it must, or die.

With eyes sharpened by gnawing hunger, the huge raptor sailed on, probing every movement below with a building urgency. Silent as a passing cloud.

★ ★ ★ ★ ★

Part I

★ ★ ★ ★ ★

Chapter 1

"Useless, you're the most no account, lazy tomcat in the State of Texas," Caleb Starr fumed as he watched a pair of field mice scurry for cover when he hoisted the heavy mineral block. "At least I named you right."

The gray, fat tabby sat on its haunches licking a paw and ignoring both Caleb and the mice that quickly found refuge underneath the mountain of brown feed sacks stacked high in the barn.

"Ain't you even gonna *try* to catch one, or did you decide to become a vegetarian?"

Caleb shook his head and tossed the weighty burden onto the tailgate of his pickup with a grunt. Sharp, searing pain shot from his lower back across his hips as if he'd been branded. There were twelve fifty-pound blocks in the bed of the truck, and this was the twelfth time in the past several minutes he had endured the all too familiar agony.

He sucked his lungs full of the stale, hot barn air, arched his back and exhaled slowly. The pain subsided into a manageable crick.

"Do not be too angry with *el gato, señor,*" Jesus Santiago said with the calm, even voice of an old man. "There are more *ratóns* and *ratas* here to dine on the free food you so generously provide than many *gatos* could possibly catch."

Caleb turned toward the wrinkled Mexican who sat in a cane-backed rocking chair inside the open doors just out of the burning sun. No one knew exactly how old Jesus was, not even the old patriarch himself. Jesus remembered when Hoover was president and the Great Depression had ravaged the land. His parents had died when he was very young. He believed he was around eight when he had followed his cousin Raul in fording the Rio Grande to seek work in the United States. His skills were limited to shepherding, an occupation that paid little; however those who hired him had asked no questions. Over forty years earlier he and his wife, Ernesta, had moved into the small worker's house. Both were still here. His wife had been buried underneath a spreading live oak in the ranch cemetery for more than thirty years. A simple wooden cross made by Jesus marked her resting place on the flank of a cedar-covered limestone ridge behind the main house. For many years the old man had been far too frail to do any kind of work. When Caleb and his wife, Laura, had bought the ranch nearly twenty years earlier, Jesus had come along as part of the deal.

"He doesn't have any other place to go," Vern Miller, who sold them the ranch, had said, "or anyone to take him in. His wife's buried here, and they never had any kids. It'd kill the old fellow to send him off, so he stays or no sale."

Caleb and Laura readily agreed, and the likeable Jesus grew to become as familiar as the hills and trees that dotted the countryside. He subsisted strangely enough on checks sent to him every month from a San Angelo brokerage firm. Over the years the wily man had invested his meager paychecks and somehow parlayed them into a decent enough sum to pay for his modest needs. These days his activities were limited to carving whistles from tree limbs with a Barlow pocket knife, reading Western novels and giving out advice to anyone who would listen.

"We will have a very bad winter, I think," Jesus said, sending a curl of willow bark flying with his knife. "All of the little animals are storing away food, and their coats are getting very long. It is not a good sign."

"At the two hundred and sixty-five dollars a ton they charge at the co-op for goat feed, I'd hate to see any of my mice runnin' around looking scraggly," Caleb said. "If we could get those goats in as good shape as everything else that eats the stuff, we'd get top dollar for the next shearing."

Jesus looked up from his half-formed whistle and focused his coal black eyes on Caleb. "Still, we are going to have a bad winter. That is a problem with people these days, they do not take the time to read the signs that *Dios* gives us. Also, why do you not wait until your strong son comes home from school to help with the heavy work? It would spare you much pain and the animals would be no worse for the wait."

Caleb pursed his lips, and the furrows on his brow grew deeper. He didn't like being reminded that Tristan was having to attend summer classes to graduate from high school. The only interests the boy had lately were watching movies on TV or playing his guitar. Tristan had just turned eighteen, and Caleb tried to tell himself it was normal to be rebellious at that age. Every time he attempted to talk with his son about his failing grades, the boy would shake out his overly long hair, stare at his feet and refuse to talk. It had been like this for two years now, ever since . . .

"The boy's job is studying, and mine is running this ranch," Caleb growled. He forced the biting black memories into his mind's waiting room and climbed into the cab of his ten-year-old pickup truck. He slammed the door and coaxed the engine to life. He grimaced as the gears gave out and growled like an angry dog when he moved the shift lever. *Damn clutch is plumb worn out,* he thought.

With a jerk the battered Chevy lurched from the barn into the glare of a cloudless west Texas afternoon. Caleb squinted his eyes and wished he hadn't broken the lens on his prescription sunglasses last month. Glasses cost money to replace, so he kept his remaining good pair on the stand next to his easy chair so he could at least watch the news or read a book. His eyesight was plenty good enough to drive and take care of the neverending myriad chores that accompanied owning twelve hundred acres of ranch land, along with leasing thirty-eight hundred more from his neighbor, Hector Lemmons. Caleb hated going back to the optometrist again. That money hungry, almost-a-real-doctor had tried for years now to get him to wear bifocals. Only bankers and bean counters wore bifocal glasses. He was only forty-six. Aside from gray temples, the beginning of a potbelly and a back that was in worse shape than his bank account, Caleb could pass for a much younger man. Bifocal glasses be damned.

Like all ranchers and men who made their living from the land, Caleb made a quick check of conditions as he drove slowly toward the south pasture and his awaiting three hundred head of Angora goats.

The Aermotor windmill alongside his frame house was spinning rapidly in the afternoon breeze. He noticed the discharge pipe that emptied into a six-foot high by thirty-foot across concrete storage tank was delivering only a tiny stream of water. This was arid country. With the heat of summer a plentiful supply from this well was necessary to keep his hundred head of Brahman Cross cattle alive and hopefully gaining some weight.

He stopped the pickup, set the parking brake and let the engine continue to puff blue smoke and slobber oil from its rattling tailpipe while he went to check out the problem. It was as he feared. The sucker rods were rattling up and down in the casing and bringing up but little water. The leathers were worn out and needed to be replaced. This was something that couldn't be put off.

Disgusted with having to call out Rollie Turner and pay for a crew to repair his windmill, Caleb grabbed at his front shirt pocket for a cigarette. Except for a ballpoint pen, it was empty. He had quit smoking over two years ago. When upset, he still reached for a cigarette.

"Horse feathers," Caleb grumbled. "A man should be able to afford a few good vices in this world. Maybe I oughta give up eating and start smoking again; at least then I wouldn't have to watch my weight."

A smile crossed the rancher's well-tanned face when he looked down at Useless rubbing against his jeans and purring up a storm. There was no telling when that cat would show up or what he might have brought along with him. Usually it was a half dead mouse. Occasionally his offerings were far more interesting, like lizards, tarantulas or a snake. Twice this spring the cat had carried two small, very dead diamondback rattlesnakes into the house. How Useless had kept from being bitten was a source of amazement to Caleb. Since then, every time the tomcat came around, Caleb was careful to make sure he hadn't brought along another rattler with him, especially one that might still have a little life left in it. A quick inspection showed Useless had showed up empty-mouthed.

"So I guess you want to ride down and watch me strain my back some more?" Caleb asked.

The mouser meowed his answer and made a beeline to jump onto the seat of the still running pickup.

Caleb turned to follow when suddenly some of the Rhode Island Red chickens that had been lethargically picking away at a few struggling sprigs of grass began squawking with alarm.

An ominous black shadow rolled across the sun-drenched earth sending the chickens into an outright panic, running with outstretched wings toward the safety of their coop.

"Damn chicken hawk," Caleb swore. "I'll fix your wagon!"

After the problem with the windmill, the rancher wasn't in any mood to lose one of his egg-laying Rhode Island Reds to some blasted predator. He strode to his truck, reached over Useless and grabbed a Stevens single shot twelve-gauge shotgun from the window rack and popped open the breech. From the jumble inside the glove box, he extracted a magnum shell loaded with number two steel shot and poked it into the chamber. As he spun to spot the hawk he snapped the gun closed and cocked the hammer.

The chicken eater had missed on its first pass and banked to swoop in for another try. *That is one big hawk,* Caleb thought as he squinted into the glaring sun and carefully led the shadowy predator's approach so the charge of shot would hit it full on.

He fired and the shotgun slammed hard against his shoulder. To his satisfaction the hawk exploded into a ball of feathers and crashed into the ground about a hundred feet from where he stood.

Useless took the explosion in stride. The tomcat jumped from the pickup, ran over to the downed bird and began warily circling it.

"No you can't drag it home," Caleb said, rubbing his shoulder with his free hand as he walked to join the cat, still carrying the shotgun.

When he got to within a few feet of the crumpled heap of feathers, Caleb froze in his tracks and stared down at it with wide, shocked eyes.

"Oh my God, Useless, I've done gone and killed a bald eagle!"

The rancher swallowed hard, then bent over and grabbed onto a leg that had talons as long as his little finger and hoisted up the dead bird. A broken wing flopped outward showing the wingspan of the raptor must have been well over seven feet. The white head dangled lifelessly, blood dripping from its hooked beak. There was no longer any question; it was a bald eagle, our national bird, not some chicken hawk that he had blown out of the sky.

"I'm sorry, old fella. If I could've seen what you were, I reckon you could have had a chicken for dinner. Damn it all, I sure hate this."

Then Caleb noticed a small black plastic box fastened to the base of one of the eagle's huge tail feathers. A short metal wire ran outward along the shaft of the feather. Its only purpose could be an antenna. A tiny red light in the center of the box flashed on and off, keeping time with the rancher's rapidly beating heart.

"Christ on a crutch, Useless, this darn bird has been wired with a locator beacon. I'd better get to cracking and bury it quick. If whoever's tracking it shows up, the shit will hit the fan for sure."

Caleb's last few words were drowned out by the rhythmic beating of an approaching red and white Bell Jet Ranger helicopter that was cruising just high enough to clear the fan on his ailing windmill.

The suddenness of the helicopter's appearance had caught him totally by surprise. He was too shocked to do anything but watch as the Bell Jet began circling. The rancher made out a man in the passenger seat of the bubble front who had a video camera pointed at him.

Caleb, so floored by what was transpiring, took a moment to realize that he was holding the dead eagle in one hand and the shotgun in the other. A tight knot formed in his gut.

"Useless, my buddy," he said over the roar of the helicopter, "reckon ol' Jesus was right about us being in for a rough winter."

Chapter 2

From the cockpit of the circling helicopter, Marsh Wheelan glared down at the eagle killer through a fog of red rage.

He knew ranchers hated eagles as much as the coyotes and bobcats that preyed on their livestock. But this shotgun-toting son of a bitch had just blown the first eagle he ever released out of the sky for absolutely no reason.

At twenty-eight Marsh held a PhD in biology from Berkeley. Six months ago he had taken a position with Run Free, the radical but well-funded environmental organization that was supported mostly by affluent movie stars and recording artists.

Releasing endangered species back into their natural habitat made for good press; grizzly bears and wolves in Montana and Idaho; eagles in Texas. All were quixotic ideas to his way of thinking. There were simply too many people in this world for the species Run Free released to possibly thrive. Beside that, he simply didn't care about anything but his image as a staunch environmentalist.

Ah, but the contacts. Marsh had carefully sought out as many well-heeled donors as he could and told them what they wanted to hear. He methodically left a hint here, a suggestion there. Marsh Wheelan was capable and intelligent, a man of action and ability. Laws needed changing. It would take a man of his talents to force those changes through the legislature.

Marsh was a man with high ambitions. With enough money and support he could be a congressman, maybe someday, even president. Politics were his first and singular love. Power, prestige and money. Foremost of all was power; the rest came along for the ride.

Now this simpleton with a shotgun had possibly done as much damage to his budding career as he had the bald eagle.

"Do you want to land?" the pilot asked over the roar of the chopper.

Marsh fixed his eyes on the shotgun in the rancher's hand. "No, we have orders not to confront anyone in what might be a dangerous situation. I've got some good videotape of him that'll hold up in any court. Just make certain of landmarks. I also made note of his license plate. Let's get the hell out of here before we get blown out of the sky ourselves."

The pilot, Wes Shelton, gave a tense nod of consent and put the Bell Jet into a slow climb to the west. He knew Caleb Starr would never shoot anyone. Three years ago he had gotten to know the rancher when he sprayed some mesquite trees for him. That was just before the man's wife had come down with cancer. If some cocky kid from Run Free, who needs a string to keep his glasses on his head, wanted to know who had shot that eagle he could find out for himself. There were lots of crops to spray in West Texas and only one bald eagle that needed following. Make that *was* one bald eagle. Wes knew which side of the bread his butter was on.

Marsh keyed the microphone and spoke in a cold, measured voice. "Release control, this is Mother Hen. I'm confirming my earlier transmission. Raptor number two-eleven is down. We are returning to base."

He winced when his supervisor's, steely voice boomed into the headset. Dianne Petrov possessed all the charms of an electric chair. "Did you talk to the man and find out why he shot the bird?"

"No Ma'am. He pointed a gun at us. It would have been too

dangerous."

"You have the event on video?"

"Everything is on tape but his confession. I also got the license plate number of his truck. The man was holding that eagle up like it was a trophy. I hope like hell they give him the max for what he did."

After a measured silence Dianne said, "That is none of your concern. I'll turn the matter over to the authorities along with a copy of your videotape. Come to the office when you get back to San Angelo. We'll talk about further releases. Perhaps we will move to the west; there are fewer people living in that direction."

"Yes, Ms. Petrov," Marsh said. He slipped the microphone back into its slot, glad to have time to collect his thoughts.

His investment banker father's harsh voice crackled in his brain. *The secret of being a winner is the ability to turn defeat into victory.*

Marsh seldom thought back on his childhood, a succession of military schools and infrequent, condescending visits from his always too busy dad. He had to give the old bastard credit though—he'd made a ton of money. A lot of good that would ever be. His daddy's entire estate was now willed to his new young wife, a twenty-nine-year-old blond bimbo. When the old fart's bum ticker finally gives out, Marsh likely wouldn't receive even a lousy million.

But the advice was sound. Marsh needed desperately to make a name for himself. The gears in his head moved with the cold, calculating precision of a cat stalking its prey as a plan formed.

By the time the Bell Jet cleared a clump of mesquite trees and glided in for a landing at Mathis Field, Marsh Wheelan wore a vulpine grin on his clean-shaven face. Dianne Petrov would have to wait a while for that conversation.

Marsh tossed the video camera and log book onto the seat of

his Bronco and sped off to his apartment. First he needed to make another copy of the tape, then place a long distance phone call or two. Not only would his scheme make a name for himself and bring in a fat check, he would have the sweet pleasure of totally destroying that eagle-killing rancher.

Authorities, Dianne Petrov and Run Free be damned. He was Marsh Wheelan, a future leader and champion of the environment. Very shortly his name would be in front of millions of potential voters.

Defeat turned into victory. For the first time in Marsh's life, his father might be proud of him.

Chapter 3

The sun was low and blood red when Caleb Starr drove his battered pickup into the town of Lone Wolf and pulled to a jerky stop in front of The Slip Up Saloon. With this single exception, the Southern Baptists had been successful in keeping not only the town, but the entire county of Lone Wolf, Texas, dry as a sackful of sand.

Back in nineteen fifty-one, Pastor Ezekial "Hellfire" Hawkins had been moved by the spirit to attend a month-long retreat at a Baptist Encampment in Louisiana.

Deek Gilmore and his wife Louise, had seized upon the opportunity of the preacher's long absence to move some spirits of their own. With the clandestine help of a few county officials who enjoyed an occasional nip or two, they managed to slip a liquor license through the powers that be. Hence the name of their bar.

In spite of fervent and frequent prayer meetings held by the nearly apoplectic Preacher Hawkins upon his return and those of his many successors calling down God's wrath upon that den of iniquity, The Slip Up Saloon plugged along unscathed.

Caleb climbed stiffly from the cab of his truck and stretched his aching back. He grimaced when he glanced down at the dead eagle crumpled in the pickup bed.

The fact that some lawman hadn't come calling on him came as no surprise. The local game warden, Bruno Leatherwood, he'd known since high school. The sheriff he'd been acquainted with his entire life. His sister, Monica Blandon, had been duly elected to that post for the past twelve years. Caleb Starr wasn't a hard man to find.

There was no doubt in his mind that he'd have to pay a fine for shooting an eagle. The fact he didn't even know it was an eagle when he blasted away or the fact that it was attacking his chickens wouldn't get him off. Hell, these days it was probably against the law to even shoot a chicken hawk.

The entire sordid affair had undoubtedly been video taped by that guy in the helicopter. Even O.J. Simpson's dream team of lawyers couldn't get him off on a not guilty plea with that kind of evidence. The best he could hope for would be a small fine. Vaguely, he remembered some rancher in East Texas getting fined five-hundred dollars for killing some eagles a few years ago.

Since what he'd done had been a total accident, perhaps the judge might show some mercy and let him off with a suspended sentence, or possibly community service. Picking up beer cans in the park would be easier than coming up with cash. After writing out checks every month to pay on Laura's staggering hospital bills, there simply wasn't any money left over for fines.

Caleb put the dead eagle out of his mind when he walked by Rollie Turner's white flatbed Dodge pickup that had the brakes and throttle installed on the steering wheel. Getting his windmill repaired so his cattle wouldn't run out of water was a more pressing issue. Rollie had lost his left leg from a land mine in Vietnam and while he couldn't drive a vehicle without special controls, the man could shinny up a windmill tower with the ease of a squirrel climbing a tree.

When Caleb swung open the door and stepped into the smoky, dark interior of the bar he hesitated a moment to blink his eyes into focus. A song was wailing from the jukebox about not letting your babies grow up to be cowboys. Caleb couldn't agree more, especially after the day he'd had.

There were probably twenty people in The Slip Up. It was a good crowd for a Tuesday night in a town of less than two thousand souls. Everyone there knew Caleb and acknowledged his presence with either a "Howdy" or smiling nod, which he quickly returned. Several voices yelled to Prairie Dog Pete Cleburne, the pear-shaped bartender, to give Caleb what he wanted to drink and put it on their tab. This happened every time he went to the saloon. Everyone in Lone Wolf knew that Caleb only escaped bankruptcy by mortgaging his ranch to the hilt and financing hospital bills until the second coming. Though well intentioned, this generosity stabbed at his heart like a driven nail.

Only during those times when dark memories drove him to seek the laughter of others or to meet someone on business did Caleb Starr enter The Slip Up Saloon.

"Hey Caleb," Prairie Dog yelled from the far end of the bar, "come over here and have a beer with Rollie. He's tryin' to get his memory to working so he can figger out what he done with his wooden leg."

Rollie Turner was plopped on a bar stool with a crutch by his side. His left pants leg pinned up tight against the stump above where his knee used to be. The windmiller was skinny enough to hide behind a barbed wire fence. From beneath a silver head of bushy hair, Rollie's perpetual smile flashed at Caleb when he approached.

Prairie Dog set a frosty mug of draft beer on the oak bar and spun the handle toward Caleb. "About a hundred of these an' you'll be on the same planet Rollie was last night."

"So, you went into San Angelo for supplies yesterday," Caleb said.

Rollie took a snort of whiskey from a bottle wrapped tightly in a brown paper bag, wheezed, then chased that with a mouthful of beer. "Yep, and I haven't had so much fun since the last time I was in the big city."

"Not everyone comes back from Angelo missing a leg," Caleb commented.

"It'll turn up," Rollie said with shrug. "Not many folks would have any use for the thing except maybe as a doorstop."

Prairie Dog Pete stood behind the bar with his arms folded up against his chest. With his shaggy blond beard and hair he gave the appearance of a fat prairie dog begging for a peanut. "The last time he got on a tear in Angelo some kids found the thing in a phone booth. They were playing kick the can with it when some cops saw 'em and took the leg away."

Caleb couldn't resist a chuckle. After the events of the day it felt wonderful. "You know, Rollie, most folks carry a spare tire for their car in case they get a flat. Maybe you oughta get an extra leg or two. Old Jesus could whittle one out of a mesquite tree that'd hold up to fixing windmills for when you get a job, like now."

"Which one of your mills is ailing?" Rollie asked, turning serious.

"The one close to the house that waters my cattle. It's only eighty feet deep so it shouldn't be a big job. I'm sure new leathers is all it needs."

Rollie knew Caleb meant he hoped it wouldn't be an expensive job. "If the casing and sucker rods are okay, the whole thing won't run much over a hundred bucks. I'll be out first thing in the morning. Don't worry about paying for it until later."

Caleb pointed at the crutch leaning against the bar. "You planning on climbing a windmill with that thing?"

"Nope. I'll get Buck Parnell's kid to do the work while I yell at him. He's dumber than a bucket of stove bolts, but height don't bother him none."

Caleb nodded in agreement. He would replace the leathers himself except for an unreasonable fear when he got over a few feet above Mother Earth. That blasted mill was thirty-three feet in the air, same as a three-story building.

"Well, sonny boy, it's good to see you out among the living for a change," Hector Lemmons said in his cackling voice as he sat down in an empty stool alongside Caleb and thudded his empty mug on the bar. The ancient rancher frowned his stubble-bearded face at the bartender. "You sleep walkin' again or could a man possibly get a beer around here. I'm over seventy years old and ain't got all the time in the world."

Prairie Dog smiled good-naturedly and went about refilling the mug. Hector Lemmons owned the largest ranch in Lone Wolf County. The old man's holdings were over twenty-three thousand acres not including what Caleb leased from him. Hundreds of producing oil and gas wells should have kept Lemmons from fretting over running cattle or sheep, yet the rancher loved the land and seldom talked about anything but the weather and his livestock.

"We sure need some more rain, boys," Hector said.

"That's for sure," Caleb agreed. This was a usual conversation in west Texas where they *always* needed more rain. "Old Jesus says we're in for a mighty rough winter. A slow, deep-soaking shower would make for good forage if he's right."

"My money would be on Jesus," Rollie interjected. "That old man predicted the drought back in the fifties. Hell, in those days half the wells around here only pumped dust. It was so damn dry even the ducks forgot how to swim."

"Those were hard times for us all," Hector said, his gray eyes glazed in thought. "A lot of good folks went broke back then. I hope to never see the likes of it again."

Prairie Dog stepped close to the bar and leaned forward. "There was a college perfesser type in here the other day. He said this Mexican thing, 'El Niño,' would make the next few years the wettest ever. Cocky little bastard, but he seemed to know what he was talking about. You guys would never believe what he was doing around here."

Hector placed his elbow on the bar and leaned his head against his fist. "And I'm bettin' there ain't no way you ain't gonna tell us all about it. Bartenders are bigger gossips than church women."

Prairie Dog grinned. "And all this time I thought you fellows just hung around because of my sparking personality, sharp wit and good service."

"It's getting piled pretty deep in here," Rollie said. "Go ahead, Prairie Dog, and spill it while you can still remember what it's about."

Humor fled the pudgy bartender's face. "The guy works for some environmentalist group called Run Free. He said they're going to start releasing some bald eagles hereabouts."

Caleb's heart fell to somewhere in his gut.

Hector's usual smile faded to be replaced by a look of astonishment. "That bunch must be workin' for the government to be *that* dad gum stupid. With all the baby lambs an' goats in these parts, that'd be like a nest of yellow jackets in the outhouse. Won't be any time before one of those eagles gets its tail feathers singed by a load of birdshot from some rancher who's just trying to protect what's his. Those things belong in Alaska where their dining habits don't cause a man hurt."

"The problem is," Prairie Dog's voice was bitter, "this guy told me there's a bunch of new laws on the books these days. Anyone kills an eagle, it's a year in prison and a hundred grand fine. Don't that beat all."

In the dim light of the bar no one noticed the color had drained from Caleb's face like his throat had been cut.

"Why that's plumb crazy," Rollie said. "A body could rob a

string of convenience stores an' not get slapped that hard."

Hector reached for his beer, shaking his head in disbelief. "If memory serves me, I think it was old Charles Dickens who wrote '*The Law is an Ass*'; I reckon ol' Charlie knew his elbow from a hole in the ground."

Caleb remained silent. He chugged the last of his beer then said through clenched teeth, "Thanks for the drink. I have some things to take care of." He hopped from the stool and was out the door before anyone could say a word.

"What do you reckon's eatin' him?" Prairie Dog asked.

"That man's had a world of problems land on his shoulders since his wife died," Rollie said. "He must have forgot to pick up his boy or something."

Hector stared at the now closed door, his expression tight with concern. "Yeah, I reckon that's all it amounts to."

Chapter 4

Caleb held open a black plastic trash bag while Bruno Leatherwood stuffed the rumpled carcass of the bald eagle inside. For all its great size, the dead raptor was surprisingly light, probably weighing no more than twelve pounds. Caleb mentioned this fact to the game warden.

"Every bird that flies a lot is mostly feathers with a little meat wrapped around spindly bones," Bruno replied. "Turkeys and chickens, now they're mainly ground birds and can pack around more ballast without causing them problems. Hawks and eagles are predators; they have to move quick as a snake and stay airborne for hours at a time."

"I heard there's some mighty stiff laws for killing an eagle," Caleb ventured, a knot the size of Texas in his gut. "Bruno, I thought I was shooting a chicken hawk. This darn thing swooped in out of the sun. It was after my laying hens."

The game warden shook the trash bag firmly to settle in the carcass, then spun the opening closed and fastened it with a plastic tie.

"Mostly, those laws are meant to keep people from shooting them for profit. In the right places, this eagle would fetch a couple of thousand dollars."

"What!" Caleb was dumbfounded. "Why in the world would anyone pay that kind of money for a dead eagle?"

"Indian paraphernalia. The feathers are used in hats and dance fans and hung on pipes. The talons make amulets. Wing bones are fashioned into ceremonial whistles that sound just like the 'kark kark' of an eagle. A bundle of feathers makes a wedding bouquet in an Indian marriage ceremony."

"I had no idea about stuff like that."

"Outlaws in places like Montana and Wyoming make a lot of extra money every year killing eagles and selling them to the Indians on their reservations. There's more demand than supply. If an eagle gets fried by a power line—that kills more of them than anything—or we come by a dead one for some other reason, most agencies of the government give them to the Indians. I'll stuff this one in the freezer where it will keep until I get orders as to what to do with it."

Caleb summoned his courage and asked flat out. "Are you going to arrest me?"

Bruno spun and faced the rancher. His steel eyes were unreadable as stone. The pale and scared look that Caleb wore reminded him of thirty years ago when he'd caught the then young man with three doves over the limit. The game warden had yelled and threatened until tears were streaming down the boy's cheeks. Then he told him to go on home and never break the law again. And Caleb Starr never had, until now.

"No," he answered with unaccustomed kindness. "I can't see why since it was an accident and you were just trying to protect your chickens. The book says even hawks are protected though. Keep that in mind. I reckon I'll just put this eagle on record as being found shot by persons unknown."

"Thanks, Bruno, but there's something you need to know. I don't want you winding up in Dutch on my account. You've got your retirement to think about."

"What in the world are you rambling about?"

Caleb reached into the front pocket of his khaki shirt, then extended his hand to the warden palm side up. Bruno's eyes widened in alarm at the small black box with a winking red light in its center.

"Holy shit, Caleb! You should've tossed that thing in the back of the first truck heading out of here going anywhere. That eagle must have been part of a release. They'll be tracking it for sure."

"Oh, you're right about it being followed. The feathers hadn't all settled before I had a helicopter circling. Some guy with a video camera probably got some really good pictures. I thought you might have had a phone call."

The furrows in Bruno Leatherwood's tanned face deepened with tension. After a heavy sigh he said, "No, I haven't heard a word, but I'd reckon we will. I'm going to write up a report, only I think I'll sit on it awhile to see how things go. You'd best check in with your sister. Maybe she's heard something."

"Thanks, I'll head over there now."

Caleb was halfway to his pickup when he stopped and turned. "I heard there's a hundred grand fine and a year in prison for shooting an eagle. Is that right?"

Bruno's pinched expression told Caleb what he'd heard was true. "Don't go slamming gates that ain't even built yet. You've got lots of friends hereabouts. The whole mess was an accident."

With that statement the game warden turned, and carrying the trash bag containing the eagle, strode toward a shed in the backyard of his home.

Caleb's throat was dry as the powdery west Texas earth he walked on when he climbed into the seat of his pickup to go visit the Sheriff of Lone Wolf County.

A white two-story Victorian house with ornate, yellow gingerbread trim housed Blandon's Funeral Parlor. It sat behind a peeling picket fence on Main Street across from the cemetery. Both of Lone Wolf's churches, The First Baptist and Saint Augustine's Catholic, were on opposite sides of the graveyard.

It was a thrifty arrangement. Locals were quick to point out that neither the preacher or the mortician had to burn a gallon of gasoline to lay someone away.

Caleb parked his pickup under an enormous live oak tree that had supposedly seen service in the past for hanging bothersome persons who had difficulty reading brands. He was careful to keep his truck on Main Street. Lane Blandon's gray concrete driveway was spotless. Monica had always been a stickler for cleanliness. Caleb didn't want to irritate her by letting his truck drip messy black oil where it would show.

The undertaker, Lane Blandon, whom everyone referred to as "Bones", had married Caleb's sister over twenty-four years ago. Their union had produced no offspring. Until recently both had lavished their attentions on their nephew, Tristan.

As Caleb walked toward the front door, he wondered how long it had been since his son had even visited. He knew exactly why. In spite of himself, Caleb stopped and gazed underneath a mottled canopy of rustling tree leaves and twinkling stars toward the graveyard. His wonderful wife resided there. A too small marble headstone marked her resting place. It was impossible to come here without having memories crash down like they were made of iron.

Cancer. Melanoma. If only she could have received treatment earlier. These words of many specialists in San Angelo and Dallas stalked the hallways of Caleb's mind like a tenacious ghost.

It had begun all so innocently. One of the hundreds of freckles on Laura's petite neck grew inflamed and angry. She was a busy lady, holding down a full time job at Hercules Oil Company, keeping a tidy home and helping out with the myriad chores that come with owning a ranch. There simply wasn't time to fret over small things like a boil. Several months passed swiftly before she saw Doctor Rexton. By then, the lesion was the size of a silver dollar.

That was over two years ago. Yet to this day Caleb couldn't drive past the cemetery on his way to town and not be inundated with memories. Tristan, however, seemed to have retreated into anger. The boy refused to talk about his problems in school or his constantly getting into fights. It was as if he was lashing out at the world as if it was the disease that had taken his mother.

"Hey, Monica, it's Caleb. His truck must have broke down or something because he's heading our way." Bones's cheerful voice from behind the screen door jerked Caleb out of his dark reverie.

For all the years he'd known him, the undertaker's appearance varied but little. He was a tall man, over six and one-half feet and lanky as a range steer that had suffered through a hard winter. The suits he perpetually wore changed in color only from light gray to dark gray. His black horn-rimmed glasses completed the image.

"At least he sort of resembles your brother," Bones said, then turned his head to look over his shoulder. "Hon, just to be on the safe side, maybe you ought to run his ID."

The undertaker always maintained a great sense of humor. Given his somber trade, many wondered how he could always joke and smile. Caleb knew humor was the only way the sensitive man could keep his emotions in check.

"I reckon it has been a spell," Caleb said, reaching to open the screen door. "You could come out and see us sometime. Your customers wouldn't miss you."

"No, but I would." Monica still wore her blue sheriff's uniform, complete with gun belt. "Someone has to cook and clean while I'm out keeping Lone Wolf a safe place to live."

Bones grinned. "If you weren't such an all fired fanatic about that *safe* part, my business would pick up."

Monica ignored him and focused on Caleb. "I just got back a

few minutes ago. There was a little fender bender out on Sixty-seven. It'll take me longer to fill out the paper work than it'll take the body shop to fix both of their cars." She strained to look around her brother. "Tristan didn't come along?"

"He'd best be home studying, or he'll have to spend six years in high school like your husband did."

Bones ignored Caleb's verbal jab and turned serious. "I sure wish there was some way we could reach that boy. He's going to have a mighty rough row to hoe if he don't come out of it. Lately Monica's gotten some complaints about him fighting."

"Where's my manners?" Monica said to change the subject. "Caleb, what would you like to drink, beer or coffee?"

"A beer would be nice."

"Grab two while you're at it, Hon," Bones said. "Shoot, we might even have more than that." His face melted into a devilish grin. "It's hard to get into trouble when you've got an in with the law."

When his sister walked to the refrigerator, Caleb noticed she had gained a few pounds. Tip Conroy, her sole deputy, was built like a bowling ball. He received his nickname when he supposedly tipped over the scales at the feed store while trying to weigh himself. No one in Lone Wolf could remember ever seeing Tip without him having a box of doughnuts handy. It was obvious Monica had taken a liking to them also. Still, with her close cropped brown hair and infectious laugh she seemed little changed from when they were kids growing up together.

The beer was golden and ice cold. Caleb made small talk, enjoyed the company and tried to postpone bringing up the subject of that blasted eagle. He had already decided Monica knew nothing about it. His mind was a crazy mixture of hope and fear. He couldn't allow himself to be lulled into a false sense of security simply because no one had called down the law on him so far.

"Sis," Caleb said firmly, "I think I might be in a lot of trouble."

Monica could feel the tension in his voice. "Are you talking financial or legal?"

"Legal."

"Tell us about it. Tell us all about it," Monica said.

Caleb did. Two more empty beer bottles were lined up on the kitchen table before he finished. Neither Monica nor Bones had interrupted his tale with a single question.

"My God!" Bones exclaimed. "They can't put a man in prison for shooting an eagle. That's crazy."

Monica twirled her coffee cup worriedly. "I really don't know. That would fall under federal jurisdiction. What I will do tomorrow is call Quentin Miller. Not only is he the best lawyer around, he's a friend of Senator Ames. Don't worry, Caleb, I'll be discreet. There's a chance this Run Free organization might let things blow over, call it an acceptable loss. I just think we'd best know our options."

Caleb scooted his chair back and stood up. "Thanks guys, I just hope this won't turn out to be a big deal."

"If we can do anything about it, it won't," Monica said.

Bones put a comforting hand on Caleb's shoulder. "You get some rest and don't stew on this. We're family, and we're always here to help. Don't forget that."

"I won't," Caleb said. He pecked a kiss on Monica's cheek, then strode outside into the sultry night. When he climbed into his pickup, he tried to keep from staring out across the moonlit cemetery but was unsuccessful.

Chapter 5

Marsh Wheelan ran his fingers over the check, like he was making love to a beautiful woman.

Only money was better than sex. Sex was fleeting pleasure. Money was a means to an end: opportunity; power. And power endured for a lifetime.

Dianne Petrov would most likely fire him in the morning. If not then, certainly soon. He could care less. Marsh had not bothered to check in with her since returning to his apartment to make a copy of the videotape. Phone calls had kept him too busy for petty details. It had been difficult to reach everyone he wanted to in short order. Messages had to be left and his calls returned. But they *had* called him back, just as he had expected them to do.

Then he had gone to meet a chartered Lear jet at the airport. The shapely but businesslike young lady reporter had quickly written him out a check for fifteen grand. He could possibly have held out for more, made some additional phone calls. It simply wasn't worth it. Marsh was a man of action. He'd smilingly accepted the check. Before the Lear cleared the end of the runway, he had been on his cell phone, punching numbers.

Famous actors and singers, proud to do their part to save the environment had given him their personal calling cards. Finally the time had come to let them know *he* was the man to turn to.

It had taken him until eleven o'clock to reach the more important ones. The west coast, where many of them lived, was two hours earlier than here in San Angelo, Texas. Before he hung up, each and every one of them knew that Marsh Wheelan was the savior of the environment. A man who only needed financial support to see their goals reached far more quickly than Run Free ever could.

Now he lay on his king-size bed and fondled the check. Tomorrow he would cash it. Today was Thursday. By the end of next week, millions of people in the United States would know his name and how he had photographed a bloodthirsty, outlaw eagle killer. All they would have to do was look at the headlines at the check-out counter.

The check was drawn on the account of *The Weekly World Probe,* one of the largest selling tabloids in the country.

He sincerely hoped his name would appear on the cover in large type, right below the picture of that damn shotgun-wielding rancher holding a dead bald eagle like a trophy.

Chapter 6

"Señor," Jesus said to Caleb when he walked over to where Tristan and the old patriarch were sitting under a yellow bug light on the open porch of Jesus's two room house. "One of the headlights on your truck is burned out. You should fix it, I think."

"From the way this day's gone, I'm surprised you aren't telling me the thing's on fire."

"No, *señor.* The bad headlight is all that is wrong with it, this night."

A nearly empty pitcher of lemonade and a dog-eared copy of the novel, *The Time It Never Rained* sat on a rusty metal table alongside Jesus's oak rocking chair.

Tristan squatted Indian style, his back resting against a porch post across from the elderly man.

The old Mexican grabbed up the novel and waved it at Caleb.

"The *Señor* Flagg in this book had many bad days also. I think he did not complain about them as much as you do."

In spite of his vexations, Caleb couldn't contain a grin. Jesus had taught himself to read English many years ago. Then he developed a liking for novels, especially westerns. The sides of his bedroom were stacked with paperback books from floor to ceiling, like a second wall. This one book he was holding so proudly had been inscribed to him by the famous author, Elmer Kelton, himself. It was the old man's pride and joy. He had nearly worn the cover out showing off the autograph to every visitor from the meter reader to the tax assessor.

Caleb wondered just how long his son had been here and hoped he'd done at least some studying beforehand. Tristan loved to listen to the old man's tales. A few might have a ring of truth to them, but Caleb suspicioned most of Jesus's stories were born behind the cover of a book.

"How did school go today, Son?" Caleb asked, careful to mask any hint of sarcasm.

Tristan shrugged skinny shoulders as he eyed the porch floor and shook his collar length blonde hair. "Fine, Dad."

"Did you finish all of your homework?"

"Yeah. Where have you been, out with Hope?"

Caleb's jaw set tight with irritation. It seemed no matter how hard he tried, any conversation with Tristan wound up in an argument. Hope Rexton was a ray of sunshine in an otherwise bleak sky. The daughter of Doctor Jake Rexton, Hope had moved back to Lone Wolf a year ago after a bitter divorce. Her only daughter was married and living in California. Hope was a registered nurse and worked for her father at his office. Over the past few months, Caleb and the lithe redhead with emerald eyes had gone to San Angelo together a few times. A movie and dancing later was all it had amounted to. Caleb had nothing to offer any lady other than a mountain of debt. What made it all the more annoying was the fact that Tristan liked Hope. The boy just seemed to enjoy riling him.

He decided to ignore the question. "I've been over to see Monica and Bones. They asked about you."

"Been busy," Tristan replied curtly.

"You haven't been *that* busy, Son. I want you to drop by on your way home from school some day next week and pay them a visit."

"Dad, first you tell me to study, then I'm supposed to run all over the place. Which one is it?"

Caleb felt his anger rising like bile. "You aren't studying now, are you? If you'd buckle down and work when you were supposed to, there would be plenty of time to go see folks who care about you."

Jesus held out his hand and clucked his tongue. "I was telling young Tristan about the famous outlaw Black Jack Ketchum. He was born and raised near here. A person should know about the history of where he lives."

Caleb was grateful to be able to change the subject, but his temper had reached boiling. "Ketchum killed a lot of men. When the law finally hung him, they dropped him so far the rope popped his head off. A darn good lesson for young'uns to pay attention to."

Tristan bolted to his feet and glared at his father. Caleb noticed he wore a tattered Beavis and Butthead T-shirt he'd been ordered to throw in the trash a month ago.

"Son," Caleb said with strained softness, "can't you even try to do what you're told just once in a while?"

Tristan dropped his gaze to his feet, walked around his dad and slouched silently off into the darkness toward the main house a hundred yards to the south.

Once the boy was out of earshot, Caleb sighed and said, "He has a lot of rage bottled up inside him."

"Si, señor," Jesus said. "But in that, I would say he may not be alone."

Caleb slid a lawn chair close to the old man and plopped down in it. He remained silent as the twinkling stars while Jesus tamped his pipe full of fresh tobacco and used nearly a book of matches getting a fire built in it to suit his tastes. The aged Mexican drew deeply on the pipe and sent a cloud of smoke toward the bug light. He was obviously waiting for Caleb to speak.

"Smoking's bad for your health."

"*Si, señor.* I am sure that someday either my pipe or something else will kill me."

A thin smile crossed Caleb's lips. It was hard to remain in a bad mood around Jesus. "Being a father's not an easy task these days."

"No, and it never was, even before these days. Young Tristan has his whole life ahead of him. I would hope he walks a good path. If I am right, he will. Sometimes it takes a while to find a purpose."

"He just has so much anger I can't get through to him."

"*Señor,* anger and pain are very much the same thing."

The truth of the old man's words stabbed at Caleb. "I reckon I could cut the boy a little slack."

Jesus started to answer when Useless jumped onto the porch with a welcoming meow, a still kicking pack rat dangling from his clenched jaws.

"That cat's one good mouser," Caleb said.

"He will have many to practice on. It is going to be a very bad winter."

"I hope you're wrong this time."

"*Si,* so do I. *Señor,* this morning I heard you shoot, then a helicopter flew low for a while. Did something happen?"

Caleb swallowed hard and hoped he spoke true. "Uh, no. Nothing at all. Well, I'd better get home. Tomorrow's gonna be a long day."

Jesus puffed at his pipe, but the fire had gone out. "I will stay out and read. If a person spends too much time inside a house they breathe up all of the oxygen before it reaches their brain. Then they can't think clearly."

Caleb stood up and grinned at Jesus. "If that's true, then maybe I ought to stay out more. My head hasn't been working real good lately."

"Have a good night, *señor.*"

"You, too. See you in the morning."

When Caleb walked off the porch, the old man was trying to build another fire in his pipe. In the distance, over the rolling hill to the north, a pack of coyotes wailed like lost souls.

Chapter 7

Monica Blandon hadn't slept well last night. The more she thought about her brother accidentally killing a bald eagle, the more concerned she became. While her duties as sheriff mostly consisted of civil, traffic, and minor criminal matters, Monica kept up with the trends in law enforcement. During the past few years, many environmental protection laws had been enacted and/or stiffened to carry heavy criminal penalties. Some transgressions against these rules commanded greater prison time than bank robbery or manslaughter. Nearly all environmental laws were enforced on a federal level by any of a number of alphabet soup agencies such as the EPA, FWS, DOA, NRC, FBI, etc.

Only one man in Lone Wolf would be able to answer her questions.

After having breakfast with her chubby deputy, Tip Conroy, and going over last night's shift report, which, except for a single speeding ticket, was blank, Monica decided to visit Quentin Miller personally. Quentin wasn't just the best attorney in town, he was the only attorney.

She parked the sheriff's cruiser, a Jeep Cherokee Wagon with nearly two hundred thousand miles on it, in front of Quentin's office. Monica climbed out and admired the impressive two-story red brick building while she collected her thoughts.

During the hectic oil boom days of the twenties, when some people believed Lone Wolf might become a larger town than

San Angelo, Thaddeous Anderson had erected the ornate structure to house his bank. Like any town built on mineral wealth, a finite resource, Lone Wolf's future depended on the area producing huge quantities of oil at a good price.

The stock market crash in twenty-nine and the ensuing depression ended both Thaddeous's bank and the future of the town. Wells that had produced a hundred barrels of oil a day trickled down to pump only five or ten. A corresponding plunge in the price of oil nailed shut the coffin of dreams.

Quentin Miller had bought and restored the decaying building back in fifty-seven. In spite of his remote location, the colorful lawyer had built a clientele and reputation that extended far beyond the boundaries of the State of Texas. He maintained a whiskey-sipping relationship with senators, congressmen, including former President George H. W. Bush, and his son, George W. Bush.

If anyone could allay Monica's concerns it would be Quentin. Now in his late sixties, he only took on cases he cared about, often *pro bono.* Since the county of Lone Wolf couldn't afford a district attorney, he had held that unpaid position for the past fifteen years.

Monica took a deep breath, walked over and swung open the massive walnut door.

"Well, good morning, Sheriff," Rosemary Page said precisely. A crusty, no nonsense retired English teacher, Rosemary had lasted nearly a year as Quentin's secretary. A record for the cantankerous lawyer. "We haven't seen you around here for a while."

"Since we've got word out that John Wesley Hardin's great-grandson prosecutes criminals in Lone Wolf County, most crooks take their business elsewhere."

"It's *gotten.*"

"Excuse me?"

"The correct word is *gotten,* not *got.*"

Rosemary could make a sheriff or a United States senator feel like they were still in grade school.

"Yes, Ma'am," Monica said. "Is Quentin in? I need to see him."

"*Mister* Miller is in his private office. I shall ring him and find out if he has time for an audience."

"Rosy, quit pullin' that *Mister* crap on people," Quentin's voice boomed from his open door. He'd been addressing his secretary as "Rosy" ever since he discovered it irritated her. "Monica, come on back here. *Rosy* will bring us some coffee."

With a satisfied smile, Monica walked around the haughty secretary's desk, noticing the former teacher now wore an expression like she'd bitten into a green persimmon, and stepped into Quentin's office. The massive room had once been the bank's vault area. A large "cannonball" safe, its warped door hanging open on one hinge, stood alongside the lawyer's desk.

Back in thirty-three John Dillinger and his gang had supposedly blown it open during a robbery. The famed bank robber later lamented that the dynamite had cost him more money than the safe had contained. Whether the story was true or not, Quentin loved it, and the ruined safe was a favorite topic of conversation.

It was generally believed, especially by Quentin Miller, that his great-grandfather had been the famous gunfighter, John Wesley Hardin. A lineage of which he was most proud. On the beautiful wainscot wall behind the attorney's cherrywood desk, between floor to ceiling shelves containing hundreds of law books, were numerous glass plate photographs of the gunman. Somehow Quentin had obtained John Hardin's law school diploma that he had received after being pardoned from the prison in Huntsville. Quentin proudly displayed his own law degree alongside Hardin's.

"Well, what brings our lady of the law out to see me on such a beautiful Friday morning?" Quentin asked. He leaned his rotund body back in his leather swivel chair and laced his fingers behind his silver-haired head and smiled while he awaited her reply.

Monica sincerely liked Quentin Miller. He was generally friendly as a puppy but could turn as tenacious as a bulldog when the occasion called for it. The lawyer always dressed like a west Texas rancher. Today he wore a red western shirt, blue jeans and a bola tie that had a fist sized chunk of turquoise held to the clasp by a pound of hammered silver.

"Quentin," her voice unusually low and halting, "I need to get your advice on a matter. Hypothetically speaking—."

The lawyer held up his hand like a traffic cop. "I don't speak hypothetical. They didn't teach that in law school. Knowing not only the what, but also the who, is sometimes critical. Hell, Monica, you know I'm a lawyer and whatever you tell me won't go past the door, speaking of which I'll have *Rosy* close behind her after she finally gets around to fetching our java."

The prim secretary walked in carrying a pewter tray that held two porcelain cups of steaming coffee. The aroma was delicious. Monica's look of appreciation gladdened the lawyer.

"It's my own private blend," he said. "I get a shipment every month flown in from Colombia. I'll tell you that it contains *some* coffee. The rest of the ingredients are proprietary, but if you like it, I'll send some over to your office."

"Why thank you. How generous."

"It *is* quite good," Rosemary said as she placed the tray on a serving cart, spun and goose-stepped out like a storm trooper, slamming the door closed in her wake.

"Want in on the pot?" Quentin asked, a twinkle in his blue eyes.

"Pot?"

"I have a bet running with a few friends that *Rosy* will either have a nervous breakdown or quit before the Fourth of July. It's even money. If the Nazi holds out, you win."

Monica fished a sawbuck from her pants pocket and laid it on the lawyer's desk.

"My money's on the Nazi."

All traces of humor fled the attorney's face. It was time for business. "Okay, now tell me what has you so concerned. As uptight as you are, I'd venture Bones got tired of waiting for someone to kick the bucket and played Kevorkian."

"No, it's my brother, Caleb."

Quentin sighed and drummed his fingers on the desk. He had gotten the doctors and hospitals to take long-term payments for Laura's bills which totaled nearly a quarter million dollars. His influence had enabled Caleb to avoid bankruptcy and hang on to his ranch. The lawyer assumed her brother's problems were financial.

"Someone putting pressure on him for money?" Quentin asked.

"No, it's not that simple. Yesterday he shot what he thought was a hawk swooping in after one of his Rhode Island Reds. Quentin, it turned out to be a bald eagle with a radio transmitter tied to its tail feathers. Caleb said a helicopter circled him and some guy inside got video tape of him holding the dead eagle. He had his shotgun with him, too."

Attorney Quentin Miller, famous for his courtroom orations, was at a loss for words. He picked up his coffee cup and studied the dark contents like a scientist poring over a Petri dish, lost in thought.

After a long, heavy silence he said, "He'd have been better off coming up one chicken short."

"Caleb said he'd broken his work glasses and hadn't bought new ones yet. Damn it, Quentin, he's afraid he'll go to prison for this. He took the dead eagle over to the game warden. Neither Bruno nor I have heard anything, but I'm afraid it's just a matter of time. Caleb said several times he would never have shot if he'd been able to see what the thing was."

"Run Free has gotten permits to release eagles back into the wild here in west Texas. They're a small but very well-funded and connected organization. Senator Hollingsworth is their counsel in Washington. That's where their headquarters are, too. I know Holling fairly well. We had dinner together at Duke Zeibert's the last time I was out to the Hill."

Monica took a sip of her coffee and smiled. It was delicious. She thought she could detect a hint of black walnuts. "Prairie Dog over at The Slip Up told Caleb he'd heard there was a hundred grand fine and a year in prison for killing an eagle."

Quentin snorted and said, "Prairie Dog generally has problems not getting the head on the bottom side of a mug of beer. This time, however, I'm afraid he may be accurate."

Monica felt like ice water was trickling down her spine. "How can that be?"

"Did you ever read the Bible, the Old Testament?"

The lawyer's question surprised her. "Yes, several times. Our folks took us to church regular."

"Then you know how many rules they had back in those days. And that was before there were any such thing as lawyers, let alone a bunch with nothing to do but think up new pain for folks. Our entire government is made up of lawyers who get elected to some political post every so many years by passing a bunch of new rules we all have to live by. The environmental movement is a strong one, and well funded. They also get a lot of press coverage. Eagles, wolves and grizzly bears are mighty interesting and exotic critters. No politician with enough brains to come in out of the rain is going to say anything bad about them. Ranchers and farmers might vote, but the environmental groups have the money and know just where to spend it to further their own interests."

"Then Caleb *is* in a lot of trouble."

"Not necessarily. What we have to do is kill the snake before it bites. I'll give Holling a call and visit with him, give him the facts of the matter. It'd be best for everyone if this mess just went away. A rancher getting arrested for shooting a predator on his own property would polarize a lot of factions. God, the news media would have a field day. Caleb'd be a Messiah trying to save the world to some. To others he'd be more evil than Hannibal Lecter."

"Do you think you can stop this?"

"Why hon," Quentin's Texas drawl was back, "this ain't my first rodeo. When I get done talking with Holling, I'm sure he'll convince the Run Free folks that just dropping this unfortunate incident will be in everyone's best interest."

Monica was feeling relieved. Quentin had that ability. It was one reason clients drove all the way from Dallas and Austin for his services. She smiled and finished her coffee.

"Great coffee, Quentin. Thanks for being a friend."

"Shucks little lady, at the rates I charge I can afford to do favors. I'll send the Nazi by with a sack of coffee later on."

Monica got up, walked behind the desk and gave Quentin a peck on the cheek.

"Getting kissed by a pretty woman beats money any day," he said, grabbing a black cigar from an oak humidor on his desk. He held it up and grinned like a fox. "Genuine Havana. I have them smuggled in with my coffee beans."

"Quentin Miller, you're incorrigible."

"I know, ain't it great?"

The sheriff had her hand on the door knob when the lawyer called after her. "For Pete's sake, tell Caleb to get his damn glasses fixed."

Chapter 8

Dianne Petrov was quite upset with her field assistant, Marsh Wheelan, who sat slumped in a chair across from her desk. He was dressed in clean, pressed camouflage shirt and pants. A pair of aviator sunglasses dangled from his neck by a fluorescent green nylon cord. He seemed unusually quiet and sullen.

It was early afternoon. She hadn't heard a peep from him since yesterday, when he'd radioed from the helicopter after raptor two-eleven met with its unfortunate demise. Dianne was a punctual person. She expected the same courtesy from her employees.

"Marsh," she said in a matronly tone, "I waited here for you until late last night. I tried to call, but your phone was busy. Would you care to explain?"

He shrugged and fidgeted with his sunglasses, all the while thinking he should have been an actor. Winning an Oscar would be a snap. "Uh, Ms. Petrov, ma'am. I'm so terribly sorry about causing you any anxiety. It's just that I was so upset by seeing that poor eagle killed. Then that rancher pointed his gun at us. For a moment I thought both the pilot and I were dead men. There are some awful people in this world. When I got back to my apartment I was so nervous I couldn't quit shaking. I took a shower, lifted the receiver from the phone and went to bed.

"This morning I took a long drive to collect my thoughts. I'm all right now, but I'm sure I'll have nightmares about that terrible incident for years."

In reality Marsh had spent most of the morning at a bank trying to get the check cashed. Fifteen thousand dollars, especially from a tabloid, seemed suspicious to the bird-legged teller. It had taken a lot of threatening and yelling on his part before a vice-president made some phone calls and finally okayed the check to be cashed. The comforting stack of hundred dollar bills was stuffed in his pants pockets as he spoke.

Dianne Petrov sighed. She didn't believe a word he'd said, but he did deserve credit for the teary-eyed performance. Marsh Wheelan was a cold-blooded little weasel who would sell his grandmother's cat for medical experiments. She hadn't reached her position in a male-dominated society without being able to read pricks like a billboard.

"Marsh," she said with just enough sarcasm in her voice to pass a message, "if you can compose yourself from seeing that poor eagle shot, perhaps we should discuss the next releases. We have six more pairs of raptors to release back into the wild. I want to avoid any more disasters. So we'll move farther west. Reagan County has less populated areas than Lone Wolf. We feel that will increase our odds of success greatly."

"Uh, sure, Ms. Petrov," Marsh said haltingly. "Yes, I believe I can manage to carry on." He reached out and dropped a videotape on her desk. "I got some really good pictures of that eagle killer. Once you view it, you'll understand why I was so terribly upset. The good part is there's enough evidence on that tape to convict him in any court."

Dianne shook her short dishwater blond hair and suppressed a grin. She was going to enjoy this. "I've had communications from our Washington headquarters. Their decision is to drop the matter. We've had considerable problems in Montana with some of the wolves we've released into the wild there attacking and killing sheep and cattle. It's bad for public relations when any of our released endangered or threatened species begins preying on domestic livestock. Run Free's counsel has concluded that prosecuting anyone who is simply defending his livelihood would not only result in negative publicity that could affect our revenue base, it might very possibly influence some court decision to go against us."

I don't think you're going to bury THIS case, Marsh thought. "That position just isn't tenable. Our environment must be protected at all cost. If some cretin cowboy can get by with blowing a helpless bald eagle out of the sky, then threatening me with a shotgun, we've already lost the battle to restore the balance of nature."

Dianne Petrov's answer came cold as wind blowing over blue ice. "Knock off the crap, Marsh. I had a long visit with Wes Shelton, the helicopter pilot. According to him, that rancher never pointed any gun at you, let alone threatened. The raptor was eliminated near a cluster of buildings. The pilot mentioned there were chickens running about. Eagles are opportunistic feeders. When birds are available, they'll eat more of those than anything else, even fish. I'm not telling you anything you don't already know. We lost an eagle because we released it in an overly populated area. I don't want to hear anymore of your insipid whining."

Marsh swallowed hard and kept silent until he could form a credible reply. *You witch. I'll see to it that you're well paid back for your insolence.* Being fired at this time wasn't in his plans. Later, when it appeared Run Free was retreating from its stated objective of protecting endangered wildlife would be perfect.

"I'm sorry to hear the pilot didn't interpret the situation in the same light I did. Perhaps you're correct that we put this dreadful affair behind us and continue with our work." He put on his practiced trust me smile. "I'm ready to continue if you are."

He gave in way too easy. The beady-eyed son-of-a-bitch has something up his sleeve. But what? Dianne Petrov knew she would need to keep a close eye on her assistant's activities in the future.

"Okay, let's go over the topo maps of the area north of Big Lake. Perhaps we can plot an area where some raptors won't have much human company."

"Certainly, Ms. Petrov. I'm terribly sorry about our little misunderstanding."

Dianne waited until Marsh had gotten up and was through the doorway before following him to the map room. Having him at her back gave her the uncomfortable feeling of being stalked.

Chapter 9

Caleb entered The Slip Up Saloon with a smiling Hope Rexton close by his side. It was just past seven on a sultry Friday evening. A scattering of black thunderclouds had been able to produce only enough moisture to raise the humidity. One week and a day had passed since Caleb's unfortunate encounter with the eagle. Tonight he felt like a little celebrating for more than one reason.

Early Monday morning, while he was putting away the last of the freshly washed breakfast dishes and nursing a cup of coffee, Quentin Miller had phoned. Somehow, someway, the silver-tongued lawyer had managed to convince the Run Free organization not to prosecute him for shooting their bald eagle. Caleb wondered deeply as to what strings Quentin had pulled to accomplish the feat. The wily attorney seemed to be able to perform more tricks than a Las Vegas magician. It was a comfort to be able to call the lawyer a friend and be able to put this incident behind him. Thankfully, only a handful of people around Lone Wolf knew anything about the eagle. Those who did would keep quiet about the matter, which was just the way Caleb wanted it.

Caleb approached Bruno Leatherwood at Trotter's Hardware Store on Wednesday. The game warden had called him aside and quietly said that he'd wrapped the dead raptor in gunny-sacks, packed it in dry ice and air freighted the remains off to the Wind River Indian Reservation in Riverton, Wyoming. Caleb tried to envision what a headdress made out of the crumpled mess of feathers would look like. He'd quickly given up and driven back to the ranch to work on a bad section of fence.

Today he'd received a pleasant but perplexing surprise in the mail. There had been the usual mountain of junk crammed into the box: a notification that he had qualified as a finalist in a million dollar sweepstakes (sent bulk rate of course); two applications for credit cards with an annual rate to die for; and the normal day's delivery of catalogues touting everything from discount cruises to leather underwear. Among the trash destined for the wastebasket, he found a single first class letter with no return address. He'd opened it to find two crisp twenty dollar bills wrapped inside two sheets of clean white typewriter paper. A hand printed, unsigned note said simply:

"Keep up the good work"

Caleb had absolutely no idea what good work he'd been doing lately but liked the rate of pay. Closer examination showed the letter had been postmarked in New York City. Caleb had never even been to New York, let alone known anyone there who would send him cash.

Not being a man anyone could accuse of looking a gift horse in the mouth, Caleb slipped the green bills into his wallet alongside a lonely five spot and drove back to his ranch shaking his head in wonderment.

A windfall of forty dollars should be put to good use, so Caleb had called Hope at work and asked her to join him for a drink at The Slip Up that evening. The bubbly redhead quickly said yes. Hope always seemed happy to go out anytime he asked.

This evening he'd been forced to pick her up in his battered truck. He would have preferred the car, but Tristan had taken it to San Angelo to see a movie. Caleb found his son having a driver's license hard to fathom. The boy shouldn't have grown up so fast. The car was Laura's old AMC Pacer, not a classy vehicle (kids at school jokingly called it "the yellow pisser"), but it certainly rode a lot more comfortably than his 4 × 4 truck.

Hope didn't seem to mind the dirty, battered pickup in the least. Tonight she wore trim blue jeans and a tight-fitting short sleeve print blouse that molded her willowy charms perfectly. With a wispy bang of flaming hair dangling over her left eye, Hope looked more like twenty than her forty-two years.

Caleb loved being in the company of a lady. The intoxicating sweetness of perfume and soft, happy laughter were utterly delightful. He knew full well these times would always be few and far between. Short of his winning the sweepstakes that had been in today's mail, he would have to remain alone.

"Hey Caleb, you and Hope come over here and join us," Bones Blandon's voice boomed. The mortician was sitting at a table by the bar with Hector Lemmons, Rollie Turner and Quentin Miller.

Hope wrapped her arm around Caleb's as they walked over.

"I don't know about this," Caleb said with feigned concern. "Sharing a table with a lawyer, an undertaker and a one-legged windmill repairman might not be a great idea."

"At least there's no stockbrokers, televangelists or used car salesmen hereabouts," Bones quipped. "I can't understand why folks don't like undertakers. After all, we're the last ones in this world to let you down."

Hope rolled her eyes and moaned while Caleb slid out a chair for her.

"Bones," Quentin said, "if you come out with anything about folks dying to do business with you, I'm going to sue you for wearing out bad jokes in a public place. We've the pleasure of having a beautiful lady in our presence. It'd be a shame to run her off with pedestrian humor."

Caleb took a moment to eye Rollie's artificial leg then scooted his chair in close to Hope. "I see you got your leg back. Where did it turn up this time, or don't you want to talk about it in front of Hope?"

"He lost his leg?" Hope said, incredulous.

"Just the one that's detachable," Prairie Dog said, as he came over to take their order. "Ol' Rollie gets a snoot full ever once in a while when he goes to San Angelo for supplies an' forgets things, like his wooden leg."

"Where did it turn up this time?" Caleb asked again.

"Some old lady saw it sticking out of a dumpster," Bones said. "I guess she darn near had a heart attack, then called the police saying she'd found a dead body. The same officer that had found the leg before received the call. Monica brought his leg back on one of her trips to the city. She said the cops went and carved Rollie's name and phone number on it to save 'em time in the future."

Hope broke into an amused smile. She loved being with happy people. That was one reason she enjoyed spending time with Caleb. In spite of his troubles and heartaches, he'd kept the ability to laugh. A vast difference from her mean-spirited ex-husband. His sole gratification in life seemed to come from hurting others, and her. After a final beating which had ruptured her spleen, she'd filed for divorce, taken back her maiden name and moved to Lone Wolf. Hope only regretted she hadn't done it much sooner.

"What would you like, little lady?" Prairie Dog asked.

"Just a draft beer," Hope replied, much to the bartender's relief. Women had the darnedest habit of ordering setups for mixed drinks he didn't have a clue how to fix.

"Same for me, and bring all of us one," Caleb said happily, plunking down one of the mysterious twenties that had come in the mail. It made him feel downright magnanimous.

Rollie Turner took a nip from the bottle wrapped inside a brown paper bag that sat on the table in front of him and grinned at Hope. "It's too bad I don't have an artificial arm too. Then I could tell folks it costs me an arm *and* a leg to visit San Angelo."

Hope chuckled and said, "It sounds like you might be better off ordering what you need and having it freighted in."

Rollie's bushy eyebrows furrowed with disapproval. "Why, and deprive all those poor barmaids of their livelihood. That would be a heartless thing for me to do."

Hector Lemmons joined in, "And if ol' Rollie ever does more than just tip 'em, Missus Turner will put knuckle marks all over his skinny body."

Prairie Dog waddled over doing a tenuous balancing act with the full tray of beer mugs. To everyone's surprise he managed to get them delivered without spilling a single one, then reached out and picked up Caleb's twenty.

Caleb motioned toward the bill in Prairie Dog's hand. "You guy's know that's the darnedest thing. There were two of those twenties came in today's mail. No return address, no name, nothing. Just a note telling me to keep up the good work."

Hector eyed Quentin Miller. "You can bet your hole card it wasn't a lawyer. They're tighter than chrome on a bumper. Our legal eagle here hasn't bought a round of drinks since Clinton was in office."

Quentin didn't respond to the old man's ribbing. His expression grew serious. "There's an old aphorism I've found to be true most of the time. It says 'beware of Greeks bearing gifts'."

"Nope," Caleb said. "Whoever it was, they're from New York City, not Greece, leastwise that's where the letter was postmarked."

Prairie Dog shrugged his shoulders. "I don't know what there is to worry about. I'd just spend their money an' keep on doing whatever it was that made 'em happy in the first place."

Caleb said, "I'd be glad to if I had a clue what tickled their fancy. Since I don't, I suppose we should just enjoy ourselves."

"Sounds like a plan," Prairie Dog said, as he headed off to the cash register.

Quentin spoke up, "Still, I'm concerned. People don't go sending out cash in the mail for no reason. However, if the world wasn't full of fools and idiots, I'd be out of a job." He pulled out his wallet, extracted a ten spot, laid it on the table and glared at Hector Lemmons. "Tighter than chrome on a bumper?"

"Gentlemen and lady of the jury," Hector replied, bringing a chuckle from the group. "I retract that statement."

The conversation drifted to the weather, or lack of it. Rollie maintained that the water table was stable and no drought appeared imminent. Hector went into great detail describing how dry it had been in the fifties and how little the windmiller knew about weather cycles.

The lawyer soon tired of the seemingly unending weather report. "Hey, Prairie Dog bring your paper over here so we can check out the headlines."

Quentin was referring to the bartenders long standing subscription to *The Weekly World Probe.* It had become a tradition at The Slip Up to spend Friday evenings poking fun at the hoaxy tabloid.

"They sure hit the nail on the head that last issue," Rollie said with a grin, while Prairie Dog fished out the paper from a drawer underneath the ornate brass cash register.

Hector winked at Hope. "Yup, they sure did, an' had the pictures to prove it, too. Hillary Clinton's actually a space alien from Alpha Centauri. She's going to run for president with Slick Willy as her running mate. Then when her new health care plan goes into effect, they're going to start dumping vitamins in our drinking water to keep people from getting sick. The catch is it'll also cause everyone to become sterile. No more kids. No more people. In a hundred years the space aliens can take over the joint and never have to fire a shot."

"I don't see anything farfetched about any of that," Caleb said seriously. "You fellows obviously have a distrust of the news media."

Quentin chuckled. "A month ago they ran photos of Elvis buying groceries at a supermarket in Lake Havasu City, Arizona. It's an obvious fact the reporters who work for that paper take their research seriously and do the fourth estate proud."

"Amen to that," Prairie Dog said unrolling the tabloid as he walked. "Without these fine folks, Friday evenings at The Slip Up would be a tad dull."

With a showman's flourish the pudgy bartender brandished the weeks headline without looking at it first.

Rollie Turner jumped nearly spilling his beer. "Holy shit."

A slight gasp issued from Hope's mouth. The attorney's and Hector Lemmons's eyes widened.

Caleb froze as if he were chiseled from granite.

Prairie Dog flipped the tabloid over to see what all of the fuss was about. He thought they were teasing him. Then he read the headline. The usually loquacious barkeep was at a loss for words.

The caption screamed in black words, "Texas Eagle Killer Caught On Videotape." Scarlet streams of blood dripped from the heading around a page-size photograph of a rancher with a defiant sneer painted on his face. The man held a dead bald eagle in one hand, in the other was a shotgun with a slight wisp of smoke drifting from the large barrel. There could be absolutely no doubt as to who the eagle killer was. The man sat at their table.

His name was Caleb Starr.

★ ★ ★ ★ ★

Part II

★ ★ ★ ★ ★

Threatening to bind our souls with secular chains:
Help us to save free conscience from the paw
of hireling wolves, whose gospel is their maw.

John Milton

All hell broke loose . . .

John Milton, *Paradise Lost*

Chapter 10

"I—I thought it was over," Caleb stuttered, his faltering voice broke the chill silence that had enveloped the group like a fog.

"Then that *is* you," Rollie exclaimed. "Oh, my God!"

Hope grasped Caleb's hand. "There must be some mistake. That shoddy paper never reports the truth." She hesitated, trying to keep her fragile control. "Does it?"

"So Caleb went and shot an eagle," Hector Lemmons said matter-of-factly. "Those phony environmentalist S.O.B.s shouldn't have gone and tossed 'em out around here in the first place. What did they expect, every rancher in the country to just grin and feed 'em baby lambs and calves? Eagles are nothing but predators that just go a killing things."

Quentin Miller kept his eyes fixed on the tabloid Prairie Dog still held. The lawyer's speech was measured, clinical. "The time for opinions has passed. Now that the dogs have been unleashed, what Caleb must do is get ready for the battle of his life. One thing we can depend on: a whole bunch of government agencies are going to be fighting over who gets the biggest piece of Caleb Starr's rear end. This matter has come down to the letter of the law. That means common sense will be thrown out the window."

Prairie Dog took another glance at the paper and shook his head. "I don't understand. If Caleb here did shoot an eagle, what's the big deal? It's just a bird, and I'm sure he must have been protecting his livestock or something."

"Yeah," Hector growled, "since when can't a man defend his

own private property?"

Caleb turned to face Hope. Her green eyes were wide and moist. "It came swooping down out of the sun after my chickens. I thought it was just a hawk. Honest to God, I didn't know it was a bald eagle. My glasses were still in the house. Then that helicopter came—"

Quentin Miller interrupted. "Caleb, as your attorney and your friend I'm telling you not to say another word about this to anyone. This town will be crawling with reporters and investigators real soon. From here on I'll do all of the talking. If anyone asks you anything, you send them to me."

Hope bit nervously at her lip, then glanced from Caleb to the lawyer. "Are you saying Caleb might be arrested?"

"Little lady," Quentin said softly, "there are many laws on the books, both state and federal, to protect endangered and threatened wildlife. It's a certainty Caleb will be indicted and arrested. Right now he's standing in the swamp with water up to his neck and the alligators are on their way."

Rollie shook his head in disbelief. "How many people read that rag anyway?"

Prairie Dog folded the paper and handed it to Quentin Miller. "Oh, about two million I'd reckon."

Only a sob from Hope Rexton broke the heavy black silence.

The sparse black thunderheads had drifted on, leaving a canopy of twinkling stars and a yellow half-moon in their wake. Wordlessly Caleb and Hope walked side by side in the pale light as the rancher saw her safely to her door. Hope lived in a small frame rental house alongside the highway on the outskirts of Lone Wolf. A white picket fence gave the cottage the appearance of something out of a Norman Rockwell painting. Hundreds of chirping crickets keeping track of the temperature while singing for a mate were the only sounds that broke the stillness.

The couple stopped in front of the stoop. Hope turned and grasped Caleb's calloused hand. He noticed twin streaks of black mascara running from her emerald eyes down rouged cheeks. He slipped a white handkerchief from his shirt pocket and dabbed at them.

"On the bright side," he said happily, "I'd venture you weren't bored tonight. Myself, I haven't had so much fun since the time the hogs ate my little brother."

In spite of everything terrible that had happened, Hope Rexton threw back her head and burst out laughing. Then, to Caleb's dismay, the redhead threw both arms around his neck and standing on tiptoes planted her ruby lips full on his. They kissed long and deep, neither wanting to give up the moment for harsh reality.

When they parted, Caleb still held her shoulders in his strong hands. In the waning light Hope could see the big man's eyes were bordered with tears. She summoned all her resolve and said, "Let's do this again, real soon."

Hope wanted to say more, say something, anything to ease the agony she knew he was enduring. Her voice broke and with a shudder she spun and vanished through the door of her house, silently as some fey creature of the night.

Caleb quickly strode back to his pickup. Lingering would only prolong the pain. And he had two other unsavory talks yet to perform. As he drove to his ranch, the thick sultry air that blew through the open window by his side couldn't carry away the lingering perfume of a beautiful lady from whom he must forever remain apart.

As Caleb had expected, Jesus was sitting alone on his porch under the familiar yellow light reading a book. Why anyone ever thought a yellow bulb wouldn't attract bugs was a mystery to Caleb. A cloud of millers and other flying insects darted incessantly hither and yon around the brightness.

He clicked on the dome light and surveyed his wristwatch. It was nearly ten-thirty. Tristan had orders to be home before eleven, but the way his son's attitude and behavior had deteriorated, Caleb figured he likely wouldn't be in before midnight.

Caleb flicked off the light then turned the key and stilled the rough idling-engine. He sat in the cab of the pickup awhile gathering his thoughts and cherishing the calm night sounds of the west Texas desert. The distant bawling of a calf told him the animal had temporally lost its mother. He could decipher the songs of country life as easily as old Jesus read a novel.

Skills such as these used to be valuable ones. A man could depend on them to see him through tough times his entire life. That was before the world had gone topsy-turvy for ranchers, farmers, oil field operators and he guessed also loggers or anyone who made a living from the land. Not so many years ago, drought and market conditions were the main concerns. Then, insidiously as the cancer that had taken his wife, the faceless, nameless "they" of the government had grown to control every facet of life. Not all government sponsored programs were bad; water conservation, rabies and mesquite control were beneficial. Yet all made inroads on personal freedom, a trade-off for cradle to grave security bestowed by a benevolent, all caring, all knowing bureaucracy.

Government by bureaucracy can only succeed by ruthless and vicious punishment of any transgressions, whether real or perceived. Even Bruno Leatherwood's rule book of game laws was thicker than the Bible. Caleb could only imagine the thousands and thousands of pages of law that contained indecipherable regulations that were meant to be enforced on the businesses and citizens of this country. This caused Caleb to remember a fat, grinning sheriff he'd seen long ago on television; "You can't make a move without gettin' busted boy," the officer would say gleefully. Obviously very happy someone had made a mistake so he could tout his authority.

Now Caleb Starr was going to be the party who got busted. Strange, he didn't feel like a criminal. He hadn't broken any of the moral codes instilled in him by parents, preachers or teachers. Still he held no doubt the law would soon make an example of him.

Quentin Miller had told Caleb to be in his office by nine tomorrow morning. The lawyer wanted to go over their options. The normally cool-headed and calm attorney had seemed rattled by that tabloid headline. Caleb figured if a knowledgeable man like Quentin Miller was upset, he should be doubly so.

You can't make a move without getting busted, Caleb thought, gazing into the night with a faraway expression. *If you can't fix it, don't let it worry you to death.* Those words were his dad's.

Both his parents had been loving, intelligent, kind. And both had been killed in a fiery head-on car crash while Caleb was in Vietnam saving the world from communism.

He shrugged off the burden of memories as if they physically rested on his shoulders and climbed from the cab of the truck. Jesus had to be informed, then Tristan.

First he shook a cigarette from a pack he'd bought at a convenience store on the way home. After a fruitless search of the pickup for matches, he went into his house and lit the smoke on the pilot light of the kitchen range. He inhaled deeply and broke into a fit of coughing.

These things used to taste good. I must have been crazy.

As soon as he caught his breath, Caleb walked over to the sink, turned on the water and drowned the cigarette. He tossed the soggy butt into the trash, thought for a moment, then added the rest of the pack. On his way to visit with Jesus he grabbed a six pack of beer from the refrigerator. At least one vice was necessary to get through this day.

"Hello, *señor.* For what good occasion do you bring beer?" Jesus said happily, placing a bookmark and setting his book aside. It was a Dean Koontz novel, which surprised Caleb. Usually the old man read only westerns. "For whatever it is, I shall give thanks. Beer is not called nectar of the gods without reason."

Caleb pulled a can loose from the plastic ring, popped the tab and handed it to Jesus. "If you're on a first name basis with any gods I'm not familiar with, I'd appreciate it if you'd give them a holler."

"No *señor,* just *Dios,* who you already know." The wrinkles in the old man's brow deepened. "Men do not usually call upon *Dios* unless there is trouble. I think this is a failing, for He should be thanked also when good comes our way. I also think perhaps that is not the case this night."

"You're a smart man," Caleb replied as he popped open another beer. "We've got a load of problems headed our way, and the Devil's driving the truck."

Jesus took a long drink, crossed his spindly legs, leaned back in his rocker and said, "It is well to always remember that *Dios* never closes a door without opening a window. Tell me of these problems."

Caleb did. In careful detail beginning with the day he accidentally shot the eagle and ending with Prairie Dog's unfurling of the tabloid with his picture on the cover.

The old Mexican finished his beer, then crushed the can with a surprising show of strength.

A flash of headlights stopped Jesus's reply. Tristan was home. Caleb bit his lip then called his son over and repeated the story he'd just told Jesus.

To the rancher's wonderment Tristan turned supportive. "Dad, I don't know what to say, but whatever comes, I'll help out anyway I can."

"I knew you would, Son," Caleb said, his eyes misty again. He handed Jesus another beer. "I'd reckon with Quentin Miller's help, the three of us can handle anything."

Jesus set the unopened beer beside his book and said solemnly, "We will need to stay together. For *El Diablo* is coming to Lone Wolf."

Chapter 11

Marsh Wheelan was livid. His name wasn't "reliable source." When he'd picked up a copy of *The Weekly World Probe* this morning and not seen his name on the cover he'd wadded the rag up and tossed it in the gutter. The main reason he'd sold that videotape of an ignorant sodbuster holding a dead bald eagle was to get his name in front of millions of people.

That little bitch had lied to him. Once she had the videotape, every promise she'd made him was forgotten. The reporter had given him her word that he would get credit for those photographs.

Damn it all, at least some of the low-lifes who read that miserable paper had to be registered voters. You just can't trust anyone these days.

Of course the fifteen grand hadn't been hard to take.

Ah, and the contacts he'd made. Some very wealthy people—the only ones who really count for anything in this world—knew his name and what he had done to save the environment.

He would likely need both the money and the contacts now.

Dianne Petrov sat across the desk from him glaring back with the cold-eyed countenance of a traffic cop. Marsh figured she'd called him in for this Saturday morning meeting just to fire him. There was no need to hide behind a facade of servitude and geniality any longer.

"Well, *Dinah,*" Marsh said with open contempt. "Do you have a real problem, or is it just that time of the month?"

Dianne Petrov refused to lose her temper as Marsh had hoped. Her reply was icy and controlled. "I don't think you can comprehend the damage your rash actions may have caused. The phone calls started yesterday when the first issues of *The Weekly World Probe* came out. There never was any question where they got those photos and who their source in our organization was. The tabloid owners agreed to send us a copy of the check they gave you. Especially when a United States senator asked them to. Also, the reporter said you were quite anxious to be given credit for the pictures.

"Our goal at Run Free is to peacefully co-exist with landowners as much as possible—."

"And those goals are wrong," Marsh barked. "You can't save the planet by using kid gloves. I've done more to save wildlife by this one action than the entire foundation has accomplished in years. That's why I've decided to resign and start my own environmental group."

Dianne Petrov's lips narrowed into a thin grin. "It's a little late for that. The records show I fired you last night. You're just here to pick up your stuff so I don't have to set eyes on you again."

"Ha!" Marsh shouted. "If anyone in Run Free thinks I give a rat's ass about being fired, they're wrong. It will only benefit me when I begin showing how a true environmental activist does business. Donors will be standing in line to support the Wheelan Foundation when I advocate tougher laws and severe gun control so defenseless creatures like that eagle can live in safety—."

"Stow it, Marsh! You're phony as a counterfeit hundred-dollar bill. About you forming your own organization, you may have bigger problems. Senator Hollingsworth and the president of Run Free are quite upset with you and your libelous actions. The damage you caused to our organization could be in the millions. There is a meeting with our law firm this morning to prepare a lawsuit that will destroy you. One sweet thing about lawyers—as long as they're fed, they're just like bulldogs; they bite down hard and never let go. Senator Hollingsworth assured me our lawyers will be well fed."

This was one eventuality Marsh Wheelan hadn't considered. His silence and pasty expression conveyed that fact.

"Now get out of my office," Dianne Petrov said, then added gleefully, "and try to have a nice day."

Chapter 12

The noted attorney, Quentin Miller, drummed his fingers nervously on the oak cigar hamper he kept on his desk. Caleb found the lawyer's silence ominous. After what seemed to be an eternity, he watched Quentin extract a long, black cigar from the hamper, snip the end off with a cutter, then use up three matches just to light it. He puffed a cloud of acrid smoke toward the ceiling and finally spoke. "My old great-granddaddy would have found the son of a bitch who sold those pictures to that shoddy tabloid and dispensed some justice from Judge Colt."

"It was me shooting a gun that started this mess," Caleb replied. "And old John Hardin *did* wind up getting himself shot."

"I know," Quentin sighed. "The sad part of the matter is the whole affair had been quietly laid to rest. When the press gets hold of something, they're worse than a pack of wild dogs. Every government agency you ever heard of and a bunch you haven't are going to be forced into action by all of the additional publicity."

"I don't understand what you mean by *more* publicity. Isn't that article in *The Weekly World Probe* the end of it?"

"No, that was just the beginning," the lawyer mouthed his cigar. "I've made some discreet inquires to Houston and Dallas. I have friends at the major newspapers there. The Associated Press has already picked up the story and is sending out reporters to verify it. Killing a bald eagle will sell a hell of a lot of papers. It's a sure bet the major television networks will be moving on it also. *Geraldo, Sixty Minutes* or *Dateline* would have a field day with this."

Caleb felt weak, as if his backbone had turned to rubber. "Oh my God."

"A little prayer to the Big Guy upstairs might be a good idea. The news coverage will give us very few options. We can plead you not guilty without looking too foolish, but with the video tape we can't win in court."

There was a copy of *The Weekly World Probe* on Quentin's desk. Caleb pointed to the snarl painted on his face in the picture. "How did they make me look like that? I've seen serial killers on television that looked kinder than I do there."

"Computers can manipulate photographs in short order. How do you think they can show Bill Clinton shaking hands with a space alien? What we need to concern ourselves with are the original photos of you lifted from that tape. Also, there's the fact that you gave the carcass of that eagle to a Texas game warden and admitted killing it. Bruno's not going to lie under oath."

"I never expected that he would," Caleb shook his head sadly. "I'm not going to get out of this without going to jail, am I? Who's going to take care of Tristan and the ranch? Jesus is too old and stove up to do the work."

"Don't go locking yourself away just yet," the lawyer said firmly. "It will be up to a judge to decide if that happens. I'm betting once we present our case, you'll not have to worry about spending any time in the Greystone Hotel."

"But what about the fines? Prairie Dog said it was a hundred grand! You know I don't have that kind of money."

Quentin held out his hand palm down. "Settle down. Everything is negotiable. The hardest part will be the waiting, but let me worry about handling the judge. I've found, for the most part, they're fair, reasonable people."

The office door swung open, and Rosemary marched in carrying coffee. She smiled at Quentin then shot daggers from her eyes at Caleb before she stomped from the room.

"I think she hates me for killing that eagle," Caleb remarked.

"Pay her no mind. Rosy drowns a kitten first thing every morning so she can start the day off right."

"Most folks are going to think I'm as evil as I look on the cover of the tabloid. A bald eagle is our national symbol. Quentin, I think I could handle jail better than having people hate me."

The lawyer took a heavy puff on his cigar. "I'm not going to sugar coat the facts. There are three factions: the first is going to be out to destroy you. These are vocal and radical environmental organizations and individuals. The second is going to take your side in defending your land—that's where those twenty dollar bills came from. This bunch will maybe pay some of your legal fees, but they're small in number and some of them will be so radical they'll cause more trouble than they're worth."

"That's only two. You mentioned three factions."

Quentin grimaced. "Here are the real problems: agents of various government bureaucracies. They're going to try to look good for the press, their superiors and that first group I told you about. I said earlier, reporters are like a pack of hungry dogs. A government bureaucrat with a rule book is the most vicious creature on the face of the earth. You'll have your work cut out for you to remain levelheaded. Don't even volunteer a single word. They'll twist it, then use it against you. Be cooperative, but no matter how nice those agents may seem, remember the only thing they really care about in this world is their career and that rule book of theirs."

"Who's going to arrest me? I couldn't take it if Monica had to."

"Right now I doubt anyone knows for certain. They're going to argue jurisdiction for awhile. The crime will most certainly be prosecuted on a federal level, so that should get Monica off the hook. You might spend a little time in the Lone Wolf jail until I get a bail hearing, however."

"Quentin, there's no way I can raise a bond. You know the ranch is mortgaged to the hilt."

The lawyer put on his first smile of the day. "Hector Lemmons and I had breakfast together this morning. He said he'd be proud to stand your bail. If I can schedule things right, you'll be in and out in less than an hour. Now get back to work, and if anybody, I don't care who or what they say they are, comes around, keep quiet and refer them to me."

"Why did Hector agree to help me? He's my neighbor."

"He's also your friend."

"Thanks for saying that. I reckon I should get home. Tristan's waiting to help me repair the roof on the barn."

"Tell Tristan hello for me and not to worry, and that goes for you, too."

Caleb finished the last of his coffee and trudged out of the office. He was careful not to even glance at the sharp-eyed secretary when he passed by her desk.

On his way home from the lawyer's office, Caleb dropped by Trotter's Hardware Store to buy ten pounds of galvanized flat-head nails and five gallons of roof patching tar. Lately the barn roof had begun to leak so bad during the infrequent rainstorms that Jesus joked that a person would probably stay drier if they remained outside.

Repairing a roof was hot, miserable work, conducted far more feet from God's firm earth than Caleb cared for. Having Tristan available to help out would be a great time to accomplish the task. The boy wasn't troubled by height in the least.

John Trotter and his wife, Dagny, had bought the long established hardware store from old Sam Williams just last year, enabling Sam to retire and attempt to catch that hundred-pound catfish he swore lived in Lake Nasworthy.

The Trotters had moved to Lone Wolf from Los Angeles, California, saying they wanted to raise their three children in a safe, rural environment. They had changed the name of the store to their own from Lone Wolf Ranch Supply, which it had been called since the twenties, and joined up with a national chain, which considerably raised the prices on most items. Still, the store wouldn't support the family in the style they desired. Dagny had taken a job in San Angelo for additional income, leaving John to tend the business.

Caleb strode up to the counter and gave John Trotter his modest order. He shuddered when he noticed a copy of *The Weekly World Probe* laying on the back counter.

"Eagles are magnificent and treasured creatures, Mister Starr," Trotter said icily. "My wife and I discussed your killing of one of those splendid birds and have decided it would be bad business to continue carrying you on our books. I'm sure you understand; we must set an example for our children."

John Trotter then handed the shocked Caleb a white envelope. "This is your current statement. Prompt payment will be required. In the future, any purchases must be on a cash basis."

Caleb's dismay quickly yielded to fury. A man can only swallow so much anger before it boils over. "You sanctimonious bastard. Here I've done business with you even after you jacked up prices, and now I'm not even welcome in your store. And to top that off, I don't even get the courtesy to tell what really happened."

Trotter backed up, ashen faced. "Don't get violent. I'll call the sheriff!"

Caleb sighed. "Wish you'd shown your colors before now. I'll get a check out to you when I get home. It'll be a pleasure driving to San Angelo. There's a lot better class of folks there to do business with."

The rancher crammed the envelope deep in his jeans pocket and stomped out, nearly colliding with Hector Lemmons at the door.

"Where's the fire?" Hector asked.

"Trotter ran me off and told me to pay my bill up. He says it'll set a bad example for his kids to do business with me after what happened."

Hector glared at John Trotter. "Is that a fact?"

"Please don't be upset, Mister Lemmons," Trotter said, fawning. "This decision has absolutely nothing to do with you. Why, you are our most valuable customer."

"Not any more I'm not," Hector growled. "It's time you learned a lesson about living in a small town and sticking by your neighbors. While you're in a bill figurin' mood, add mine up, too."

Caleb couldn't help but feel satisfied when he climbed into his pickup for the drive home.

Tristan and Jesus were in the shade of the open barn door when Caleb pulled up and shut off the engine. In spite of his arthritis, the old man always pitched in to help when he could. The long extension ladder was already in place for repairing the roof.

"Dad, I'll do all of the work up there," Tristan said, nodding his head upwards. "All you'll need to do is hand me up the material."

"You know something, Son," Caleb said, "it's been a mighty long time since we've gone fishing. That roof won't leak any until the next time it rains. Dry as this summer's been, it likely won't rain before fall."

Tristan's face melted with disbelief. "Do you mean it?"

"Sure, lets all take the day off. Jesus, if you'll help Tristan get the tackle ready, I'll go take care of a little matter in the house. Then we can drop by the store and get some fried chicken, potato chips and cold drinks. We'll make a time of it. Perhaps we'll catch enough for a big fish fry tomorrow."

"That will be nice," Jesus said with a smile. "I have some frozen chicken livers and two cartons of worms in my icebox. It has been a long while since we have gone fishing, but I think the worms will still be all right."

Caleb made a mental note to buy some fresh worms when they stopped for groceries. "I'll only be a moment. It don't take long to write out a check."

Tristan watched as his dad headed off toward the house. "You know, Jesus, I never can figure out what he'll do from one minute to the next. The last I heard we'd be pounding nails the rest of the day."

"Your father has many troubles. We should help him to forget them if we can. Fishing is always good for the soul."

"I'll bet you a quarter I'll catch a bigger one than you will," Tristan said happily.

"Your money will come in handy. My pipe tobacco is nearly gone. Now, my young friend, let us get our fishing poles ready so we can eat catfish tomorrow night."

Chapter 13

A mirror-like moon hung among glittering myriads of stars as the trio drove toward the town of Lone Wolf on their way back to the ranch. Jesus was immensely proud of himself. Not only had he caught a good-sized channel catfish that weighed at least six pounds, he also had filleted out dozens of plump sun perch and placed them in the cooler.

Caleb and Tristan's best efforts had been returned to the river to grow up. Neither minded. Just spending time together by the slow-moving water had been reward enough.

"The secret of catching a big fish is to chew black tobacco and then spit some on the bait," Jesus said knowingly. "The fish cannot resist such sweet temptation."

"I'd rather have a girlfriend than a catfish," Tristan said with a feigned shudder, reminding Caleb just how much and how quickly the boy had grown up.

"*Si,*" Jesus said with a twinkle in his eye. "But in my day the *señoritas* were not so picky as they are these days. A man who chewed tobacco and caught big fish to eat had many flowers to choose from."

Caleb chuckled. "Jesus, are you trying to tell us Ernesta used to let you chew tobacco?"

"Oh no, *señor.* She was one of the picky ones. A rose without thorns would not be as beautiful. Still, to catch a big fish, it is necessary to chew tobacco."

The road they traveled on, a gravel access to several concrete dams along the Rocky River, exited to the highway where the only motel in town and the Lone Wolf Inn Steakhouse sat side by side. Tonight the parking lot was packed with late model cars.

"They are very busy this night," Jesus remarked, staring at the unusually large number of vehicles.

"Yeah," Tristan said. "There must be a party or something going on."

More like a lynching, Caleb thought, wondering if he was the only one who noticed that most of the license plates on those cars were government issue.

The heavy silence that rode with them back to the ranch told Caleb that he wasn't alone in his observations.

Caleb's Lone Starr Ranch set back a mile from the highway at the base of a low limestone ridge covered with stunted cedar. Alongside the main road there was a pipe gate at the entrance that could be closed and locked but never was. A steel grated cattle guard kept any errant cattle that evaded a fence on ranch property. Someone entering a ranch for nefarious reasons was nearly unheard of in Lone Wolf County.

Tonight, however, a white van was parked in front of the main house, bathed in moonlight. Two men, one of whom had a potbelly and long scraggly beard, were leaning against it, smoking. At the pickup's approach they bolted to attention and threw down their cigarettes.

The slender and clean shaven of the two, who wore a tie and suit jacket in spite of the heat, ran toward the truck. A metallic object in his hand glistened in the yellow light. The chubby person threw open the back door of the van and reached inside.

Caleb's first thought was the man running toward them clasped a gun. He bolted from the cab and placed himself between the perceived weapon and his son and Jesus. Closer inspection disclosed that instead of a gun, the man with a tie held a cordless microphone. Squinting through the dim light, Caleb read the words lettered neatly in red on the side of the van.

WRBC BROADCASTING
Mobile Television Studio
Houston, Texas

Caleb swallowed hard, knowing what was coming. He was angry that these reporters had violated the sanctity of his home. The act of trespassing on private property simply wasn't done in west Texas. These people obviously needed a remedial course in country etiquette.

"This ranch is private property," Caleb said firmly.

The man with the microphone ignored him and plunged ahead to within a few feet of where Caleb stood.

Suddenly, twin floodlights on a shoulder mounted camera held by the bearded man illuminated Caleb and the pickup. The rancher blinked his eyes into focus and found himself staring into the face of the reporter. He was just a kid, maybe in his early twenties. In the glare of the spotlights, his eyes were flat and lifeless as his expression.

The young man twisted his head toward the van. "Let me know when we're rolling, Jim."

"You're on," a voice shouted from behind the glare.

The reporter now stood at Caleb's side and faced the camera with a chiseled smile. "We're broadcasting from the Lone Starr Ranch where a bald eagle was allegedly blasted from the sky just last week. The killing of this protected icon of freedom and our national heritage was caught on film by a man from Run Free, an organization dedicated to the preservation of endangered wildlife. Mister Caleb Starr, owner of the ranch and the man who was caught on tape, gun in hand, immediately after the eagle's demise, is by my side."

The microphone was thrust in Caleb's startled face. He couldn't understand how this newsman knew who he was, then he realized his picture had been in front of millions.

"Mister Starr, please let us hear *your* version of this terrible incident," the still nameless reporter said.

Everything had happened so fast, so sudden, that Caleb didn't have time to think before he spoke. This was exactly how the news crew had planned it. Rattle them and ruin them was Layton Deevers's motto. He hadn't become the youngest investigative reporter the station ever had without being very good at getting a story. Layton idolized Geraldo and modeled his own weekly thirty minute exposé, *Inside Texas,* after the famous journalist's style.

Caleb blurted, "Uh, I—I really didn't know it was an eagle."

"Then you do admit you killed it?"

"My lawyer, Mister, uh, Miller, Quentin Miller. I wisht you'd talk to him."

"This is the time to tell the viewing public your side of the story, Mister Starr. A wise man would make good use of it," the reporter said in calm, even words.

"You're on my land. I'm asking you real nice to leave," Caleb said, gathering his thoughts.

"We have come a long distance to interview you, sir. Surely you're not afraid to speak the truth."

"No, gol darn it, I'm not. This just isn't right. Now I'm not asking, I'm telling you to get off my ranch."

A door squeaked open behind Caleb, and Tristan appeared by his side. "You heard my dad. Leave right now, or I'll call my aunt. She's the sheriff, and we'll have you arrested."

The reporter's face molded into a satisfied smile. He shoved the microphone toward Tristan. "Young man, would the Sheriff of Lone Wolf County be your father's sister?"

"Yes, Sir," Tristan answered politely and honestly, just as he had been taught to do.

Don't even volunteer a single word. They'll twist it, then use it against you, Quentin Miller's good advice jolted Caleb like a lightning bolt. Desperately, he tried to think of some way to head off the damage he knew had been caused to Monica.

The reporter was quicker. He spun to face the camera. "Ladies and gentleman, we now know that the alleged eagle killer's sister is the sheriff of this county. Could that be why the laws protecting our national symbol have not been enforced? This and other questions surrounding this shameful incident will surely be the focus of investigators. Has nepotism allowed landowners to scoff at environmental laws or will justice win out?"

"Get off my land," Caleb growled through clenched teeth.

"Mister Starr, we are still awaiting your version of the story. Certainly you want to tell our viewers what happened that hot afternoon to incite you to act as you did."

"Not another damn word," Caleb spat as he stepped close to the man, his fists clenched. "You've been warned to pack up and get!"

The reporter had been in tight situations before, yet was often successful in coaxing an account from angry people. Sometimes getting them mad was the key. He stared at the rancher like a rattlesnake eyeing a field mouse.

"Mister Starr, with all due respect, only guilty people refuse to talk on camera."

"I told you I'm not saying anything more."

Caleb heard a door slam on the pickup. From the corner of his eye he saw Jesus limp around to the bed of the truck. The old Mexican reached over the tail gate and lifted out the catfish that still had enough life left in it to thrash wildly on the chain stringer.

"Perhaps *señor,*" Jesus said, "these *pendejos* need some

encouragement to do as you ask and leave your fine ranch."

Caleb and Tristan watched in disbelief as the old man began twirling the fish like a lariat while heading for the now wide-eyed reporter.

"The fins of a catfish have a poison," Jesus said. "It will cause much pain."

"I'm being attacked!" Layton Deevers cried. "Jim, Jim tell me you're getting this," he said backing quickly toward the van.

The spotlight jiggled with the cameraman's laughter. "It's just a fish," the man behind the glare said.

"My God, get us out of here, these people are crazy!" The investigative reporter made one quick stand, composed himself and said to the camera. "This is Layton Deevers reporting from the ranch of the alleged eagle killer Caleb Starr. As you can see we are being forced away by threats of violence."

Deevers narrowly averted a swipe from the catfish before he jumped into the van and slammed the door shut. The cameraman flipped off the floodlights. Even in the pale moonlight, the bearded man's grin was plain. He nodded with satisfaction at Jesus, laid the camera away, climbed into the driver's seat, started the news van and calmly drove away.

"I'm sorry this happened," Caleb said.

"That young *gringo* has no *cojones,*" Jesus remarked, obviously happy with himself.

"Yeah," Caleb replied, "only it isn't wise to go swinging things at folks like those even if it is only a half-dead catfish. They can cause a passel of trouble."

Tristan placed a hand on his dad's shoulder. "At least they're gone."

"Yes, Son, but I'm afraid this is just the beginning, not the end."

Jesus surveyed his catfish in the moonlight. "I am glad I did not hit that *pendejo* with my good fish. The meat might have gone bad."

Caleb grew morose and silent. *They'll twist it, then use it against you.* After a long moment he hoisted the cooler from the pickup, causing a sharp pain to shoot up the middle of his back.

As he trudged to the house with his burden, Caleb had an inward impression that he knew how a woman who had been raped must feel.

Chapter 14

The harsh ringing of the telephone on the stand by his bed shook Caleb awake. It had been a night of fitful sleep, plagued with disjointed nightmares, none of which made sense in the light of day. He did remember being pursued by a screaming eagle the size of a small airplane. It had fiery, angry eyes and talons long as swords. Just as the curved claws were ready to rip him to shreds, he had been jolted to consciousness by the phone.

A quick glance to the ticking Regulator wall clock showed the time to be after six. He should be out of bed by now anyway. He never wanted to talk to a soul until he'd had a cup of black coffee in the morning.

Caleb made certain he was speaking into the correct end of the receiver, then said groggily, "The person on the other end of this thing had better not be trying to sell me something."

"Caleb, this is Monica," his sister's concerned voice answered. "We need to talk. Are you by yourself?"

"Of course I'm alone," he said, recognizing too late the sharpness in his voice. The very idea that he might have a lady in the bedroom with him was ludicrous.

"I meant, can we speak openly?"

"Uh, sure, Monica. What's the problem?"

"It's plural, Caleb. I mean there's all kinds of problems standing around the station guzzling coffee as we speak. There's over a dozen Feds in my office. Six are FBI. The others are from different agencies, a couple I've never even heard of before. I'm in the john talking on my cellular."

Caleb suddenly felt very awake. "I supposed this would happen a little later on. Are they coming to arrest me?"

"I'm sure that will happen, but I don't have a clue when. All they're doing right now is asking a lot of questions and arguing among themselves. My guess is whoever winds up with jurisdiction here gets a gold star on the paycheck or something. Only one of them seems like he's got sense enough to pour sand out of his boots: A big black man from the Austin FBI by the name of Jefferson Tate. Thank God he seems to be taking charge. Tate's the only one in the bunch with common sense. A few of the young ones are scary as hell, wearing Kevlar vests and packing machine guns around easily as most people carry their lunch."

"My God, do they actually think I'm dangerous?"

"A bunch seem to *wish* you were. The rest are going by the book."

"I reckon I'd better give Quentin Miller a call."

"Already done. I phoned him before I called you. He's getting dressed and coming down. You're to stay put until he gets in touch."

"I will. Monica, I'm so sorry about all of this."

"You can be sorry later. Right now we have more important things to worry about." She hesitated then said, "Don't do anything crazy. Some reporter from Houston filed an assault report on you and Jesus. John Trotter at the hardware store told the FBI you threatened his life. Watch your temper, little brother."

"Monica, that reporter was on my ranch and refused to leave. Jesus just swung a catfish at him is all that happened. Trotter's lying through his teeth—"

"A catfish?" the sheriff interrupted. "Tip took the report as assault with a deadly weapon. Look I've got to go. We'll get into this later. In the meantime, try to keep from making things worse than they already are."

"I'll do my best, but honestly, anymore it seems like everything turns out wrong. I'll wait for Quentin's call. Bye, Sis, and thanks."

When Caleb put the receiver down, he noticed his hand trembled. Now, harmless old Jesus was wrapped up in this sordid mess. How could that aged Mexican swinging a catfish at some snot-nosed, arrogant reporter who was trespassing be written up as assault? The government couldn't be stupid enough to treat a catfish as a deadly weapon.

They'll twist it, then use it against you.

On second thought, they just might be that stupid. A system that had become so dominated by rabid politicians and self-serving interests it could send a man to prison for a year for protecting his chickens was capable of nearly anything.

It's just too damn bad Jesus got involved. The old man must be eighty years old. He doesn't need this shit.

Caleb put on his robe, went to the kitchen and flipped on the coffee maker. Every night before going to bed he always prepared the morning coffee. He never understood how anyone could start the day without a few cups of java to get their heart started.

Tristan could sleep in for awhile this morning. Generally, getting the boy out of bed was a considerable chore. The way this day was headed, he'd likely need the extra rest.

On a normal day, Caleb would click on the small television on the counter and watch the news. That didn't seem like a prudent move now. Instead he threw open the windows and while the coffee pot gurgled, Caleb luxuriated in the gentle breeze, listening to the soporific creaking of the windmill. He saw a few of his Brangus cattle watering at the tank. Even by the velvet glow of a newborn sun he could make out their sleek coats and knew they were doing well.

This was his element. A place on this earth where he belonged and also loved. Caleb Starr held no higher ambitions than to work his ranch, in peace with the world.

It was a hard life, with long hours and few rewards that could be added up by an accountant. Yet it was a lifestyle that had built this country, then seemingly been forgotten. Briefly, Caleb remembered a bumper sticker that had been popular several years ago, "Don't complain about farmers with your mouth full."

Caleb was taken from his thoughts by Jesus hobbling out the backdoor of his house. He watched as the old man opened the gate and went into the garden area surrounded by a high fence to keep the deer out and turned water to his spreading patch of watermelons. Perhaps a few might be ripe by the Fourth of July. It would be doubtful. Usually that melon was bought in San Angelo. Then toward August, all of Jesus's watermelons came ready at the same time. Laura used to cut the green rind into squares and make sweet pickles from them—.

You're getting old when everything good is only remembered.

Jesus noticed Caleb standing in the window and waved. In a few minutes he would be over for coffee. The lonely old man joined him most mornings. Normally they would talk about ranch problems while Caleb kept prodding Tristan to get dressed and ready for school.

Today the conversation would be about some very large problems.

The coffee pot sputtered its last gasp. Caleb took two large porcelain mugs from the cabinet and poured them full of the steaming brew, black and strong. The way God meant for coffee to be drunk.

Jesus rapped politely on the screen door. Caleb shouted his customary "Come on in."

The aged Mexican shuffled over to the kitchen table, slid out a chair and plopped down as Caleb set a cup of simmering coffee in front of him.

Jesus blew a fog of steam from his mug, then sighed, "*Buenos dias,* my friend. I do not think my melons are growing as they should. We are going to have a bad winter. When this happens it messes everything up."

"We need to talk about what happened last night."

"There is no problem, *señor.* I put the fish in a washtub, and he is still very much alive. I will wait until the grease is hot and the cornmeal ready before I cut him up. They taste much better that way."

A flash of anguish stabbed at Caleb. The old man had no clue he'd done anything wrong by swinging the fish at that obnoxious reporter.

Assault with a deadly weapon. In a pig's eye. How could anyone who knew vinegar from honey claim such a thing?

Still, he had to come out with it. "Jesus, there's something you need to know—"

The harsh jangling of the telephone interrupted. Caleb decided it must be Quentin and wondered how the lawyer had acted so quickly. There was no reason to keep anything from Jesus so he grabbed the wall phone in the kitchen.

"Hello," he said softly.

"This is Bruno Leatherwood. Caleb, the shit's hit the fan about that blasted eagle. I tried to reach you last night, but you weren't home. The Federal Wildlife Service has agents out here investigating. For some reason, their computers showed you to be a dangerous person, and they've called in the FBI for enforcement. I've had dozens of calls from government officials and news reporters asking me the truth about that story of you killing a bald eagle. My God, I can't believe all the hoopla about this. An airliner crashing into a school wouldn't cause any more attention. Caleb, I had no choice but to tell them the truth."

Shock caused any words to wedge in Caleb's throat. The worst scenario he had imagined was having to turn himself in to possibly a couple of Federal Game Wardens. This whole thing had gone insane. The FBI had been called in for enforcement, some lousy computer reported him to be a violent man. That was laughable. He hadn't been in a fight since high school. And even back then he'd done what he could to avoid trouble.

Then Caleb was stuck with an ancient pain. He *had* killed his fellow man before. But that was during war time, many years ago in a stinking hellhole called Vietnam. The very government that was now after his fanny over a dead bird had shoved a rifle in his hands and told him to use it. Caleb Starr had been raised to be a patriot. He never questioned his orders. The red scourge of Communism had to be stopped, and he did his part without reservation. It looked now like his combat experience was to be used against him.

"I don't know what to say, Bruno," Caleb finally said. "Monica called and told me the sheriff's office is crawling with Feds. Quentin Miller is on his way there now. About my shooting that eagle, don't worry about anything but the truth. I was always taught you're better off to stick with that. One thing I would like for you to do, if you can, is find out just why they think I'm such a threat. Is it because I was a soldier or what?"

"That information should be in our computer system. I'll try to get online and check it out before some other idiot calls and ties up the phone. Caleb, I'm truly sorry about all of this."

"I know Bruno, thanks. Call me back if you find something."

"You got it."

Jesus pushed away his cup and frowned. "I do not think this is going to be a good day for a fish fry."

"No, my friend, I don't believe so."

"This thing with the eagle I do not understand. It was simply an accident. Don't they of the government have real criminals to catch? Surely, a man cannot be fined and thrown into prison for such a trifle."

"Quentin Miller said there's thousands of new laws enacted every year. An entire firm of attorneys can't keep up with what's legal or not. I suppose that's the reason most politicians are lawyers. Even the losing side collects a couple of hundred dollars an hour. They're just making sure all their little lawyer buddies have a good income. But to answer your question, according to the letter of the law, I could spend a year in prison for shooting that eagle."

"Dad, that can't happen. I need you and Jesus needs you," Tristan said, his voice tight with grief.

Caleb spun to face his son. He hadn't known the boy was up and dressed, standing in the doorway behind him. "Tristan I don't know how this mess got so out of control, but we have a great attorney on our side. Quentin will—"

His words were suddenly drowned out by the heavy beating of helicopter blades. The walls of the house shook and dust billowed in the morning air as the large craft dropped to the earth behind Caleb's pickup. More thunder from the ridge behind the house could only be from a second helicopter landing there. The trio ran to stare out the window.

An assault force of a half-dozen men, all wearing camouflage suits and black bullet proof vests jumped from the 'copter and scrambled for cover. Every one of them carried an automatic weapon that they quickly pointed toward the house and its stricken inhabitants.

Caleb grabbed Tristan by the shoulder and threw him to the floor. Jesus needed no urging. The old man was already under the kitchen table.

"Madre de Dios, señor," Jesus said loudly over the roar of the

departing copter's. "I think it is as I feared: *El Diablo* has arrived!"

Caleb didn't answer. He was too busy wondering why the vests of the assault force were lettered DEA. Hell, the strongest thing he ever had in the house was aspirin. What in the name of everything holy were agents of the Drug Enforcement Administration doing attacking his ranch?

Chapter 15

At least they're not blasting the place full of holes like what happened at Waco, Caleb thought. He knew wooden walls wouldn't stop rifle bullets. If anyone out there got trigger happy, they were all dead. Being careful to keep under cover, Caleb inched his way up the wall to the phone, grabbed it and dropped back to the floor. Thankfully the buttons were on the receiver. He punched nine-one-one, knowing the call would be answered by Monica or at least Tip Conroy. Someone there had to know why this was happening.

"Sheriff's department." His sister's voice was a comfort.

"My God, Monica, what the hell is going on? Some helicopters just dropped an assault force with machine guns. They've got the house surrounded. Their vests are marked DEA."

"Is everyone all right?" Monica was obviously shocked and concerned.

"No one's shot yet, but that bunch outside didn't drop by to ask us to church."

Caleb overheard yelling in the background. Shouted curses. Denials. Then a man's voice come over the receiver. He had a distinct Southern drawl and growled like a provoked bear.

"Mister Starr, this is Field Agent Tate with the Federal Bureau of Investigation. Are you certain the men surrounding your house are Drug Enforcement personnel? We have no knowledge of that fact."

"So far they haven't tried to get acquainted. They sure as hell have DEA written on their vests and are packing automatic rifles. If they're not Feds we're in a lot more trouble than I thought."

"Damn!" Agent Tate exclaimed. "Don't do anything to start an incident."

"No one here's planning to upset them any. The only gun on the place is in the back window of my pickup and that's where it'll stay."

More arguing. Then Tate's gruff voice returned. "Are you admitting to me that you are in possession of a firearm?"

Caleb's frustration grew. "No, damn it. I told you my shotgun's in the pickup."

Yelling in the background again. Thankfully Monica came on the phone. She would make more sense than the FBI agent.

"Caleb, the FBI files show you to be an ex-con. They just told me this. I said it wasn't true, then punched up your record on our computer. The blasted thing verified the fact. There's no way I can explain. Quentin Miller's here now trying to convince them, but if that bunch of Feds outside your place has the same information—"

A bullhorn's blaring from outside took Caleb's attention.

"This is McKenzie of the Federal Drug Enforcement Administration. The house is surrounded. There is no way to escape. Throw your weapons out the door and leave the dwelling with your hands raised and you will not be harmed. If you do not do as instructed we *will* open fire."

"Señor," Jesus whispered from his hiding place under the table. "I think they are pissed off about something more than a dead bird."

"I'd reckon you're right about that," Caleb said.

Tristan lay stretched out on the floor. Only a quivering lower lip betrayed his frayed nerves. The rancher felt a burst of pride that his son was holding up so well. Caleb's mind was spinning trying to decide the safest course of action. There was no denying anything could set those Feds to shooting. He had to protect Tristan and Jesus at any cost.

"Caleb, Caleb, pick up." Monica yelled from the receiver.

"We just got orders to come out or get shot," he answered. "Monica, if something goes wrong, please watch after Tristan."

Caleb laid the phone down, ignored his sister's pleading and carefully stood, holding his hands palm out. When he stepped to the window only a screen separated him from the Fed's rifles that were aimed at his heart.

"We're unarmed," he shouted. "There's just my son and an old man in here. We don't have any guns to throw out."

His immediate answer was the ominous click of an automatic rifle being cocked. A sound he'd heard several times in Vietnam. It made his blood run icy. He could make out the faces of two of the agents behind their plastic face shields. The pair crouched behind his pickup. They were just boys, eyes wide with tension and adrenalin. Caleb knew that one slight, nervous twitch from an index finger meant he was a dead man.

"Keep your hands where we can see them," the bullhorn sounded. The man holding it was standing behind a big live oak tree, the rising sun glinted off his shield, rendering his features invisible.

"Everyone out there stay nice and calm," Caleb said loudly, trying to keep even a hint of tension from his voice. "I'm going to walk around to the door nice and slow. Then Tristan—that's my son—and Jesus will follow me outside. We're all going to do as you ask, and we're going to move real slow, so don't get trigger-happy."

"We don't believe your story about not having any weapons. If anyone so much as hiccups, you're all toast," the man with the bullhorn proclaimed.

"Believe what you want, but it won't look good on the six

o'clock news if you fellows kill two unarmed men and a young boy."

A long silence. To Caleb, standing in plain sight of the riflemen, it felt like an eternity.

Then the bullhorn man spoke, "If you come out clean, no one will get shot. You have thirty seconds. Don't even think of trying to screw with us."

Caleb kept his hands raised and turned to his son. "Tristan, you and Jesus do just as I do. We're all going to walk out that door, and no one is going to get hurt."

Caleb wished he felt as confident as he sounded. Jesus crawled from under the kitchen table and stood with a grunt. Tristan came to his feet alongside the old man. The boy's face was alabaster. "Dad, why are they doing this?"

"That's what we're going to find out. You two stay behind me with your hands up and don't make any fast moves."

"*Señor,* we are like molasses in January," Jesus said.

Caleb, keeping his hands high, walked to the open door and pushed the screen door open with his foot. He swallowed hard then stepped outside with Tristan and Jesus in tow.

"Down! Down! Down!" the bullhorn man shouted. "Keep your faces to the ground and your hands out."

The three dropped to their knees and stretched out.

"*Go! Go! Go!* Secure the prisoners. Check the house." Faceless voices yelled. Heavy boots thundered on dry dirt. Caleb felt a rifle barrel stuck in the middle of his back. Strong hands yanked his arms back to the cold embrace of handcuffs.

"Prisoners secured, Sir." A new voice shouted.

"Go! Go!" Footsteps crashed through the house.

After a long moment of more yelling, "There's no other parties, sir. We have a stable situation."

Caleb was jerked to his feet. Tristan stood ashen-faced alongside Jesus. Both were also handcuffed.

"Who's in charge here?" Caleb said.

"I'll ask the questions," a man snapped, walking toward them, rifle held at port. "My name is McKenzie. That's all you need to know. Make it easy on yourselves—where's the stash and refueling station?"

"Huh?" was all Caleb could say through his open mouth.

"Don't play dumb with me, sir. We know all about you and what goes on here."

"Then maybe you oughta tell me what's going on," Caleb said.

Quick as a rattlesnake strikes, the man slammed the butt of his rifle into the pit of Caleb's stomach, bringing him to his knees. "So you're going to be a smart ass."

"Dad!" Tristan exclaimed and made a lunge to come to his father's aid.

An agent jumped in front of him. "Keep to yourself!"

"It's okay, Son," Caleb wheezed. "Some men get a charge out of beating up on handcuffed people who can't defend themselves."

"Call for transport," McKenzie snarled to no one in particular. "We'll sweat the truth out of them later. I don't think this man will make the mistake of trying to jump me *again.*"

"Sir," a young agent said to McKenzie, "we haven't been able to find a thing to verify our information. Perhaps this ranch isn't a drop."

"Williams, you men are to take this place apart board by board. I want you to check out every nook and cranny. Then you'll do it again. Do you understand me?"

"Sir. Yes, sir." The agent replied smartly, then ran to join his colleagues.

Caleb stood straight with difficulty and glared at McKenzie. "My sister's the sheriff, and there's an FBI agent on the phone in the kitchen. His name is Jefferson Tate. Maybe you should do yourself a favor and go talk with him."

McKenzie's scowl was replaced by a perplexed expression, but his attitude remained. "What the hell are you doing on the phone with the FBI? This is a DEA operation."

"I simply suggested you should talk to the man."

"Davis," McKenzie shouted, "check the phone and see who's on the line. Be careful it's not rigged to a bomb first!"

There was a long silence, then muted talk from the house. Finally Agent Davis returned. "Sir, there is a man on the phone identifying himself as Jefferson Tate. He claims to be with the Austin Branch of the FBI. He's requesting you to talk with him and then transport the prisoners to the jail in Lone Wolf. Sir, he says there is a problem."

Federal Agent McKenzie's face matched Tristan's paleness. "Jeff Tate! I've worked with him before. He's a good man. What in hell is going on here?"

Jesus glared at McKenzie. "I think that would be a nice thing for all of us to know."

Chapter 16

In a first class hotel room near the Alamo and the Riverwalk in downtown San Antonio, a willowy blonde lay face up, spread-eagled on the king size bed. Leather cuffs attached to shiny silver chains gripped her wrists and ankles. The girl wore only a pink half-bra that cradled her bare breasts delightfully and a matching silk garter belt.

A hooker who shopped at *Frederick's of Hollywood.*

She was plainly frightened. Her eyes were wide with fear, like those he had seen on animals being herded up the killing chute at a slaughterhouse. At least she would remain silent. A hard rubber ball crammed into her mouth and held firmly in place by a black leather strap assured that.

Marsh briefly drank of the girl's heady perfume and her fear. Then he turned his attention back to the laptop computer sitting on the desk.

Ah, the power of a computer. Years ago he had become an extremely proficient hacker. This skill had assured him his college degrees. His grades had left something to be desired. Breaking into any computer system was never a problem for a man of his ability. Once, for a few wonderful hours, he had even entered the database for the Central Intelligence Agency.

Marsh had the passwords for Run Free's databank, making it an easy task to jumble their records and foil, for awhile at least, their determined attempts to file a lawsuit against him.

The most pressing problem was to keep his reputation as an

environmentalist intact. That eagle-killing rancher had to be destroyed to accomplish this goal. Marsh's actions of selling the videotape must appear laudable. All he needed to do was be a champion of wildlife until he could spring onto the political scene. This petty incident would be soon forgotten.

Once he knew the rancher's name, it was a simple matter to hack into the Department of Motor Vehicles and tax records from the county. Then he had Caleb Starr's social security number. After that it was child's play.

The Federal Wildlife Service now had a long file on Caleb Starr entered into their database showing him to be a dangerous and repeat offender, a known trafficker in eagles and endangered species.

Then, he had entered the FBI files and altered them to show Caleb Starr had an extensive criminal record. Ten years in Huntsville prison for manslaughter of an IRS Agent was a neat touch.

Best of all were the computer files of the Drug Enforcement Administration. Caleb Starr was now a well-known drug dealer with a clandestine landing strip for airplanes and helicopters to refuel on their way north from Mexico. His ranch was a drop point for every conceivable drug and a veritable fortress that could only be taken by great force.

To make certain things would go his way, Marsh had then downloaded *their* altered files and faxed copies to law enforcement agencies, television stations and newspapers for a thousand miles.

More fat for the fire.

He exited the database of the *New York Times* where he had planted a wonderful story of how an environmental activist by the name of Marsh Wheelan had single-handedly exposed an outlaw Texas rancher who killed bald eagles for profit. He needed to break into one more government agency's records to complete his task.

That could come later.

Now it was playtime.

Women were meant to be dominated by men. It said so in the Bible. Many times.

Marsh stood up and slipped off his black robe. He wore nothing underneath. He carefully placed the robe on the back of his chair to keep it from becoming wrinkled.

The bound whore began moaning with fear and thrashing her head from side to side. He wasn't going to hurt her any more than she'd agreed to.

But she had been *very* well paid.

The blonde struggled against the chains when he extracted a little toy from the desk drawer.

Strange, he thought. *A person would think a girl in her profession would have had something like this used on her before.*

No matter.

She was chained and helpless. He was in control and aroused.

Power is the world's greatest aphrodisiac. Whoever said that had known what Marsh Wheelan was all about.

Chapter 17

Monica Blandon had never seen Quentin Miller's neck flush red before. She didn't think that was a good omen. The sheriff nervously watched the proceedings through a one-way mirror fitted into the wall of the interrogation room. The small cubby hole office wouldn't begin to hold all of the federal agents who wanted in on this. Her brother, Tristan and Jesus were sitting at the table, still handcuffed. She wanted to be by Caleb's side but knew having Quentin there was more important.

At least no one had gotten killed or badly hurt. One member of the DEA assault force was in a San Angelo hospital getting cactus spines plucked from his legs. During all the excitement, the young man had misjudged and jumped from the helicopter too soon and landed in a spreading clump of prickly pear. Monica doubted the agent would repeat that error again soon.

"I don't give a rat's rectum what your computers tell you," Quentin Miller's bombastic courtroom voice bellowed from the open door. "I know, personally, and for an absolute fact, that Caleb Starr was here in Lone Wolf peacefully running his ranch when you're saying he was locked down in Huntsville prison. We have to be dealing with a case of mistaken identity here."

"Mister Miller, we're checking out that possibility now," Jefferson Tate drawled.

Monica's respect for the silver-haired FBI Agent kept growing. He was a huge man, but his eyes were kind and his voice calm. Tate seemed as perplexed as everyone else, only he appeared to be genuinely interested in finding out facts.

"I say we haul 'em all up to Lubbock and sort it out there." Alton McKenzie of the DEA seemed unable to accept the possibility he hadn't broken a major drug ring.

Quentin's steel eyes bored at McKenzie. "I suggest you read the Constitution of these United States. Then I advise you to ponder on the possibility that Senator Ruth Ames, who I know personally, might call your boss and arrange for a transfer to Reykjavik or some other seaport. Perhaps you could find a helpless iceberg or two to raid up there."

"Gentlemen, we're not trying anyone here," Tate said calmly to Quentin. "We just need to get our ducks in a row. Alton deals with really nasty customers and comes across a tad gruff on occasion."

"He rammed my Dad in the gut with a rifle butt after he was handcuffed," Tristan said, his voice nearly breaking.

"The man tried to jump me," McKenzie shouted.

"A handcuffed man tried to assault you?" Quentin turned and asked Caleb, "Did he strike you?"

"Yes sir."

"And were you handcuffed at the time?"

"Yes."

Jefferson Tate's eyes rolled toward the ceiling. A few agents in the room decided they had urgent business elsewhere.

"Beating a prisoner in federal custody is inexcusable," Quentin said. "I'm going to require statements, under oath, from everyone who was there. Mister McKenzie may not have to worry about being transferred to Iceland after all."

DEA Agent Alton McKenzie shuffled his feet and bit worriedly on his lower lip. "Uh, perhaps we could work this out right here."

"Are you going to be all right, Caleb? Do you wish to see a

doctor?" Quentin asked with the gravity of a priest giving final rites.

"I reckon I'll be okay."

"Now, Mister McKenzie," the lawyer said, "do you have any evidence, whatsoever, or did your raid on the ranch uncover anything that could possibly cause charges to be brought against either the minor, Tristan Starr, or Jesus Santiago?"

Alton McKenzie cleared his throat, then sputtered, "No, we found nothing at the ranch, nor on our records regarding those two."

Quentin stared at Jefferson Tate. "Your turn. Same question."

"Nope, nothing here either," the black man replied.

"Then, may I please inquire as to just why the hell they're in handcuffs?"

"Davis!" McKenzie snapped, "get over here and release the boy and the old man. I never told you to bring them in cuffed in the first place."

The expression DEA Agent Davis wore when he removed the manacles said he would have no qualms with Quentin's idea of transferring his boss to Iceland.

Jesus rubbed his wrists. "*Señors.* I think I left the water running on my watermelons. This should be attended to. Too much water will rot the roots."

"We can't just leave you here, Dad," Tristan said placing his hand on Caleb's shoulder.

"Yes you can, Son. This mess might take awhile to figger out. I'm afraid you're being asked to grow up a little faster than I planned, but we have a ranch to run. Animals need taking care of, and there's no one but you and Jesus I can depend on."

"*Señor* Caleb," Jesus said, "do not concern yourself. Young Tristan and I will have no problems. I will not read another book until the south fence is repaired, and the goats and cattle are tended to."

"Dad," was all Tristan could manage to say without tears.

"Come, let us do your father's bidding," Jesus said. "Perhaps *Señora* Blandon will drive us home."

Jefferson Tate spoke up, "We've got a lot more men around here that have less to do than the sheriff does. I'll have an agent take care of it."

A slight smile crossed Jesus' weathered face. "Thank you, *señor.*"

Caleb watched in silence while his son and Jesus were ushered from the room. He was proud Tristan was holding up so well. And there was no way he could ever repay Quentin Miller.

"Now, *gentlemen,*" the attorney said firmly, "with that matter resolved we can focus our attentions on my client. Would you please be so kind as to state your charges?"

Alton McKenzie spoke up, "The Drug Enforcement Administration has files showing Mister Starr is a well-documented drug dealer."

Jefferson Tate cocked his head. "Do your records indicate he was ever imprisoned in Huntsville for ten years? The sentence was for manslaughter."

Agent McKenzie frowned. "No, no criminal record at all, just that an extensive investigation gave information there was a large cache of drugs on his ranch."

"And you found nothing?" Quentin asked.

McKenzie shook his head. "No. Nothing at all, but we are still searching." He quickly added, "We *do* have a warrant."

Jefferson Tate looked worried. "You know, Alton, the fact that our computer records don't agree suggests a problem."

"Well, hallelujah," Quentin said. Someone has finally seen the light."

"You're right, Jeff, something *is* wrong here," McKenzie said sheepishly. "Our computers should agree."

A tall, bean-pole thin man with jet-black hair and watery

blue eyes stepped forward. "I'm Randall Whitehead with the Federal Wildlife Service out of Del Rio. What you fellows are up to, I don't have a clue. We're here investigating the killing of a bald eagle. A story was published on this matter in a tabloid, and a state game warden confirms this incident. Our computer files show Mister Starr has been convicted many times for violating the Endangered Species Act and is known to deal in eagle paraphernalia."

"That's a lie," Caleb roared. "I've never done anything against the law except shoot that one eagle."

Quentin Miller's face grew pale. "My client is under great duress."

"Well, *I* heard him confess," Randall proclaimed. "That's enough for me to arrest him."

"Caleb," the lawyer said quickly. "Did any of these men read you your rights?"

"No sir, they didn't."

Quentin grinned at Agent Whitehead. "Have you ever, in your vast law enforcement experience, heard of a little something called Miranda? Any *alleged* confession without that matter being taken care of first is inadmissible."

Jefferson Tate's eyes shot dark daggers at Alton. "Your bunch hauled those people in here handcuffed and never Mirandized a one?"

"Well," he stammered, "we *were* going to once we found the drug cache."

"Shit and shinola," Tate mumbled. "We're coming off here like the Keystone Cops."

Randall Whitehead clucked his tongue and said to Caleb. "You have the right to remain silent . . ."

While the Federal Wildlife Agent completed reading the court-ordered warning from a plastic card he had produced from his pocket, Monica walked in and stood beside Quentin and Jefferson Tate.

"Thanks for letting the boy and Jesus go," she said to the FBI agent.

"No problem, ma'am," Tate said. "But I'm afraid your brother might have a set of troubles we didn't know anything about."

"We're even," Monica said, "because no one here had a clue about all of the charges you Feds had cooked up against him."

"That's what has me concerned. We all should be tuned into the same channel, but we're sure as hell not. Our FBI background check, and also yours, showed Caleb to be an ex-con who did hard time in Huntsville. And I believe you and Mister Miller when you tell me he was here in Lone Wolf, while the records show him in prison. Alton's Agency and now the FWS have totally different files on the same man. Something's mighty rotten in Denmark." Jefferson Tate's bushy eyebrows slanted into a frown as he stared at the FWS agent. "What about this eagle killing thing. Is there any truth to that?"

Randall Whitehead poked his Miranda card back into his pocket and glowered at Tate. "A picture of Starr holding a dead bald eagle was on the cover of the last edition of *The Weekly World Probe*. The local game warden, I think his name's Leatherwood, verified that Starr turned in an eagle to him. That's enough to charge him with a federal crime in my book."

Tate snorted. "I'm not surprised to find out the FWS subscribes to that rag. But since no one in the Bureau reads it, we couldn't have known about the publicity. All the FBI was called in for was to help apprehend a potentially dangerous criminal." Tate glanced down at Caleb and shook his head. "The next time you folks at the FWS soil your drawers over someone popping an eagle you might at least *try* to handle the situation yourselves before calling us in to hold your hand."

Randall Whitehead shouted, "The DEA believed Starr was dangerous too."

"Gentlemen," Monica interjected, "bickering isn't going to accomplish anything."

"Shucks," Quentin said, "I was beginning to enjoy this."

"No, the lady's right," Jefferson Tate said. "We need to find out the truth of the matter." He rolled his head towards the open door and yelled, "Lindsey, have you gotten hold of Huntsville yet?"

A young man walked in. Monica couldn't help but notice how much alike the Feds looked. Most were in their thirties, all wore close-cropped hair and trim suits with ties. Aside from Tate, not one had ever shown a resemblance of a smile.

"Yes, sir," the agent said. "They have no record of anyone by the name of Caleb Starr ever being incarcerated there."

"Shit," Tate said.

"Oh, shit," Alton McKenzie exclaimed.

Quentin Miller shrugged his shoulders and sighed. "We told you so."

"Listen here," McKenzie said. "We're not about to let a dangerous man walk because of some computer glitch."

Monica glared at the DEA man. "Did you or any of your agents find anything at Caleb's ranch to verify your information?"

Alton McKenzie made no attempt to mask his cold fury. "No—not yet."

Randall Whitehead's voice was heavy with sarcasm. "The Federal Wildlife Service has both evidence and a law enforcement officer's statement that a crime has been committed. This is enough for *us* to make an arrest. Perhaps with some diligence and luck, the FBI and the DEA might accomplish as much."

Jefferson Tate's massive arm kept a red-faced McKenzie from lunging at Whitehead. "Alton! Let it go. We're all on the same team here." He glared at the FWS agent. "Let's try to act like professionals here."

Randall Whitehead kept his eyes on McKenzie's knotted fists. "You're right, Agent Tate. I apologize for my remarks."

Quentin Miller stepped over to Caleb and placed a hand on his shoulder. "Now maybe we can focus on my client. He has a son to care for and a ranch to run."

"Caleb Starr is under arrest," Randall Whitehead said firmly. "He's not going *anywhere.*"

The lawyer's steely eyes surveyed the room. "Okay, so we have a charge of violating game laws here. That is a bailable offense. Anyone want to up the ante?"

McKenzie said, "Today is Sunday. Starr can't be arraigned until a federal judge can schedule a hearing, which will take days. By the time that happens, the DEA will have a lot more to charge him with than breaking some petty game law!"

Caleb jumped to his feet and glared at McKenzie. Even though the rancher was handcuffed, the DEA agent stepped back, his face pale. "It's too bad you weren't in Germany back in the thirties. Hitler would have taken a shine to the likes of you. There's never been any illegal drugs on my ranch and there never will be. I fought for my country in Vietnam and have always been proud to call myself an American—until now."

Quentin Miller stepped between Caleb and the DEA agent. Then he faced McKenzie. "We have had enough of your groundless accusations and threats. Either make your charges at the arraignment, or I'll have you up on charges for assaulting a prisoner."

Alton McKenzie's face turned to a seething expression of rage. He glowered at the lawyer for a moment, spun and stomped out of the interrogation room.

"Mister Miller," Jefferson Tate said, "I'm sorry for Alton's behavior. He's really a good man, but his own daughter died from an overdose of heroin a couple of years ago. I assure you, however, he will only follow the book."

"That's a comfort to know," Quentin said. "I'm calling a halt to this inquisition. Monica, if you could get Caleb settled down in a nice quiet cell and fetch him something to eat, I'll try to get Judge Matthews on the phone and schedule a bail hearing for tomorrow."

Jefferson Tate took a key from his pocket and unlocked the handcuffs from Caleb's wrists. "I think we all need to settle down and check things out. This whole affair is one big mess for some unknown reason."

Randall Whitehead focused his eyes on Monica. "I expect your brother to be at that arraignment."

"He'll be there, sir," Monica said.

She slid her arm around Caleb's and gently escorted him to a jail cell. The sheriff of Lone Wolf County was glad to be away from the mass of Federal agents. None of them could witness the tear that trickled down her cheek when she locked her brother behind a heavy iron door.

Chapter 18

Hope Rexton couldn't believe what she was hearing when the radio announcer, his voice sharp with tension, described a drug raid on a ranch near Lone Wolf, Texas.

"Details are still sketchy, but we understand three men were arrested at the scene where a dozen or more agents of the Federal Drug Enforcement Administration conducted a surprise raid this morning.

"The ranch is supposedly owned by a longtime resident of the area, Caleb Starr, who is currently under investigation for the alleged killing of a bald eagle earlier this month. It is not known at this time if Starr was one of the individuals taken into custody during the raid. Stay tuned to this station for further developments as they become available."

Hope clicked off the radio and set the hot buttered cruller on a plate beside the glass of orange juice. Her appetite had fled.

It was just past noon, and Hope had been enjoying a lazy summer Sunday. She had slept late, then made a pot of coffee and watched television while stretched out on the couch in her fluffy bathrobe. There had been two old black and white Humphrey Bogart movies on, *Casablanca* and *The Petrified Forest.* Hope loved Bogart and savored every line of both films. After a long, hot shower she'd dressed and prepared a very late breakfast. Then she had turned on the news.

Caleb had explained to her about the eagle. The whole affair was just a terrible accident. How his picture had wound up plastered on the cover of a cheap tabloid was as much a mystery to him as it was to her.

Something deep in Hope's intuition told her the tabloid article and the federal drug raid on his ranch were related. Not for one second did she believe Caleb could possibly be involved in anything so monstrous as drug dealing. From bitter experience Hope had learned to recognize what lay in the heart of a man. Caleb was her friend. And he had a young son who must be devastated by all of this.

Hope quickly pulled on her tennis shoes and laced them. She grabbed her purse on the way out the door.

The white Mustang convertible roared to life and the redhead's tires spun gravel as she sped out the driveway on her way to the Lone Starr Ranch. Hope had no clear idea of what she could do once she got there. Only one thing was certain: friends take care of each other. And Caleb Starr was her friend.

A pair of jet-black Ford automobiles were leaving Caleb's ranch when Hope turned into the long gravel driveway. The cars were filled with stern-faced men. They slowed and stared at Hope, making her feel as if they were mentally comparing her face with wanted posters.

She fought down the urge to smile and wave at them using her middle finger. Somewhere in the statutes there was undoubtedly a law against flipping off a federal agent.

When Hope pulled the Mustang to a dusty stop in front of the house, she knew something was desperately wrong. Even the air felt heavy and oppressive.

Jesus stood outside the open kitchen door, leaning heavily on a cane. His leathery face echoed sadness. Hope climbed from her car and walked to his side. She had never known the old man to use a cane and grew more concerned.

"Are you alright, Jesus?" she asked.

"No, *señora.* I am sorry. This is not a good day."

"Where's Tristan?"

"The young man is inside. We do not know what to do."

"Tell me. I'm here to help."

"*Señora,* the *federales.* They kept us out here while they tore everything apart. Then they just left without so much as an explanation. *Cabrons!*"

Hope patted the distraught man on his shoulder as she stepped inside. Once she surveyed the destruction, Hope Rexton had several stronger epithets than *cabrons* to describe the agents and the havoc they had wrought in their fruitless search for drugs.

A tornado couldn't have done much more damage. Drawers and cabinets hung open, their contents heaped on the floor. The propane range had been slid out and dismantled. Bare nails and sun-faded outlines on the walls marked where pictures and family photographs had been removed and tossed onto the jumble. Kitchen canisters had been opened, flour and sugar dumped, after first being tested for cocaine, she assumed.

The French Connection movie flashed through Hope's mind. In it, the Gene Hackman character had torn apart a new luxury car in his relentless search for drugs. The fact that he was successful made the wreckage palatable. The question of what drug enforcement agents do when they come up empty-handed had been painfully answered. They simply walk away. No apology, no repayment for damages. Nothing. It was left for the hapless victims of a futile search to put their lives back together as best they could.

Something like this can't happen here in America, land of the free. The Constitution guarantees against unreasonable searches.

Sorry about tearing your home apart. Too bad we didn't find anything. We're outta here. Have a nice day and remember to pay your taxes so we can get a big pay raise.

Anger flowed through her veins like fiery brimstone.

A scraping noise deep in the house shook away her acid thoughts. Hope had never been past the kitchen before. Ranchers commonly conduct most of their socializing and business there.

She threaded her way around the overturned sofa and dismantled television set and entered what she assumed was Tristan's room.

Instead of the expected teary-eyed boy, she found a young man with a granite expression sliding drawers back into an oak dresser. He shot a quick glance in her direction and continued with his task.

"I'm so sorry," Hope said.

"It's not your fault," Tristan said without slowing down.

"Your father wasn't responsible for causing this."

"I know that. All I can do is try to put the place back together before Dad gets home. He's got enough problems without having to clean up this mess."

Hope smothered a sob and tried to think of something to say when the rattling of an approaching diesel engine took both their attentions. Tristan placed a T-shirt he had just folded on the bed and went with Hope to see who was there.

Rollie Turner and Hector Lemmons wore expressions of disbelief as they stood in the destroyed kitchen.

"Those bastards!" Rollie spat. "Those rotten bastards!"

Hector was silent for a moment, then focused on Tristan. "Boy, I've known your daddy longer than you've been alive, and I'm telling you straight: he's a good man. A far better man than the people who did this."

Jesus hobbled in on his cane. His lower lip quivered as he rolled ancient rheumy eyes around the room. *"Con permiso, amigos."* He bent slowly and picked up a picture with a trembling hand. "There is much to do."

Rollie Turner stepped over and took the picture from the old man. With his artificial leg the windmiller walked with only a slight limp. "You're right, Jesus. There's a lot to do." He placed a hand under the old Mexican's shoulder. "And you've got your work cut out for you. I've got a cooler full of beer that I'm going to put on your porch. There's going to be a lot of thirsty folks here this afternoon. Your job's to see that they're taken care of."

Jesus started to answer but only nodded his silver-cropped head. Hector, Tristan and Hope watched as the pair hobbled out.

"Well there ain't no use bawling over spilt milk," Hector said. "I'll get on my cell phone and call the missus. Then I'll rustle up our hired hands and a few others."

"This will be a lot of work," Hope said.

"Yup," Hector replied. "I've heard about rock bands wrecking a hotel, and they always manage to put those places back together. Reckon we can too. Standing around gawking wide-eyed like a cow looking at a strange calf ain't gonna do the trick."

Crickets were chirping their nightly mating call when the many friends, neighbors and relatives of Caleb Starr had finished their task of putting the ranch in order.

Monica had been unable to leave her duties as sheriff, but her husband, Bones, and the portly deputy, Tip Conroy, came to help.

The heaviest work had been in the barn where tons of feed sacks had been slit open and searched, their contents spilled on the dirt floor. Hector had sent one of his hired hands to his ranch to fetch a pickup load of empty gunnysacks.

"I just knew those things would come in handy some day," he'd said.

Several men had shoveled, raked up and re-bagged all of the expensive goat feed so none was lost.

The gray tomcat, Useless, had shown up to see what all of the action was about and chased a few mice that were checking out the unexpected windfall of food that had come their way. It gladdened Tristan to see the cat return. When the helicopters roared in, Useless had bristled up like a bottle brush and darted off into a clump of mesquite trees.

Hope made a final survey of the restored ranch house then joined the milling crowd on Jesus's porch where Rollie's well-attended cooler had been refilled many times during the long, hot afternoon.

Over twenty men and women had shown up to help, many of whom Hope did not know. Four of the men were Hector Lemmons's hired hands. She had overheard the rancher offer to pay them double for working on Sunday. They had vehemently refused any money at all. "Nobody would think of being paid for helping someone clean up after a twister. I can't see any difference here," one had said.

Jesus seemed to have regained his spirit. The old man's cane had disappeared into the depths of his house, which had been slightly ransacked. A smile was on his furrowed face when he handed out either a beer or soda pop to anyone who asked.

As was usual for rural Texas, some people here were tee totaling Baptists, but when a neighbor needed help, all squabbles such as the sinful drinking of alcohol were laid aside until the crisis had passed.

Rollie Turner popped the top on a cold beer. "I reckon Caleb will at least recognize the joint now. Those pricks with ears from the DEA sure did a number. I don't know how the government can get by with running over folks and not have to pay for the damage they cause."

Hector Lemmons snorted. "Dad-gummed liberal Democrats

is what the problem is. Ever dad-blasted one of them is a dad-burned lawyer and never did an honest day's work in their life. All they want to do is suck on the government tit all their worthless dad-gum lives."

Hector noticed Quentin Miller. The attorney had shown up mid-afternoon and begun shoveling feed. Lines of sweat streaked his dusty face.

"Present shysters are excepted," Hector added quickly.

"Don't stop on my account," Quentin said with a broad grin. "I enjoy a good tirade. Besides, I'm a registered Republican who never did work for the dad-blasted government. And ever since lawyers starting advertising, half of the profession turned into either ambulance chasers or politicians, so I can't fault your logic."

"There was no call for anything like this to happen. I do not care what their motives were." Quentin's prim secretary, Rosemary Page, joined.

Her hatchet face was accented by her gray hair pulled back tightly into a bun. Rosemary's initial anger over Caleb's shooting of the eagle had melted when the lawyer brought her to the ranch to let her see firsthand the destruction wrought by the DEA in their relentless search.

"I have completely rearranged Mister Santiago's books. They are now alphabetized by the author's name," Rosemary disclosed.

Jesus rolled his eyes sadly. He knew that finding any book he wanted would now be an arduous task. Nevertheless he said, "*Gracias, señora,* for your kind help. I am indebted to you."

Rosemary's lips turned into a resemblance of a smile. *"De nada, señor, se siente mejor?"*

The secretary's perfect Spanish surprised Jesus. "*Si,* I am feeling much better now."

Quentin Miller stared at Rosemary with lowered eyebrows. "I

didn't know you could speak Spanish."

"You never asked. For you erudition, I am also fluent in German, French and Hebrew."

Hector Lemmons shook his head. "Well, I'll be a suck-egg dog. Quentin's done got himself a regular perfessor working for him these days."

"A retired professor of English to be exact, Mister Lemmons," she answered and snatched a can of beer from Jesus's hand and popped the top. *"Salud,"* she said to Jesus then slugged down a healthy swallow.

Hope Rexton stepped up and faced Quentin Miller. A sultry evening breeze whipped at a wild tress of flame red hair that dangled on her worried brow. Everyone's expressions grew serious at her approach. They knew Caleb Starr's problems were far from over.

"I talked with Judge Matthews on his cell phone before I came out here," the lawyer volunteered. "He was on the golf course like I'd thought. He'd just bogied the ninth hole. Once I'd filled him in on the situation, he agreed to work in a hearing for three o'clock Tuesday afternoon. Caleb will be a free man after then."

"I feel so sorry for him," Hope said. "This nightmare is far from over. A lot of people will believe Caleb is a drug dealer, no matter what. That eagle incident started all of this. I can't help but wonder if everything that's happened is somehow tied together."

Hector placed a calloused hand on her arm. "Missy, Caleb's got a passel of friends that's gonna stick by him come hell or high water."

Tristan, who was on the porch beside Jesus spoke up, "Mister Miller, I think Hope might be right about Dad's accidentally shooting that eagle starting all of this. What's your opinion, sir?"

Quentin cocked his head. "That's already being checked on.

Unfortunately Miss Rexton is correct about these matters taking a long time to be resolved, but they will be. There's an old saying 'the truth will out'."

Rosemary Page was obviously impressed. "Why, that's from Shakespeare's *The Merchant of Venice.*"

"Si señora," Jesus said firmly. "Also but remember in Act Four of that same book, the law was ready to slice a pound of flesh from nearest a man's heart. I wish that to not be the case here." His words brought a look of awe to the secretary's face.

Rollie Turner broke the heavy silence that had settled on the assemblage like a black cloud when he announced proudly, "We don't have a thing to worry about with Quentin Miller on our side."

The lawyer forced a smile and decided he needed a beer.

Chapter 19

"There's absolutely no question about it," Jefferson Tate said to Alton McKenzie in a hushed tone. "Our computer's firewalls were breached."

The two federal agents sat at a small table at The Slip Up Saloon. It was a busy Monday night for the only bar in Lone Wolf. The men were uncomfortably aware of the baleful stares given them by the few locals in attendance. Most of the gathering consisted of nattily dressed federal employees or members of the press hoping to glean some tidbit of gossip to use in a story. After the events of this day both men needed to have a drink and talk, sardonic glares or not.

The pear-shaped bartender with a scraggly blond beard approached carrying a metal tray that held two sweaty long neck bottles of beer, ending their conversation.

Tate tossed a five spot on the metal tray. "Keep the change."

The big man's stoic expression remained unchanged as he spun wordlessly and trudged away.

"God, I hate shit-kickers," Alton grumbled.

"I'd say they probably feel the same way about us. After what's hit the fan around here, I can't blame them."

McKenzie sighed and his face grew taut. "Yeah I know, but Jeff, this shouldn't have happened. We only acted on what we thought was solid information."

"So did General Custer."

Alton McKenzie took a long drink of beer without so much

as a grin. The man possessed no sense of humor. "So the FBI files were hacked in the same manner as were ours?"

"It appears so. A trace showed the entrance originated at a pay phone in San Antonio, Texas, then to London, Tel Aviv and back to Washington, D.C. where it originally appeared, for awhile, as if the violation came from inside our own organization."

"Whoever did this was one slick, smart son of a bitch. We're supposed to be impregnable. I'd love to get my hands around his neck. We put a lot of manpower into that assault."

"His?" Tate questioned. "Do you know that for a fact?"

"No, I just assumed it was a man. I've got to stop that. These days it's equal opportunity for all criminals, ladies included."

Agent Tate's swarthy brow furrowed. "I'll bet the DEA's files were violated by the same person or group as was ours. Why they picked on this Caleb Starr, we can only speculate."

"It was that goddamned eagle he blew away. Some environmental groups are plenty radical. Remember the FWS had their files altered too. Only there, the planted information was totally different."

"Alton, I really don't believe any mainstream organization had a part in this. I've talked with the Run Free people who released that bird. They were going to drop the whole matter. It appears that Starr didn't even know he was shooting an eagle and the thing *was* after his chickens. I remember my own dad on the farm where I grew up on in Mississippi used to shoot chicken hawks. Hell, so did I. We never gave it a second thought."

Alton McKenzie spun his bottle of beer nervously. "Times change. Back in the old days, our worst problem was pot. Now we have to deal with cartels that have a bigger budget and are better armed than we are. If we're lucky enough to nail one shipment, a dozen more of that rotten shit sneaks past us. Stuff that makes pot seem harmless: horse, coke, PCPs, speed and

God knows what else."

"It's a tough world these days, coming down hard on some innocent rancher doesn't help matters. Take a look around at the faces of the folks who live here. These people hate us and they don't trust us. If we're ever going to control crime and you're going to plug those holes in the border where drugs flow like water, we need the support of these people, not their anger."

"That son of a bitch, Caleb Starr, committed a federal crime when he killed that eagle. He's not some innocent citizen in my book. Force is what gains respect these days."

Jefferson Tate finished his beer with one long swallow. "There's the letter of the law and then there's the spirit of the law. We're building more prisons all of the time and still can't keep up. I read a while back that putting up new prisons is the fastest growing segment of our economy."

"And it damn well should be," Alton said firmly.

"I'm not sure about that. Any doctor will tell you it's cheaper to prevent a disease than cure one. There may be a lesson here. Education, work programs and rehabilitation might work better than steel bars in a lot of instances. How will we really know until it's tried? I'm just glad to be retiring next year. Thirty years is plenty long enough for me. After that I'll be glad to let someone else worry about the problems of law enforcement."

Surprise washed across Alton McKenzie's stern face. "Christ, I didn't know you were planning to leave the service. You're a good agent, Jeff. We need more men like you, not less."

"The missus and I have already bought a small farm near where my folks used to live, south of Tupelo. I'm going to plant a garden, sit on the porch in the evenings and sip on a mint julep while the world keeps right on spinning without my help."

"I wish I could do that, but there's no way. I'll probably keep doing my job until some punk blows me away over a nickel bag. I can't stop. I owe that much to Dawn."

Jefferson Tate swallowed hard. He knew it was time to change the subject. Alton McKenzie would never recover from his daughter's death. And arresting drug dealers was no longer a job to him. It had become an obsession.

"The arraignment for that rancher is scheduled for tomorrow afternoon," Tate said, his voice intentionally mellow. "I assume you will be there?"

"I've been ordered to. The entire thing is a petty matter to me. Starr is guilty as Judas on killing that bald eagle. When that's out of the way, I'm going to Del Rio and meet with a snitch whose palm I've been greasing for some time. I don't want to waste any more time around this place."

"I can't help but hope the judge goes easy on him."

"You're getting soft, Tate. A law breaker of any kind is still a criminal. Never, ever forget that."

"Well," the FBI agent said, "thankfully those decisions are up to a judge and not us."

McKenzie pounded his empty beer bottle on the table and shouted to Prairie Dog, "Hey, how about some service over here!"

The portly bartender frowned and said, "Don't get your underwear in a bunch. I'm working as fast as I can."

Jefferson Tate couldn't conceal a thin smile when the fat saloon keeper began washing and drying glasses, very, very slowly.

Chapter 20

Paper plates and plastic utensils to eat with should be reserved for picnics, Caleb thought as he listlessly picked at his food. And he certainly wasn't at any picnic.

He had never been in jail before and found the experience degrading. His sister and Tip Conroy had gone out of their way to be nice, but Caleb Starr no longer felt like a human being here in the cramped concrete and steel cage.

First had come the fingerprinting, then the mug shots. A board with numbers on it held to his chest. His worn boots had been taken from him and replaced with slippers. He was perplexed when Tip had asked for his belt.

"It's just the rules," the deputy had explained. "Some folks hang themselves in a jail cell, you know."

On this, his second night of incarceration, Caleb understood what Tip Conroy had meant. *An entire year. There was no way anyone could spend that long in a place like this without at least considering suicide.*

He slid the half-eaten platter of fried chicken, mashed potatoes and gravy with a side of green peas through the slot in the bars so no one would be in any danger from him when they came to pick it up.

Then Caleb clicked on the little nine-inch black and white television set Monica had brought. Two channels with a grainy, flickering picture was the best the rabbit ears antenna could pick up through the thick walls. At least it kept his mind occupied.

Twice, he'd stomached watching the news from San Angelo. Caleb Starr had become the biggest story since a tornado wreaked havoc back in May of ninety-five. Quentin Miller had brought him a copy of the newspaper and said the DEA had cleared him of any drug dealing.

It's just not fair. Being arrested warranted headlines. Being found innocent, that's relegated to page eight, alongside an article about some flower show.

Then he remembered the eagle. He *wasn't* innocent on *that* charge.

But being locked away and treated like some monster for only protecting his chickens seemed asinine. He hadn't hurt anyone or stolen anything. That was what people were put in jail for. Not shooting a predator, and even that had been an accident.

Caleb had felt sorry he'd killed that bald eagle even before the helicopter showed up. A simple hundred dollar pair of glasses would have prevented this whole mess.

Too late for that now.

Whenever he thought back on the drug raid and how they'd accused him of being not only a dealer in that terrible business but also an ex-convict, his guts twisted into knots.

My God, how can I face Tristan and Hope? No one wants to associate with a criminal.

A heavy clang of the bolt being thrown to unlock the steel door that opened to the six cells—of which all were empty, save his—shook Caleb from his dark reverie.

At first he thought it was probably just Tip, coming to pick up the remains of dinner. Then his heart plummeted to somewhere near his ankles when the deputy announced, "Hey Caleb, you've got a mighty pretty little lady here to visit you."

Hope. The thought of her seeing him caged like some wild beast brought bile to his throat. The lithe redhead walked to his cell door wearing what Caleb knew must be a forced smile.

"At least you're an easy man to find these days," she said cheerfully, lessening his tension. "My uncle was a real rounder. Everyone in the family used to say the only time they were certain of his whereabouts was when he was in jail."

"It does work that way," Caleb answered.

"Do you want a chair Miss Rexton?" Tip Conroy asked from the open doorway. "We've got plenty of those metal folding ones. I'll be glad to fetch you one."

Hope kept her emerald eyes fixed on Caleb. "No thank you. I'll just stand. That'll make it easier for me to slip him a file."

The deputy chuckled. "You folks have a nice chat." He turned and walked away, keys rattling.

They were alone now. Caleb stepped close to the bars. The intoxicating scent of sweet perfume rose above the pervasive stench of Lysol. He began to feel like a human being again.

"How's Tristan holding up?" he asked.

"Better than you'd expect. He's a wonderful young man. I drove out to see if he wanted to come in with me. Jesus said he was at school, like you'd want him to be."

"That's good to hear. And the ranch, are things all right there? Old Jesus probably has more than he can handle."

Hope struggled to maintain her cheerfulness. She had spoken earlier with Quentin Miller. Caleb hadn't been informed of the destruction wrought by the DEA search. The lawyer thought it would cause needless worry.

"Hector Lemmons and some of your friends have been helping him. Everything's fine."

Caleb's oppressive thoughts came crashing back. Some of the people he had seen on television being interviewed by a reporter believed the hideous killer of an eagle, our national symbol of freedom, didn't deserve to live, let alone have any friends.

"I can't understand why they're doing that. I should be out of here tomorrow. For a while anyway. If Quentin has any luck, maybe he can hold off my going to prison until Tristan graduates and I can sell off the livestock and maybe the ranch."

Hope Rexton poked her hand through the bars and gently stroked his cheek. "Caleb, don't you go and give up. You've got the best darn lawyer in the state of Texas. And more friends than you realize. We're all going to fight for you, but we need your help."

A speck of dust must have gotten in his eye, Caleb thought, as he felt a tear trickle down his right cheek. "Hope, I don't know why you bother with me. Even if by some miracle I get out of this fix, all I'll ever be is a broke rancher."

"My uncle, the rounder I told you about, was a wise person. He always said that a man can only eat so many steaks, drink so much booze and sleep with so many women. After that it's all greed. Collecting things is easy. It's being happy that's so blasted hard to do in this world, and I'm happy when I'm with you—so there."

Caleb reached up and grasped her soft hand. He blinked away the moisture from his eyes and gazed at her for a long while, until he could find his voice. "Thanks for coming down here. I didn't realize just how much I needed you."

"Well, big fellow, you're going to be stuck with me for a while. I brought a deck of cards. Let me get one of those chairs from Tip, then I'll clean your clock on whatever poison you name. Blackjack, poker or whatever."

As the redhead pulled back her hand and spun to fetch a chair, Caleb said, "This uncle of yours, whatever became of him?"

Hope giggled like a schoolgirl. "Oh, eventually he went to seed. These days he's a stock broker in Dallas."

"I'm sorry."

"Yep. The whole family feels awful about that. Well, limber your fingers up and put on your glasses because I plan to cheat."

★ ★ ★ ★ ★

Part III

★ ★ ★ ★ ★

I had not known sin, but by the law.

Romans 7:7

I know of no method to secure the repeal of bad or obnoxious laws so effective as their stringent execution.

Ulysses S. Grant

Chapter 21

Tip Conroy jerked his aviator sunglasses off and stared wide-eyed through the bug-splattered windshield of the sheriff's cruiser. "If I was a chicken, I'd lay a double-yoked egg. Look at that mess, Caleb!"

Sitting in the back seat behind a grated metal screen to protect the driver and handcuffed to fulfill the regulations, Caleb Starr stiffened with shock and dismay. He had expected a few reporters to be on hand to cover his arraignment. What he beheld with astonishment surpassed his worst nightmares.

The federal building of Tom Green County was surrounded by trucks and vans, clearly marked to advertise the networks they represented. Satellite dishes mounted on their roofs pointed through openings between buildings, spreading pecan and oak trees toward distant orbiting relay stations that would instantly beam his court appearance around the world.

The stately tan brick and stone structure had been transformed into a veritable Who's Who of Journalism. CNN, ABC, NBC, CBS and the Fox Network along with dozens of lesser known television stations and newspapers were in attendance.

A hangman's noose dangling from a limb is all it would take to complete this picture, Caleb thought. *The press has already got me tried and convicted. I know Quentin's a good lawyer, but what I need here is a miracle. To the best of my knowledge, there has been a real shortage of those things lately.*

Tip shouted, "Drop down in the seat. We might get lucky and

they won't spot you until I can pull up to the prisoner's entrance. It's on the side of the building."

Caleb did as the deputy suggested. The word *prisoner* stung like a red wasp. The one saving grace was that Monica hadn't driven him in. Tip knew how much it would hurt her to bring Caleb to San Angelo, so after his night shift he'd volunteered for the distasteful task.

Tip Conroy's attempted luck was not to be. Most of the newsmen sent to cover the eagle killer's arraignment were seasoned veterans. They were used to having people try to dodge them and knew the tricks of their trade.

The moment the vehicle's worn brakes squealed to a halt, microphone carrying reporters backed up by cameramen descended in droves. Caleb didn't want to be photographed hiding like some cornered animal. As quickly as he could with his hands cuffed behind him, he rolled upright in the seat. The rancher held his head high. When an officer opened the door, Caleb climbed out and stood tall, meeting the reporters eye to eye. The journalists began yelling at him in disarrayed unison. Their shouted questions blended into a building roar like an ocean wave breaking onto a rocky shore.

Caleb could only understand some of the bellowed entreaties from faceless voices.

How do you feel about being arrested?

How do you explain the drug raid on your ranch?

Do you expect to be found not guilty?

The distraught rancher was trying to decide how to answer their idiotic questions.

Why, I just love jail. Being a drug dealer is more fun than going to Disneyland.

Quentin Miller appeared by Caleb's side and thankfully spoke for him.

"Ladies and gentlemen of the press, my client will not make

any statements at this time. This is an arraignment hearing—not a trial. Later my office will issue a release a—"

Something hard struck the side of Caleb's face and splattered. The handcuffed man jerked back just in time to see an egg sail past him to shatter on the impeccably tailored suit of a reporter.

"Down! Down! Down!" Law enforcement officers yelled. Strong arms came from nowhere and shoved Caleb and Quentin to the concrete.

"Get that bastard!" a voice shouted.

"He's got a gun!" another intoned. "NO! NO! There's two of them! Get down on your faces, scumbags."

The arms that had pushed Caleb down now helped him to his feet. He turned to stare into the face of the huge FBI agent, Jefferson Tate.

Quentin rose and surveyed the source of trouble. At least a dozen uniformed officers, some with drawn pistols, surrounded a pair of scraggly looking men who lay stretched out on the hot asphalt parking lot. One rolled his hate-filled eyes toward Caleb. "You goddamn eagle killing bastard. God will get you for what you did!"

Jefferson Tate sighed and shook his head. "Damn radical nuts. Every time there's a controversial case like this one, you can put money on the fact that at least a few wackos will show up. Problem is, sometimes they can be deadly." The FBI man shouted to the gathered officers, "Were either of them armed?"

"No, sir," one replied. "One had a carton of eggs and the other a jar of red paint or maybe blood. I'd guess they were planning on throwing it on the prisoner. For a moment that jar glinted in the sun and sure looked like a weapon. These guys are lucky as hell not to have gotten shot."

"Book 'em," ordered a sheriff's deputy with sergeant's stripes on his short-sleeved shirt. "The charge is assault. Then fingerprint them and run those men through the computer. They'll think twice before they pull anything else in this town."

At least a dozen television cameras recorded the attackers being handcuffed and carried away. They refused to walk. All the while they screamed curses and threats at Caleb Starr.

A young reporter stepped forward and shoved a microphone in Caleb's egg-splattered face. "How do you feel about this incident and the charges of killing a bald eagle?"

Tip Conroy draped his pudgy hand over the microphone and glared at the newsman. "Sir," he said with feigned calmness, "if you persist in interfering with due process of law and harassing my prisoner, I'll be forced to place *you* in the same cell with those very interesting people. Then you can ask *them* all the questions you'd like."

The young reporter swallowed hard and for a brief moment allowed his bafflement to show, something every journalist dreaded in front of cameras. He quickly regained his composure and wordlessly melted back into the milling crowd.

Jefferson Tate flashed a satisfied grin at Tip, then wasted no time ushering Caleb into the shelter of the federal building.

The west Texas sun was at its zenith for shooting down blazing heat from a cloudless sky. Inside was pleasantly cool, but to Caleb the place was permeated by an atmosphere of impersonality. Even the smells reminded him of the jail cell in Lone Wolf.

"Sorry about those assholes hitting you with an egg," Jefferson Tate said. "That should never have happened."

Tip Conroy looked at the FBI agent. "Can I take those handcuffs off now?"

Quentin Miller spoke up, "I don't want my client being hauled in front of a magistrate in chains, or splattered with an egg. Let's show a little human decency here."

Tate started to answer when Randall Whitehead of the FWS,

Bruno Leatherwood and Alton McKenzie stepped into the corridor.

Whitehead glared at Tip. "The cuffs stay on. That man is *my* prisoner, and I say what goes and what doesn't."

Quentin's neck took on a red flush. Before he could speak, Jefferson stepped between him and Randall. "You know the damn regs, Whitehead. It's up to us or the judge to decide if a prisoner is a threat or not. Now look, this man's been maligned by bad information that was somehow hacked into our computers. Starr has no record, and he's been struck by eggs. I'm taking the cuffs off and seeing to it that he gets cleaned up. It's my responsibility.

"Don't screw with me, or the next time your bunch calls me in for enforcement or back up, I just might have poor eyesight and even worse judgment."

Randall Whitehead shook with anger. "Everyone here is a witness. The FBI has taken charge. If the prisoner gets a gun and starts shooting people, it's not my fault."

"Lighten up," Bruno growled. "I've known Caleb all his life. It will be all right."

Alton McKenzie waggled his head and walked off. "Goddamn shit kickers."

Tip wore a satisfied look when he removed Caleb's handcuffs and placed them in a leather pouch on his belt.

Quentin, Tip and the FBI agent escorted Caleb into the men's room where a good portion of a roll of wet paper towels were used in an attempt to clean away the egg mess.

"Reckon that's the best as we can do," Tip said sadly, eyeing Caleb's stained shirt.

Jefferson Tate fixed his dark eyes on the rancher. "I want you to know, once you make bail I'm going back to Austin. You did nothing to deserve what's happened to you. Not only do I wish you the best, I promise the Bureau is going to do everything in its power to track down whoever hacked into our computers and see to it they get their just desserts."

"Thank you," Caleb said. "I appreciate that. I just wish a lot more people felt the way you do. Being hated is a mighty hard cross to bear."

"All storms eventually blow over, Mister Starr. Remember that," Tate said.

Quentin Miller said to Caleb, "Well, lets get down to the business of setting you free."

The aged and sparsely furnished hearing room had been constructed in nineteen-eleven when San Angelo was a much smaller town. The cramped quarters were never meant to hold the huge number of newsmen and onlookers who wanted to be present for the arraignment.

Caleb had been told by Quentin, Monica and others that the crowd would be a mixed bag of special interest groups thrown together with every news media imaginable.

Quentin had said ten thousand dollars had come to his office for Caleb's defense fund from an organization calling itself Save The West.

Along with the check had come other mail. Two letters had contained death threats. Four more declared warnings of violence against both the lawyer and Caleb. One was a polite invitation to appear on *Dateline.*

A look at the milling horde that filled the room and spilled out into the halls told Caleb his friends had been terribly correct in their predictions.

Caleb Starr took a seat alongside Quentin and Jefferson Tate at one of two worn walnut tables that faced the imposing, vacant judge's bench. Randall Whitehead, Bruno Leatherwood, Alton McKenzie and a clean-cut older man wearing an expensive-looking suit took residence at the other table.

Quentin Miller leaned close to Caleb's ear. "Christ, the Pope showing up along with Elvis and Jimmy Hoffa wouldn't have drawn a bigger crowd."

The FBI agent overheard. "Hoffa will definitely be a no-show. Even we're not certain about Elvis."

The rancher appreciated their attempts to lighten the moment. In spite of every effort, Caleb's heart thumped in time with an unheard heavy metal band while his guts writhed in his belly like a sackful of snakes.

A door behind the magistrate's bench swung open. A withered and stooped security officer, who appeared to be long past retirement age, sauntered in.

"Hear ye! Hear ye!" the aged man announced. "This court is now in session. The Honorable Magistrate, Paul Thomas presiding."

The roaring din of conversations dwindled, then ground to silence when the magistrate entered and took his place behind the high, varnished oak bench. He grabbed a gavel and struck the counter three resounding blows.

"There will be order and silence in this courtroom," he bellowed. "I will order the security officer to immediately eject anyone who violates this order."

Caleb glanced at the doddering old man wearing the security uniform and decided any ejecting would be left for someone else to attend to. The rancher was taken aback by the judge's appearance. Not only was he young, probably on the sunny side of forty, he lacked the expected black robe, wearing a business suit that would look more in place on a banker.

Paul Thomas cleared his throat then began thumbing through a stack of papers. When he finally found what he was looking for, he extracted it from the pile and dropped it to the floor. Caleb couldn't help but notice the judge's hand trembled.

This guy is more nervous than I am, Caleb thought. *He's probably never seen so many cameras outside the building before. And he knows no matter what he decides, there will be a bunch of unhappy people to criticize him.*

The security officer shuffled over, stooped with obvious effort and retrieved the paper for the judge who grabbed it and began reading the document.

Quentin, sensing Caleb's discomfort, reached over and patted his arm, but remained silent.

After a long moment the magistrate said loudly. "I have before me docket number M-8644J9. The Federal Wildlife Service versus Caleb Wayne Starr. This is a bail hearing on the charge of the killing of a threatened species to wit: one bald eagle. Is the defendant present?"

Quentin Miller answered, "Yes, your honor, and let the record show he is represented by counsel."

"Thank you, Mister Miller. And is the Wildlife Service also represented in this court?"

"They are your honor," the unknown man alongside Randall Whitehead said. "I am Jeremy Laird, a prosecuting attorney from the department, and we also have a state game warden present who was a witness to Mister Starr's confession and received possession of the deceased species from the defendant."

"Your cart is way ahead of your horse, Mister Laird," the judge said firmly. "The trial will come a bit later, if that's all right with you. This is simply a bail hearing."

"Of course, your honor," Laird answered. "These people are here in case you wish to ask them any questions."

"This simply being a matter of granting bail and having nothing to do with the guilt or innocence of the defendant, I can only commend your optimism."

Quentin Miller stood. "If it pleases your honor. We request that the defendant be released on his own recognizance. Mister Starr is a property owner with a son still in school. Except for a period of service with our armed forces in Vietnam, he has been a lifetime resident of Lone Wolf County. There is clearly no risk of flight or failure to appear."

Magistrate Paul Thomas surveyed the crowded room. "This courtroom must be an outing for optimists today. However, I am distressed by all of the publicity this incident has caused. I also understand there was erroneous and damning evidence planted in the computers of various government agencies against Mister Starr. This falsely planted data led to a DEA raid and search being conducted on the defendant's ranch that resulted in considerable damage with no illegal drugs being found." Thomas stared down from his bench at Alton McKenzie. "Is this correct, Agent McKenzie?"

The DEA man coughed. "Uh, yes sir. We found nothing illegal at Starr's ranch."

Caleb Starr felt his muscles tighten. His spine was like an icicle. *I remember now. That bastard ordered my place torn apart. I didn't think it possible. There were no drugs on my place. Not now, not ever. They wrecked my home! This isn't right!*

Quentin put a heavy hand on Caleb's shoulder and jumped to his feet, his face tight with anxiety. "Your honor. My client was taken from his ranch in handcuffs. He was unaware—until now—that his home had been ransacked. His neighbors and friends, myself included, spent many hours restoring order. Mister Starr has already suffered grievous injury at the hands of overzealous government agents. We pray that your honor will take this into consideration in his decision to grant bail."

Quentin dropped back into his chair and whispered in the fuming rancher's ear. "Caleb, please! Don't blow up. I know I'm asking a lot from you, but now is the time to grit your teeth and let me handle things."

Caleb squinted his eyes closed and knotted his fist. Then, to the lawyer's relief, he sighed with resignation and nodded his head in consent.

Anything you say or do, they'll twist it, then use it against you. A simple man can't win against the government. They have more resources than God.

Some in the crowd were plainly upset by the possible leniency they inferred from the judge's remarks and Quentin Miller's words. A building murmur of discontent swept the crowded room.

The magistrate whacked his gavel loudly. "I've already warned that there will be order in this court. I repeat. We are not here for any purpose other than the setting of bail. If this hearing turns into a circus I *will* clear the courtroom. Anyone who interferes with these proceeding will be charged with contempt of court."

A plain-faced, khaki-clad young woman standing in the back shouted, "At least the charge would be right. Any court that doesn't throw the book at some low-life who killed one of our precious wild eagles deserves nothing but contempt."

The judge's face flushed, and he pounded his gavel on the bench like he was killing a scorpion. "Officers, arrest that woman and anyone else who doesn't follow my orders to keep their mouths shut!"

Two uniformed police quickly appeared and dragged the now cursing and fighting woman down the long corridor.

The security officer stood alongside the judge's desk and watched the proceedings with obvious satisfaction.

After a few moments, quiet and order returned to the hearing room. "In case anyone else in this court wishes to make a statement," the magistrate growled loudly, "I want them to know we have a lot of empty jail cells ready and waiting." His angry eyes surveyed the room. Aside from an occasional cough, no one had a word to say.

"Mister Starr, will you please stand?" Paul Thomas requested.

Caleb and Quentin Miller rose in unison.

"Ladies and gentlemen, there is no reason under law to delay or argue over these proceedings. In a matter such as this, the releasing of a prisoner on bail, pending trial, is a prescriptive right guaranteed by the constitution. There will be no further discussion. Given the circumstances and facts presented, I hereby set bail in the amount of five thousand dollars."

Another solid whack of his gavel put a period to the moment.

"Your honor," Quentin said loudly over the now roaring crowd. "Mister Denver Gonzales, a bondsman I'm certain you know, is in attendance." The lawyer nodded to a swarthy, skinny man with a bushy moustache. "Arrangements have been made with him to secure the immediate release of my client, should it please the court."

Federal Magistrate Thomas surveyed the growing bedlam. "Anything that will put an end to this mess pleases the court. See the clerk on your way out. You know the procedure." The judge lifted his gavel, stared at it a moment, then shook his head sadly and declared, "This court is adjourned!"

Chapter 22

Marsh Wheelan pushed down the twin silver handles of the ornate opener and extracted the cork from a bottle of Mouton Rothschild with a satisfying pop. The vintage was nineteen seventy-eight, which had been a fine year for the vineyards of France. He twisted the cork free of the spiral screw and passed it critically under his nose. Passable, but not excellent. The aroma lacked the anticipated zest. He sighed with disappointment, then placed the bottle on the black marble counter top for it to breathe.

There would soon be far better wines available to soothe his discriminating palate.

Annoyed with the mediocre bouquet of the wine, Marsh walked outside and stood on the balcony of his newly-rented condominium overlooking the Pacific Ocean on Mission Beach.

San Diego was a delightful city. An enchanting, lively area, befitting a person of his many talents. Swaying palm trees framed an azure panorama that extended into infinity. He breathed deeply of the fresh, clean salt air as he surveyed the sidewalk below from his prime third-story residence.

A pair of young girls skated past on roller blades. They wore the skimpiest of thong bikinis that did little to cover God's bountiful gifts.

Ah, this was the good life. Just rewards for a man not afraid to grasp opportunity.

Marsh had decided to dine out tonight. Perhaps the fishermen who worked the bay in their small boats had been lucky. Fresh corvina grilled and covered with slivers of almonds along with a side of buttered, steamed asparagus, would make a scrumptious repast.

His reasons to celebrate were multitudinous. Being several states away from dismal Texas where that pesky Run Free group seemed determined to find and sue him was one.

Those ignorant jerks. Didn't they have the intelligence to realize how much free publicity he had given them? The bald eagle that sodbuster killed had given them millions of dollars worth of media attention. And it was entirely due to his diligence.

Hell, they should be sending him a check, not trying to cause problems.

Everything he'd done had turned out *so* well.

His perseverance in exposing Caleb Starr as a possible drug-dealing scofflaw of environmental codes had made him appear laudable.

Less than an hour ago, Marsh had completed his final task of the eagle situation. Once again his powerful laptop computer and shrewd intellect helped him hack into the files of another government agency.

That impudent rancher in Lone Wolf had a lot more trouble headed his way.

Big trouble.

The Environmental Protection Agency now had a red-flagged, take-instant-action charge against him.

Sodium Monoflouracetate, more commonly known as Compound ten-eighty, had been outlawed in the United States since nineteen-seventy-two.

But not in Mexico.

This delightful poison was so potent that an amount smaller than a pinhead would kill a coyote where it stood.

Developed for predator control, Compound ten-eighty had been widely used in the fifties and sixties for eliminating ground squirrels, prairie dogs and coyotes. Mixed with a bait of grain or meat, the effect was instantaneous and invariably lethal.

The carcass of a dead goat, laced with this deadly chemical would attract any passing eagle. They are well known as eaters of carrion. A single peck of the deadly meal, and there would be a very valuable eagle ready to be bagged and sold for a tidy profit.

It had cost Marsh Wheelan over two thousand dollars to obtain a half-liter of the lethal substance and pay for its distribution. His operative's orders were to use a small amount, then surreptitiously place the bottle and its remaining contents in Caleb Starr's barn.

A judicious investment of his hard earned money.

When the Environmental Protection Agency's inspectors, following his explicit directions, found first the bottle of Compound ten-eighty, then, in a remote part of Starr's ranch, a gutted goat, its body laced with the poison, his task would be complete.

Marsh Wheelan would garner even more praise for exposing the vicious destroyer of threatened and endangered wildlife.

The secret of being a winner is the ability to turn defeat into victory.

Already he had begun to pluck at the fruits of his labors.

Hale Cross, one of the most popular country western singers of all time, had been very generous in his support of the new Marsh Wheelan Foundation, a tax exempt corporation.

Marsh had met the outspoken environmentalist at a Run Free meeting and obtained his personal telephone number. A few well-timed calls had assured him the musician had noted the television coverage of the vile Texas eagle killer. Modestly, Marsh made sure the celebrity knew he was the one responsible for exposing the rancher's desecration of our national symbol.

Saving our planet and protecting helpless and endangered species had become a religion with Marsh Wheelan. He was the man to call to get the job done.

Hale Cross wanted Marsh to supervise the release of a pair of grizzly bears into the John Day Wilderness area of eastern Oregon. A stunningly scenic and rugged area. Cross's motives were quite understandable to Marsh. It was money.

The musician had a new album and video planned to hit the market this fall. The title was to be *Ballads of the Wild and Free.* A ghastly name to Marsh's thinking.

No matter. The singer had paid The Wheelan Foundation well to have the appropriate permits issued. With Marsh's computer hacking skills, that task was so simple as to be ludicrous.

In short order, every government agency in Oregon from the Forest Service to Fish and Wildlife would believe the grizzly bear release had been their idea all along.

The bears had to be introduced by helicopter; no motorized vehicles were allowed to mar such a pristine wilderness area.

Once the grizzlies were released, Hale wanted Marsh to camp and film the bears while they frolicked in their new habitat.

Set to music and song, the sight of these majestic animals romping free in the wild, as they had in days of old, would sell millions of copies.

Ah, the money and contacts that would garner. Marsh Wheelan's name would be on the credits. Power is built from such bases. And power was all that mattered.

The two bikini clad girls skated by again. This time they slowed and waved at him, giggling. Marsh admired the way their large breasts jiggled in the warm California sun.

One of the nice things about living in San Diego was its proximity to Mexico. A short drive, and he could indulge his discriminating urges without the bother of cleaning up the hotel room later. Maids were such snoops in the United States. He hated the task of packing bedsheets to a Laundromat and fretting over removing all of the stains.

In Mexico, well placed *mordida* took care of those little irritations.

Ah, Mexico. He watched until the laughing, bouncing girls had disappeared from sight then he returned to the kitchen and poured a glass of the Mouton-Cadet. Carefully he rolled the wineglass and observed how the film clung to the sides of the glass. Adequate was the best he could say for what had turned into a most disappointing vintage.

Those voluptuous, nearly naked girls had changed his plans for the evening. The corvina could wait. A hot tide of passion raged in his loins.

Tonight would be Mexico, and playtime.

★ ★ ★ ★ ★

Part IV

★ ★ ★ ★ ★

Ye immortal gods! Where in the world are we?

Cicero

Lord, what fools these mortals be.

Shakespeare

Chapter 23

A meager thundershower had drifted over the vicinity of Caleb Starr's ranch leaving behind a freshness to the sultry air that only added to the rancher's feeling of freedom.

It took nearly two hours to satisfy all of the technicalities of the bail requirements. In such a high profile case every "T" had to be crossed and every "I" dotted perfectly.

Once the papers were signed and approved by Judge Thomas, Quentin Miller had quickly ushered Caleb into his vintage nineteen sixty-nine Mercedes-Benz two-eighty convertible and roared off to Lone Wolf. A pair of news vans that had tried to keep up and get some more footage of the eagle killer gave up their pursuit once the lawyer sped to over one hundred miles per hour.

"Shucks, I don't have to worry about getting a speeding ticket today," Quentin had quipped with a sardonic grin. "Every cop in the area was at the hearing."

As the red Mercedes slowed and turned onto the gravel driveway that led to the ranch house, Caleb breathed deeply of the sweet air and tried to shove the nightmare of the past few days into a corner of his mind. He was home again, on his own land. He had a son to raise and a ranch to run—things that were more important than stewing on his own problems.

"Thanks, Quentin," Caleb said sincerely. "I couldn't have gotten through this without you."

The lawyer downshifted into second gear to keep an errant

stone from chipping the paint. "Don't forget that Hector Lemmons went your bail, and Hope has stuck with you through this media circus. A lot of folks are on your side."

"I'll never forget that. But a person sure never knows who their friends really are until something terrible happens. Quentin, I don't know how long it will take, but I'll see you are paid for your efforts."

Quentin cocked his head. "I'm already ahead, to my way of thinking. Do you have any idea how much free publicity I've gotten from this affair? Rosy's getting calls from all over. Folks are either wanting to hire me or shoot me. A lawyer can't ask for better than that. At the rates I charge, one good client will keep me in cigars and steaks for quite a spell. Come to think on the matter, I'd better shut up or you'll likely send *me* a bill."

Caleb smiled happily. Then he looked up the gently rolling hill to the approaching house. His smile faded like a black cloud blotting away the sunshine. "*Now* what in the wide world of hell are they up to?"

The lawyer slowed and surveyed the profusion of government cars and trucks with a grim expression. He pulled the Mercedes to a stop underneath the shade of a spreading Live Oak Tree. "Caleb, I want you to stay in the car and most of all, keep your temper in check and your mouth closed no matter what."

Caleb nodded with a sigh of resignation and slumped into the leather seat.

Quentin Miller climbed out, pulled a cigar from his jacket pocket and took a long time lighting it while he sized up the situation. When he saw Caleb's old 4 × 4 pickup hooked behind a wrecker, he winced as a bolt of comprehension struck like lightning. This should have come as no surprise.

Bruno Leatherwood stood dourly watching the proceedings. Beside him was the Federal Wildlife Service Agent, Randall Whitehead, who wore an expression of obvious satisfaction.

Bruno strode to meet the lawyer's approach.

"Quentin, I'm sorry about this, but it *is* the law," Bruno said.

"And it's a law that was never intended to be abused like this," the lawyer said, poking his cigar at the game warden like an accusing finger.

Randall Whitehead glowered and shouted, "We have the right to confiscate this vehicle and the weapon used in the commission of a federal crime. You know that, Miller!"

Quentin's neck turned crimson. He covered the distance between himself and the federal agent with five crisp steps.

"Marshals, I need your assistance here!" Whitehead barked at two young men in suits who quickly sprang to his side. "I am being threatened."

"You needn't worry about sticks and stones breaking your bones," Quentin said through clenched teeth. "But where a lawyer is concerned, words *can* hurt you."

"All I'm doing is my duty," Whitehead snapped.

"And obviously enjoying every minute of it. People with your attitude is what gives the government its lovable reputation. This could have at least been put off until after the trial."

Randall Whitehead said coldly, "Well, I deemed it an appropriate move under USCS 706 Subsection C. This act gives us the right to seize this vehicle and weapon pending the prosecution of any person arrested for violating the Migratory Bird Act."

Quentin swallowed hard and took a step backwards. He shot a glance at Caleb who was still slumped in the seat of his Mercedes. "May God save us all from bureaucrats who can quote their rule-book like a preacher reading the Bible."

Agent Whitehead motioned to the tow truck driver who sat in the cab with the diesel engine rattling. "Take it away," he shouted, "all the way to the impound yard in Lubbock, just like we discussed."

The scraggly driver nodded and everyone present watched as Caleb's pickup followed the black wrecker down the gravel road.

Quentin turned to face Whitehead. "I assume your business here is complete."

"For the moment." The federal agent seemed indifferent to the lawyer's presence. "If I can uncover any evidence that Starr had any intent to sell the one eagle we know he killed or any others, we *will* bump this up to a felony charge."

"It's just too bad you don't have any real job to occupy your time," Quentin said with a shrug. "Now that your little task is done, I would like to see you and your—minions—off my client's private property."

"Yes, we'll be leaving now. Let me assure you, Mister Miller, that this action was legally taken and search warrants in a case such as this one are quite easy to obtain."

With that statement, Randall Whitehead turned and climbed into a Suburban with white government license plates. The two suited federal marshals joined him. Then the vehicle kicked up gravel with its rear tires as it spun to move out. Three other sedans followed in its wake.

"God, I really feel bad about all this," Bruno Leatherwood said, his gaze focused on Caleb. "I wish this whole mess would just blow over." The game warden thought the burly rancher who still sat hunched in the car looked smaller than he'd remembered.

Caleb Starr kept his gaze straight ahead into a bank of low hanging black clouds. "My granddaddy used to say, 'a person might as well wish in one hand and spit in the other for all the good it does'."

Bruno shook his head sadly, went to his truck and drove off after the Suburban.

Alone now, Quentin Miller walked over to Caleb. He took a

long moment to find his words. "They'll be mighty sorry they did that. Reckon your old truck will leak so much oil the impound yard will be one hell of a mess in short order."

In spite of himself Caleb cracked a thin smile. "Yep, it'll do that all right." He climbed from the Mercedes and rolled his eyes to the house where Jesus and Tristan had just appeared on the porch. His smile fled. "I sure don't know how a man's expected to run a ranch without his truck." He turned to the lawyer. "Or are they going to take my land, too?"

"No, they can't do that," Quentin said firmly. "And there's a fair chance the judge will return your pickup." He hesitated. "But I wouldn't want to bank on it. I'd forgotten that some laws meant to stop drug dealers had been expanded to allow the government to confiscate vehicles used in the commission of other crimes also."

"All I did was keep my chickens from getting killed. For the life of me I can't figure why it got so crazy. I'm facing prison and a hefty fine there's no way I can pay, and now the bastards took my truck. The newspapers and television reports make me look worse than a serial killer. Quentin, I don't know how much more of this I can take."

Quentin motioned with his head toward Tristan who had streaks of tears on his cheeks. "Caleb, you have some darn good reasons to survive this. I'll do what I can to help and so will your friends. Right now you need to toughen up like John Wayne would have done and see to your family. Hope said to tell you she'd be by this evening and bring along a fried chicken dinner. I'm going to my office and do my job. You do yours."

When Quentin Miller drove away he studied his rearview mirror. Caleb was on the porch hugging his distraught son. The lawyer hoped his words of encouragement would turn into reality, but the way this case was going he held a multitude of doubts. A light drizzle began to splatter on the windshield. He thought of stopping and putting the top up, then thought better of it. Driving in the rain fit his mood.

"Here you go big fellow," Hope Rexton said as she placed a bowl of chicken scraps on the floor in front of the purring tomcat.

"Reckon the mice and rats hereabouts will be safe for a spell," Caleb commented. "A cat with a full belly's worthless as a politician a week after winning an election."

"Oh, but he's so much sweeter than some old windbag," Hope cooed, while scratching Useless behind his ears.

"After that good dinner I'd purr myself if somebody rubbed my back," Caleb said.

Hope flashed him a coy smile, walked over behind Caleb and began to knead his shoulders.

"I think I shall go to my house and read," Jesus said scooting back from the dining room table and standing. "Thank you, Missy, for the good dinner. Now I'll go return to my book and see how Preston Lewis gets his people out of a very bad fix. He is a really good storyteller, you know."

"Have a good night," Caleb said quickly. He was looking forward to spending some time alone with Hope. Tristan had taken the car into town to attend night school and likely wouldn't be home for a few hours. Thankfully, no one had mentioned a word about the events of the day. It felt wonderful to be able to forget his problems for a while. Having a pair of soft hands massage his shoulders while he basked in the aroma of sweet perfume was a taste of pure heaven.

The screen door slammed lightly, and Jesus shuffled away into the night.

Hope spread her fingers and stroked Caleb's arms. She bent and nuzzled her ruby lips to his ear. "I'm so glad you're home."

"What's wonderful is having you here. After everything that's hit the fan because of me I don't know why you bother."

Hope unsnapped the top two buttons of his short sleeve shirt, slid her hands to his bare shoulders and continued massaging them. It felt to Caleb as if she wore velvet gloves.

"Your heart's in the right place. That's what counts. I wasted a lot of good years with a man who cared nothing about anything but himself and making money. You care about me and others, Caleb Starr. That's all any woman needs from a man."

"I sure don't have anything else to offer except my caring."

Hope withdrew her hands and caressed his cheeks. "That's more than I've ever had."

Caleb's reply was cut short by the harsh ringing of the wall phone.

"Dad-blast that thing," he grumbled as he stood to answer it. "If someone's trying to sell me another credit card, I'm liable to reach through the line and wring their scrawny neck."

"Hello," was all the rancher spoke into the receiver before the color drained from his face. "I'll be right there."

Hope knew something was desperately wrong. "What is it?"

"It's Tristan. That was Monica. He's been taken to San Angelo by the ambulance. She said he's been beaten up and is in bad shape. Damn it, Hope, I don't even have anything to drive."

"Where did they take him? What hospital?"

"Community General."

"We'll take my car," she took the telephone from Caleb's trembling hands and placed it back on the hook. "He'll be all right. You have to believe that."

"Hope, the way things have been going lately, I've got a terrible feeling about this."

"Come on," she said leading him to the door. "Let's get there and take care of your son."

Chapter 24

Monica Blandon's face was taught with tension and anger when Caleb and Hope met her in the hospital waiting room.

Bones set a half-full Styrofoam cup of coffee on the table and stepped beside his wife. "I just can't believe it. Things like this just don't happen in Lone Wolf."

The presence of the undertaker caused Hope to gasp, "Oh, my God!"

Bones tried to force a comforting smile. "Tristan will be all right," he said firmly. "I just came along with Monica. She's pretty upset about the incident."

"You bet I'm upset," the sheriff said with a sharp edge of bitterness to her voice. She swallowed and continued in a more soothing tone, "Caleb, your son's in surgery. Like Bones said, he'll be okay, but it was touch and go for awhile. He has some broken ribs; one of them punctured his right lung."

Caleb's face was like stone. "Who did this? How did it happen?"

Monica sighed and studied the pattern in the waiting room carpet while she gathered her thoughts. "From what we've been able to learn, Tristan had just left night school and was climbing into his car when three men wearing camouflage clothes grabbed him and started pounding on him with baseball bats. One girl saw the incident and screamed. If she hadn't, I don't want to think about what might have happened."

"Who were they?" Caleb asked coldly.

"Strangers. The girl had never seen any of them before. I *will* get my hands on them. When I do those thugs will wish they'd never been born."

"She means it too," Bones said. "Tip's out right now scrounging up the rope to hang 'em with."

"I wish we could still do that these days," Monica spat.

Caleb shook with rage. "They'd still be getting off too easy. Tristan's just a boy. He's never gone and hurt anyone. What on earth could have caused something like this to happen to him?"

Bones sighed and slid an arm around Monica's waist. "Well, the girl who stopped the attack,"—his voice was hesitant—"she heard them cursing Tristan while they were beating him."

Caleb's eyes narrowed to mere slits. "Well?"

"They were yelling that eagles and wildlife have their rights, too. If anyone harmed any of God's creatures, that person deserved to die, and they were avenging angels of the helpless."

"Damn radical nuts," Caleb fumed. "There were some arrested at the hearing today. I just never dreamed anyone could sink so low as to take their frustrations out on an innocent kid. Tristan had nothing at all to do with that eagle getting killed."

Hope snuggled close to Caleb and gave him a hug. "There's a lot of crazies running around loose these days. Some convince themselves killing a doctor who performs abortion will get them into heaven. If you can follow warped thinking, it's not much of a reach to conclude that whoever beat Tristan believed they were sending a message to everyone when they attacked him. These people obviously place a higher value on eagles and wolves than their fellow man."

"The law will still take care of them," Monica said. "At least that much common sense is still in effect."

"Mister Starr?" a lady with short dishwater blond hair walked toward them. Hope noticed she was smoothing out a band-aid in the bend of her left arm.

"Yeah, that's me," Caleb said guardedly.

"I just wanted to tell you how sorry I am about all of this," the lady said. "My name is Dianne Petrov. I work for the Run Free Organization."

Monica was the only one not stunned into silence. "Why are you here?"

Dianne Petrov seemed disheveled and plainly concerned. Hope thought that if this was an act, the woman who had been at least partially responsible for causing Caleb's problems deserved an academy award.

"When I got a call about what had happened in Lone Wolf I checked with the hospital and found out the boy needed blood. I know it wasn't much, but I felt it was something I had to do."

Caleb emotions were a jumble. "Thank you, ma'am," he said with a nod.

Dianne Petrov's moist eyes darted back and forth between Caleb and Hope. Her lower lip began to quaver then she choked back a sob and darted through the waiting room doors.

"Well, don't that beat all," Bones commented after a moment. "Here we were running down enviro nuts and now one of the biggest nuts on the tree comes and gives Tristan some blood and says she's sorry."

"Some questions don't have easy answers in the world we live in today," Hope said.

Caleb was still staring at the door through which Dianne Petrov had fled. "I'd reckon you went and hit that nail square on the head."

Jefferson Tate was leaning back in his swivel chair studying a tractor brochure when he was jerked back to reality by the jangling of his phone. Now that retirement loomed close, he found himself wanting more and more to get out from behind this desk in a corner of the stuffy federal building, climb on a tractor and make things grow.

He sighed, slid the sales brochure into a drawer and picked up the receiver. "Federal Bureau of Investigation, Special Agent Tate speaking."

"Mister Tate, this is Will Jameson of the Environmental Protection Agency here in Dallas."

Jefferson liked the man's easy drawl. He was likely a native Texan or at least had been in Dallas long enough to not snap out his words like so many people in the government did. "Yes sir, how can we help out the EPA this fine day?"

"Have you ever heard of a banned poison that was used for predator control over forty years ago called Compound ten-eighty?"

"Nope, can't say that I have."

"We have a priority message that a rancher in your district is using some of the stuff to kill eagles. It's the same old boy that's been in the news lately. Our records show that you and an Alton McKenzie with the DEA were involved with a raid on his ranch last week. The fellow's name we're investigating is Caleb Starr."

Jefferson Tate bolted upright, his dreams of farming forgotten. There were many aspects of the Starr case he found troubling, especially the information that had been hacked into the government computers. "The DEA ran their raid on Starr's ranch independent of us. We were called in to assist the FWS. Let me ask you, Mister Jameson. Is the source of your information solely in your computer banks?"

"Everything's on computer these days," Jameson drawled. "May I ask why you're concerned about our source?"

The FBI agent carefully explained the erroneous data that had been planted against Caleb Starr.

There was a moment of silence while Jameson punched keys on his desktop. He whistled into the receiver, "Who-ee, it looks like our boy, Starr is a real outlaw. He's a well known trafficker in endangered species and has done hard time in Huntsville for killing an IRS agent, of all things." He chuckled, "The IRS thing I'd reckon we could overlook, but not the rest of it."

Jefferson Tate smiled. His first impression was correct. Jameson wasn't going to go off half cocked. "Let me assure you that aside from killing that eagle, Caleb Starr has no prior criminal record."

"The information we have is that there is a pint of ten-eighty hidden in his barn."

Jefferson Tate worried his cheek between his thumb and forefinger. He held little doubt that the banned poison was in Starr's barn. He also had no doubt that Alton's raid would have found it if it had been there earlier. The Drug Enforcement people wouldn't have missed anything that obvious. Someone had a vendetta against Caleb Starr. Someone with money and ability. Whoever they were they had committed a federal crime by breaking into the government's computers. That gave the FBI every reason to go after them. "Mister Jameson—"

"Just call me Will."

Tate smiled again. "Okay Will, I think this matter needs to be kept under wraps for awhile. No publicity, nothing the media can get their grubs on. Could you meet me in Lone Wolf tomorrow—say around ten—at the Lone Wolf Inn? It's the only motel in town, so I won't be hard to find."

"Then what? I'll have to take some action about the ten-eighty."

"Let's cross that bridge when we come to it. I'm certain your poison is there, and I'm also certain it's been planted. Caleb Starr has had his season in hell for some reason; I don't want to cause him any more trouble. Aside from that, I want to nail the son-of-a-bitch who's been hacking into our computer systems. You can bet your last nickel that when we find them, you'll have the real culprit that's been messing around with that nasty compound."

"Sounds reasonable to me. I'll hop a commuter plane to San Angelo and pick up a car there. Give me your cell phone number, and I'll call you if there's any change. I've never done any real detective work before, but I think I might enjoy it."

Tate gave the EPA official his cell number and added, "The one guarantee I will make is the restaurant there has the best dog-gone mesquite grilled steaks you ever wrapped your lips around."

"See you tomorrow."

Jefferson thought for a moment. Then he punched up the phone number for a man he wanted to be with them when they drove to Caleb Starr's ranch tomorrow. He hit the speed dialer.

A voice answered, "Hello, this is Agent McKenzie speaking."

Chapter 25

The rising sun was a fiery glow peeking above the rolling hills on the eastern horizon when Hope Rexton dropped an exhausted Caleb off at his ranch and sped away to get ready for work. After Bones and Monica had left, both of them had spent a sleepless night at the hospital, drinking bad coffee from a machine down the hall, talking and worrying.

Around two o'clock in the morning a doctor had came in still wearing his green surgical scrubs. Caleb thought he looked too young to have even graduated from college.

"Tristan is resting in intensive care," the physician had said with an assuring manner. "We repaired the pneumothorax—that was the hole in his lung—but were unable to get the bleeding under control and were forced to remove his spleen. Don't worry about that. It's an organ he can live perfectly well without. He'll make a full recovery and likely be able to leave the hospital in a couple of weeks."

On the heels of the surgeon had come a hatchet-faced, silver-haired woman packing a clipboard. She politely asked for Caleb's insurance information. When told there was none she had shot daggers from her steely eyes and stomped off. Paying what would undoubtedly be a staggering hospital bill had given the overwrought rancher a new set of worries to add to his growing collection.

Old Jesus came shuffling from his small house to meet with Caleb who stood wondering who had come to visit. There was a late model Dodge diesel pickup parked in front of the barn.

"*Señor* Lemmons and one of his hired men came by very early this morning," Jesus said to Caleb's unasked question. "He told me about young Tristan being in the hospital, and then I knew why you and Missy Hope had left so fast last night. I do not understand all of this happening over a dead bird. It makes no sense to me."

"Not much of anything makes sense lately." Caleb scanned the area. "Where is old Hector anyway?"

"He is gone. I am to tell you the truck is yours to use for as long as you need it. *Señor* Lemmons seemed very angry about what had happened to yours."

Another familiar burning lump found a home in Caleb's throat. "He didn't have to do this."

"*Si señor,* I am certain of that too, but he was in such a mood, *I* was not going to point that fact out to him."

Caleb sighed, "I'm sure lucky to have friends like Hector and you. It seems like I can't keep from getting further and further in Dutch. Thankfully, Tristan will be fine, but now I'll likely have to sell the place to pay for his hospital bills. I'm afraid that even Quentin Miller may be running low on miracles."

Jesus clucked his tongue and cocked his head in thought. "Uh, *señor,*" he said with hesitation, "young Tristan's hospital bills may not be such a problem."

"What do you mean?"

"Well, the young man came by to visit on his way home from school many months ago. He had an envelope with forms for insurance that is available. He mentioned that he did not wish to show it to you because it would cost money. It was not much and boys do break arms and such in their play. Please do not be angry with me, *señor,* that I paid for it without your knowing."

A person would think I'd be used to having bombshells dropped on me by now, Caleb thought as that burning lump in his throat built up steam. *Jesus most likely has trouble putting food on his own table without paying for my son's insurance. Hell, I'm his father, yet Tristan must think I'm too poor to take care of him.*

Jesus continued, "The insurance papers I have on my table. I showed them to *Señor* Lemmons, and he says since the boy was hurt on school property that there will be no problems."

Caleb Starr's face was a mask of stony dignity as his eyes darted back and forth from the elderly sheepherder to the new pickup truck.

"Thanks," was all he could manage to say as he trudged off to the shelter of his home, keeping his gaze focused on the dusty earth.

Jesus watched Caleb's departure stoically. Then the old man shuffled off to start the windmill pumping and water his garden. The day was building up to be a west Texas scorcher. Already the zucchini squash leaves were wilting.

The old patriarch understood well why Caleb had left so abruptly. No man wishes to be seen to shed a tear. That would cause an added distress. At least he wasn't angry with him, and Jesus knew how badly his friend needed that pickup truck to drive.

Chapter 26

Marsh Wheelan had to keep reminding himself to watch his speed. Thankfully the Mexican border was miles behind, but it certainly wouldn't be prudent to get stopped for speeding. The California Highway Patrol was noted not only for being picky about traffic laws, but also being quite observant.

What if some nosy cop happened to notice a splatter of blood he'd missed during his hurried attempts to clean himself up and started asking questions . . .

He had never killed anyone before. But ah, the rush of sensations that still coursed through his veins. They were a fascinating mix of sensuality, fear and power. Most alluring of all was the heady sense of power.

The fact that the diminutive Mexican whore had died so easily was simply further proof of man's superiority over women.

Marsh took a deep breath and eased off the accelerator pedal. The needle on the speedometer dropped back to within the posted speed limit. He flipped on the right turn signal of his green Ford Bronco and moved out of the fast lane.

There was a Grateful Dead CD in the player. He punched it on, and the rhythm of the blaring rock music began keeping pace with his throbbing heart as Marsh Wheelan relived the most memorable experience of his life.

The dusky-skinned girl with long raven hair couldn't have been much over twenty years old. She had told Marsh that she was a mere sweet sixteen. But all women, whether they were whores or not, lied about their age.

In a smoked filled, noisy bar, an American hundred dollar bill had widened the girls doe eyes and made an easy task of luring her into his hotel room. Then he had to promise her another hundred dollars to allow him to tie her up, spread-eagle, to the bedposts.

The whore had obviously entertained some kinky clients in the past. She wore a subtle smile while Marsh secured her naked body with silken nylon cords he had brought along for this purpose. As quick as a snake can strike he had rammed a black rubber dildo down her throat before she could realize what was going to happen to her and scream for help.

Then the *real* fun had begun.

The first time Marsh could remember being aroused was when he was a mere boy. There had been an old B-grade western movie on the television. In one of the scenes a woman had been bound to the tailgate of a wagon. Her dress was ripped open to expose her naked back. Then a snarling man with a black bullwhip had slashed crimson stripes across her creamy white skin. To Wheelan, the most stimulating of all had been the woman's screams of fear and agony.

It was a shame that he had to settle for whining and thrashing about. Listening to the symphony of screaming would have to wait until he was rich enough to afford a place miles from any curious ears.

Ah, but the dreams of times to come.

Marsh admitted to himself that he had gotten a little too carried away with the whipping. The whore's swarthy skin glistened with blood when he finally took her. He thought his lovemaking skills were the reason for the girl's intense bucking and moaning while he enjoyed himself and jammed the sex toy deeper into her throat. Instead the slut had been choking to death.

Ah, but the sensation it had given him.

If only he had had the foresight to videotape that wonderful affair.

No matter. The memories would last a lifetime. A dead whore turning up in a cheap hotel room in Mexico could never be traced to him.

Marsh punched off the CD player. The silence helped him to collect his thoughts.

It was time to move on. The Run Free organization was still trying to find him and serve that annoying lawsuit. *The bastards.* And after all he had done to further their cause.

A thin smile washed over his face when he thought of that eagle killer going to jail. The stowing of a jar of Compound ten-eighty on Caleb Starr's ranch had been a stroke of pure genius. Now, with that sordid affair finally behind him, he could focus on things that really mattered.

Hale Cross had advanced a goodly sum of money for the filming of his music video. Since the grizzly bears were to be released in Oregon, heading north would be a prudent move.

Once he returned to his condo he would shower, change into some nice clean clothes, load up his Bronco and leave this very night. Only a sluggard dawdled when opportunity beckoned.

It was amazing what a person could find on the Internet these days. A ranch in the foothills east of Los Angles that furnished animals for movies and television shows happened to have two grizzlies for sale. The bears were tame, of course. Old and toothless. Just what he was looking for. Marsh Wheelan was not fool enough to risk harm to himself by filming bears that might turn on him. It was a sad fact that these grizzlies would certainly perish when left on their own.

That was of no consequence. Hale Cross's video was what mattered. He couldn't be bothered worrying over the fate of two scraggly old bears. There were far more important interests to consume his time. Using his image as a staunch environmentalist as a springboard to politics and power was his shining goal.

The exit ramp to his condo was fast approaching. He allowed himself one last fleeting memory of the wonderful experience with the whore. He *did* owe her his thanks. She had given him a taste of what absolute power was all about.

Soon, very soon, he would have the kind of power he had always dreamed of. And lately Marsh Wheelan had been having some very good dreams.

Chapter 27

Hector Lemmons drained the last golden drop of beer from the long-neck bottle and rapped the empty on the scarred oak table. "Hey Prairie Dog, better rustle us up another round over here," he shouted to the portly barkeep, then grinned wryly. "And guess what, our local shylock's actually gonna pony up for this one. I'm wonderin' if we oughta observe a moment of silence to let everyone here absorb the enormity of this momentous occasion?"

Quentin Miller leaned back in his chair and feigned a look of deep concern at the white-haired rancher. "Why I'm only doing my part in looking out for other folks' good health. Doctor Rexton can't patch up a burned out liver like he can fix a broken arm you know."

Hector snorted, "There's a passel more old drunks out there than there are old doctors. I'd have reckoned a better line of defense coming from a noted penny-pinchin' barrister than a lame excuse like that one."

The lawyer chuckled. "You should know better than to expect a direct answer from a man of my profession. I'd break a sacred and sworn code of ethics if I came right out and admitted that I'm actually a cheapskate who prefers to do his drinking when other folks are paying the tab. I spent years in law school learning how to skirt the truth. It would be a pity to let all of that good training go to waste."

Rollie Turner shook a kink out of his artificial leg. "It gives me a cold chill to think on just how many lawyers there are infestin' this country." Then quickly added, "Present company excepted, of course."

Prairie Dog Pete ambled over to the table carrying a tray full of beer bottles and began setting them out. His eyes narrowed as he focused speculatively at Quentin. "How's things looking for Caleb Starr these days?"

A tense silence settled over the assemblage like an oppressive fog, signaling an end to their lighthearted banter. Caleb's ongoing troubles over his killing that bald eagle were on everyone's mind, only no one wanted to be the first to bring up the subject. Now that Prairie Dog had breached the matter, there could be no more postponing the inevitable.

Quentin Miller stiffened, knotted his hand into a fist and rested it under his chin, obviously planning to measure any reply carefully.

Hector Lemmons shrugged his shoulders with disgust. "That man's had shit served up to him on a shingle. A bunch of wackos nearly kill his son. Then some crackbrained laws thought up by a bunch of nincompoops allowed the government to steal his old pickup truck.

"There's not a mother's son of them government, low-life, dry gulchin', spineless, gutter crawlin', polecat flunkies that's got enough common horse sense tucked away in their narrow minds to pour sand out of their boots. All they want to do is sit on their dead asses and quote from some rule book that's got more laws in it than Carter has little liver pills. The sad part is, ever one of them is an educated idiot. Now there's not a worse kind of idiot that the good Lord ever allowed to wander around on the face of his green earth than the educated variety. I'd say that if God allows Washington to keep on gettin' by with its shenanigans, he owes the folks of Sodom and Gomorrah an apology."

Rollie Turner took a sip of beer and regarded the irate rancher with a serious expression. "Why Hector, we're all friends here. If you're upset with the government for some reason, come right out and say so. There's no reason for you to pussyfoot around on the subject. Holdin' in your true feelings might upset your digestion."

Prairie Dog had other customers to wait on and wanted to get to the guts of what was going on so he could tell his own version of the facts later. He stared at Quentin and clucked his tongue with impatience. "Is Caleb actually gonna have to go to jail for shootin' that durn bird that was fixing to munch on his chickens or not? Seems like every day I hear a different story. If you ain't got a plan by now that'll get him off, I'd reckon his goose is done cooked. Be one hell of a shame if that happened."

Everyone within earshot looked expectantly at the lawyer causing him to shift nervously about in his chair. Quentin opined to himself that he felt like someone being cross-examined in court who preferred not to give a truthful answer. "All I can say at this stage of the game is that I simply don't know what the outcome will be. The laws on this matter are both harsh and chiseled into granite somewhere back in Washington. It's an indisputable fact that Caleb did kill an eagle. What's unfortunate is the situation could have been handled if the fourth estate hadn't become involved."

Prairie Dog's bushy eyebrows narrowed in puzzlement. "How in the whole dad-blamed world did somebody's estate come to muddy the water? They sure couldn't have been from around here. Leastwise nobody's turned up their toes that I've heard anything about."

Hector Lemmons sighed and shook his head sadly at the bartender. "It's a cryin' shame you missed out on getting a government job. You'd have fit right in. To add to the storehouse of solid information that gets less use from you than a clean bar towel. The fourth estate is the news media."

"Oh, I knew that," Prairie Dog replied somewhat sheepishly. "I just had to think on it for a minute was all."

Rollie Turner spoke up, "Don't let his chidin' bother you none, Prairie Dog." He glared at the lawyer. "I find it plumb refreshing to be around folks that aren't hindered by an overloaded intellect."

"Caleb's trial date has been set," Quentin Miller said softly, bringing a steely silence to the saloon. "It'll be in twelve weeks. The Feds are moving fast on this one."

"When did all this come about?" Hector finally asked. "We ain't heard a word about it."

"I just got notified this afternoon," the lawyer grimaced. "There's some bad news. They've moved the case to Lubbock, and the FWS has a judge by the name of Kurt Gerhard to preside. Gerhard is a left wing extremist and is out to make a name for himself. I'm pulling in every marker I can to try and get a change of venue, but I doubt that will happen."

Prairie Dog tucked the metal tray he'd carried the drinks on under his arm and studied the plank floor. "It just ain't right to send a man off to jail and fine him more money than most of us'll ever see for shootin' a blasted bird."

Quentin sat up straight with a sigh. "Like I said, it's way too early to say how things will turn out. This is a high profile case, and there's a lot of pressure to make an example out of Caleb. That wasn't just a bird he shot; it was a bald eagle. They're our national symbol and a protected species. Anyone who is associated with this trial will get a lot of news coverage. Nothing draws out radicals quicker than a television camera. I'm betting Rosy could fill a shoe box with all of the hate mail and threats I've received from simply representing Caleb."

Hector said, "There's a boy lyin' in a hospital bed in San Angelo that's proof some of these nuts ain't all talk."

"Caleb's sure had a truckload of problems dumped on him," Rollie Turner remarked. "I surely hope he can tough this out."

"He will," Hector said forcing a smile. "Hell, ever dad-blamed storm blows over eventually."

"Yep, I'll drink to that," Quentin Miller said grabbing onto his beer. "I didn't become the best darn lawyer in Texas by going around losing. This is shaping up to be a tough bronc to ride, but this ain't my first rodeo. I plan on kicking some government butt in Lubbock."

Hector, Rollie and Quentin clicked their bottles in a toast. When people lose their faith, the battle is already lost.

Dianne Petrov dabbed a Kleenex to her puffy red eyes then wadded it into a ball and added it to the overflowing wastebasket beside the couch. She grabbed the remote control and punched the red "off" button putting an end to the mindless chatter and irritating canned laughter of some television sitcom.

The hot West Texas sun was floating high in a cloudless azure sky, yet she still wore a rumpled housecoat over her pajamas. Her sick days with the Run Free organization were running out. This problem, however, was of minor consequence compared to the raging moral struggle that had been playing tag with her soul.

If only that damn eagle had flown off in some other direction, none of this would have happened, Dianne thought for what she knew must be the thousandth time.

Only it hadn't. The demise of raptor number two-eleven at the hands of that rancher was still making national news.

At first Dianne had believed—hoped—the matter would be quietly handled on a local level. The man who shot it needed to pay a fine to teach him a lesson for his disregard for wildlife. Wolves, eagles and hawks all had their place in the ecosystem and a right to exist unmolested.

Then Marsh Wheelan's rash actions and the resulting storm of media attention had forced her to study the rancher and come to terms with why he had acted as he did. That was the dawning of her dilemma.

Caleb Starr hadn't killed that eagle out of malice, nor for profit or pleasure. He had acted as he did to protect a flock of red, egg-laying chickens that were near his home. Also, the rancher was far from a wealthy man. Her research showed Starr was deeply in debt and making only a meager living from the cattle, goats and sheep that grazed on the sparse grass of the Lone Starr Ranch. A fine of the magnitude dictated by law for killing an eagle would be a crushing blow for a man like him.

Dianne had always supported and even applauded the multitude of laws that had been passed by state and federal legislatures to protect and preserve endangered and threatened species. These laws were well intentioned, and no reasonable person could condone the extinction of any of God's creatures when it was scientifically possible to avoid such from happening.

In the case of Caleb Starr and Raptor Two-Eleven things had gone horribly wrong.

And Dianne Petrov knew she was the only person aware of why the flurry of government actions and news media attention had been given to this incident.

More specifically, she knew exactly *who* was responsible: that weasel, Marsh Wheelan.

The Run Free organization was attempting to sue Marsh for the damage he had done from his selling of the videotape of the incident to *The Weekly World Probe.* No one but her had a clue that Marsh was responsible for all of the rest. The DEA raid on the ranch, the FBI involvement. Government agencies had descended on Lone Wolf, Texas, like water from a burst dam.

Marsh Wheelan had been busily working to further his own

ambitions by any means available to him.

I've decide to resign and start my own environmental group. Marsh's words echoed inside her head like a familiar nightmare.

Dianne had made enough inquiries, both discreet and otherwise, to learn of the erroneous information that had been hacked into the computers of various government agencies regarding Caleb Starr. Marsh Wheelan not only had the motive and morals to do such a thing, he also had the ability. The cocky little punk's skills with a computer were uncanny.

The best approach for the future of her career would be to keep silent. At first, she had decided to do just that. After all, Starr *did* kill an eagle.

Then his innocent son, Tristan, had been nearly beaten to death. She remembered vividly seeing the battered boy lying in that bed when she donated blood. Shortly thereafter she had seen Caleb Starr in the waiting room and read the anguish in his leathery face.

Dianne took a sip of tepid black coffee, then punched numbers on her phone with a trembling finger. She kept her resolve until a woman's voice answered.

"Lone Wolf County Sheriff's Department. This is Sheriff Blandon speaking."

With a sob Dianne broke the connection and threw the cordless phone onto the couch. She had tried before to tell what she knew with the same results.

Dianne cursed her lack of courage. She leaned back on the sofa, found the remote and clicked on the television. Perhaps there would be a movie on, something that might let her forget the burning memory of Tristan Starr's battered face—at least for a little while.

Chapter 28

Caleb Starr savored the delightful lingering aroma of sweet perfume as he sat at the kitchen table listening to the gurgling coffee pot. Hope Rexton was still noisily fidgeting about in the bathroom, leaving him to his thoughts. It had been a long while since he had cause to wonder what in the world a woman finds to do in there that takes so darn long to accomplish.

Not that he minded. Waking up in the morning to a beautiful lady sleeping by his side was welcome as a warm summer rain in the desert. And just as unexpected.

He frowned when a twinge of guilt stabbed at his conscience. He wondered if this is how a man feels when he cheats on his wife. In all of the years he had been married, Caleb had never strayed from his marriage vows.

Get it out of your head. Laura's been gone for a long time now.

Then Caleb pondered if the misgivings he felt were because he was involving Hope in a situation she need not suffer through. A woman shouldn't embroil herself with a man whose future appeared as bleak as his.

The coffee maker gave out a loud sputter as it always did to signal its work was done. He stood, went to the cupboard and grabbed his mug, then with a vulpine grin extracted a second. It dawned on him that he didn't know if Hope liked cream and sugar in hers. To be on the courteous side, he filled a pitcher with milk and set it on the table alongside the sugar bowl. While he awaited Hope's appearance, Caleb sipped on his steaming coffee and replayed the wonderful memories of last night in his head.

The lithe redhead had dropped by after work and accompanied him to San Angelo to visit Tristan in the hospital. It felt wonderful to be able to make the drive in a decent truck that had a working air conditioner. When Hope had scooted over and snuggled close by his side, it had reminded him of happier times, long past.

It hadn't taken but a few minutes for Hope's sparkling emerald eyes and infectious smile to cause him to forget his multitude of troubles. She bubbled with enthusiasm like the optimist whose glass was always half full, never half empty.

Tristan's attitude and greatly improved condition had completed Caleb's enjoyable journey to cheerfulness. His son's main concern seemed to be getting out of the hospital and returning to his studies so he could graduate.

The young doctor who had operated on Tristan came by and pored through a stack of notes held fast inside a metal clipboard.

"He's doing quite well," the physician had said with a satisfied nod. "Actually a lot better than I'd expected, considering the amount of trauma that was inflicted. The bruises look worse than they really are. All we need to do now is keep an eye out for infection. The blood work checks out good, however, so there is no reason for any undue worry." He flashed a sly grin at Tristan. "If you'll promise to stay out of any more bar fights, I'll probably let you go home in a couple of days."

Buoyed by his son's unexpectedly rapid recovery, Caleb had draped an arm around Hope's shoulders on the way home and drew her close.

"Why don't we drop by The Slip Up for a drink?" he'd asked.

Hope nuzzled his ear. "That sounds wonderful, but I have a bottle of really good wine on ice in the cooler I brought along especially for this evening. I was thinking maybe we could spend some time—alone."

When they'd driven up to the house, he'd been pleasantly relieved when Jesus had quickly retreated. The old patriarch had given them a wave, then went inside and flipped on the reading light beside his easy chair. Perhaps, Caleb had mused, the wily fellow could read signs other than the weather.

They had wound up drinking the bottle of wine in bed. Hope and he had shed their clothes and melded their naked bodies together with all the passion and vigor of much younger lovers.

Pillow talk and lovemaking had kept them awake long into the blissful night. Caleb was gratified to find his equipment was still in good working order. Even his rickety back seemed to have made a miraculous recovery.

"Well, you're looking mighty chipper this morning," Hope said happily from the doorway, shaking him from his pleasant reverie. "If I didn't have to go help Dad in his office, I'd see if I couldn't give you cause to act a little more tuckered out."

Caleb grinned at her and shrugged his shoulders innocently. "I'd venture that car of yours might have a dead battery or maybe a flat tire or two. Something like that could hold you up for a spell."

Hope was already dressed in her white nurse's uniform. She glided over and pecked a kiss on his cheek. "Later, tiger," she cooed. "I'll be here tonight."

She poured a cup of coffee and left it black, just the way he liked his. Rays of golden morning sunlight played along the soft features of her face and twinkled in her deep green eyes. Caleb felt as if he were the luckiest man in the entire state of Texas, with Louisiana and New Mexico tossed in for good measure.

Hope went to the stove and busied herself frying up bacon and eggs for breakfast. Caleb moseyed over to survey his ranch from the kitchen window. His heart fell to somewhere near his kneecaps when he spied Jesus ambling about. To his relief, instead of coming to visit, the old man had grinned and given him a thumbs-up. Then went to work in his garden. Jesus might be packing the weight of many years, but he remembered a man and woman needed to be left alone on occasion.

Caleb was sopping up the last remnants of his eggs with a piece of toast when the phone jangled.

"You know," he muttered, getting up to answer it, "if I quit sending that outfit a check every month, I'd bet this wouldn't keep happening."

From the deep lines that grew across the rancher's face, Hope knew the call wasn't a pleasant one. He only said a few terse "Yes sirs" and an "I understand" into the receiver before placing it back on the hook.

Hope stared into her coffee cup and waited for Caleb to speak.

"That was Quentin Miller," he said after a long moment. "The trial date for my shooting the eagle has been set for October. It's going to be held in Lubbock for some reason. He told me not to worry, but there was something in his voice that told me I have plenty to be concerned about. I'd best go visit with him later today. Quentin might be a darn good lawyer, only I can read him like Jesus does a book. I'm afraid a whole building full of shysters might not be able to get me out of this fix."

Hope stood, went to his side and gave him a sheltering embrace. "Hey, big guy, don't go getting into a funk on me. We'll handle this together." She looked up into his worried face with a sweet smile and said softly, "No matter what happens, you'll still have hope."

Caleb watched with moist eyes as she climbed into the red Mustang and drove off, leaving behind a white cloud of caliche dust in her wake.

After another cup of coffee to collect his thoughts, it was

time to get on with the day's work. When a person owns a ranch, problems, no matter how grave, couldn't be allowed to interfere with its operation.

When Caleb walked out on the porch, Jesus came hobbling over. At first he thought the old man was coming to rib him about last night. Jesus's serious expression told him otherwise.

"*Señor,*" Jesus said pointing with his index finger toward the tree-covered ridge behind the main house, "there are many buzzards circling a short ways away. Something must have died over there. I hope it is not one of your fine cattle."

Caleb squinted into the distance. He had yet to get another pair of glasses. Still, he could make out black forms against an azure sky. The old man might be correct in his assessment. Only the Brangus cows were in that pasture.

"I'll go check it out," Caleb said. "Maybe we'll luck out, and it'll turn out to be a deer that got caught up with by a pack of coyotes or something like that. I'd surely hate to lose a decent cow, even if they're not bringing enough money these days to pay the dad-blasted phone bill."

The road through the north pasture that led to where the buzzards were circling was little used and choked with mesquite and greasewood bushes. These would certainly scratch Hector's nice pickup truck. Caleb went to the barn and fired up the John Deere tractor that had a front-end loader on it and headed off to see what the birds had found so attractive.

On a treeless knoll he saw it, and his blood ran cold. Tied with ropes so it could not be dragged off was the skinned carcass of a partially eaten goat. Littered haphazardly about it were the bodies of at least a dozen turkey vultures along with a few ravens, two coyotes and ironically, a dead golden eagle.

The goat had obviously been laced with a deadly poison and placed there to cause him more grief. He cursed aloud those who would do such a thing. From recent experience he had learned not to tarry in such a situation.

Within a half hour Caleb had transported the dead animals, using the loader bucket to a burn pit near the ranch house. A gallon of gasoline and a heap of dead mesquite limbs blazed in the growing heat of a July morning.

Soon all traces of the damning evidence would be obliterated forever. Once the fire had consumed the carcasses, the tractor would be used to cover over any traces of what had occurred.

Many ranchers jokingly remarked the best way to handle problems with predators in this day and age was to "Shoot, shovel and shut up."

In the light of his recent bitter run-ins with the law, Caleb Starr couldn't have agreed more with that statement.

The sharp pealing of the door bell coursed through Dianne Petrov's ragged nerves like a jolt of electricity. She grabbed up the remote control to shut off the blaring television set. Her hands trembled so badly that she dropped it onto the couch. A second try successfully brought a chill silence to the apartment.

Don't be so jumpy. It's most likely a salesman or some zealot passing out Watchtower magazines. If it is, I'll send them packing.

Pulling her rumpled housecoat tight, Dianne stood and steeled herself to meet whoever was calling. The possibility had been building that the Run Free Organization would send someone around to check on her. Since Marsh Wheelan had left, besides herself, there was only an attendant on duty to care for the raptors yet to be released. Timetables had to be adhered to. If she was unable to carry on with the program, another would undoubtedly be sent to replace her.

If only I could get the battered face of Caleb Starr's son out of my mind, she thought. *Marsh Wheelan caused that to happen just as surely as if he himself had wielded the club. That sniveling little weasel used every trick in the book to blow this whole eagle killing incident way out of proportion—all for his own benefit.*

A building fury at her former assistant added force to Dianne Petrov's stride and etched determination in her face. It was time to shed her pent up feelings of guilt and focus on getting her life back on track. It was just too difficult to shake a feeling of responsibility for Wheelan's vile actions.

Dianne didn't bother to use the security peek hole to check out who was there. She slid back the brass dead bolt with a firm hand and swung the door open wide.

Sheriff Monica Blandon met Dianne's startled gaze with a friendly nod and disarming smile. "Ms. Petrov, ma'am, I'm truly sorry to bother you at home, but I believe you've been wanting to speak with me."

It took a long moment for Dianne to collect her thoughts. She hadn't expected a uniformed officer of the law to come calling, let alone the Sheriff of Lone Wolf County. "How, uh may I ask why you think that?"

Monica Blandon's smile widened. "Lone Wolf might be a small town stuck out in the sticks, but we do have a lot of modern toys, like caller ID."

An unexpected cleansing tide of composure and relief swept through her veins. "Excuse my manners, Sheriff, please come in. I have a pot of coffee made, or if you prefer, hot tea would be no problem."

"A cup of black coffee will be fine," Monica replied stepping out of the building heat of the sun. "I love hot tea, but it's been a while since I've been offered any. Here in west Texas, few people drink tea any way but iced."

"Earl Grey is my personal favorite. Take a seat and I'll boil us up some."

"That sounds delightful, only don't go to any trouble on my account."

"Oh, trust me, it's not. We're going to need to spend quite a little time together. I'm going to tell you what has been going on since that eagle was killed. I'm also going to tell you how it was blown out of proportion. And then I'll give you the name of the person who caused this entire incident to become the sordid affair that it has."

Chapter 29

Will Jameson of the Environmental Protection Agency appeared very much as Jefferson Tate had imagined he would. The man was likely somewhere on the sunny side of fifty. Any battle ever waged to contain his bulging waistline had met with obvious defeat long ago. His perpetual smile, genial personality and shiny bald head reminded the FBI agent of Willard Scott, the personable television weatherman.

"Y'all mentioned that they broil up a mighty tasty steak here?" Will questioned as the duo entered the Lone Wolf Inn. "I've been thinking about a decent T-bone all morning. Those blasted puddle-jumper airplanes bounce around too much to do any reading."

"You're right about those small commuters. I swear some pilots go miles off course just to hit some good turbulence." Jefferson gave a sardonic smirk. "As far as the food here goes, if you don't think it's the best in Texas I'll put the tab on my expense account instead of yours."

Will greedily eyed the salad bar that was built to resemble a Conestoga wagon, while a plump middle-aged woman wearing a painted look of graciousness came to seat them. "Looks mighty tempting. Defenders of the public good need a treat on occasion."

Jefferson Tate said in a low tone, "Around these parts folks are just happy when they don't get all the government they pay for."

Will Jameson's habitual smile melted into a countenance of stoic granite. He said nothing until they had been seated in a remote booth and the waitress left to get their drinks. "I know what you mean. There was a time when I was proud to work for the government." His eyebrows drew together in a worried manner. "That was back when I felt like we were out to help people. Nowadays, with the multitudes of rules and regulations we have to enforce and the procedure in which we have to do it, folks are plain afraid of us. And probably rightfully so. If we look close enough we can usually find something wrong to warrant a penalty fine. I'll turn fifty-five in two years. Then I'm going to draw my pension and practice up on my golf game and try to perfect happy hour as an art form."

"I'm taking early retirement myself," Jefferson said as he noticed Will's grin return. "The wife and I bought a small farm not too far from where I was born over in Mississippi. It'll be a good feeling to watch things grow and to be out of the law enforcement loop. Sometimes I wonder if I'm simply burned out. Then maybe it's not the government that's the problem at all. It may just be the times we're living in. Change has always been hard for folks to deal with, and things lately seem to change so fast it's plain hard to keep up."

Will rolled his eyes in thought. When he spoke, his words came out measured. "When you finally retire to that farm of yours, I suspect it would be a wise move to go out of your way to let any chicken hawks be. If my information about this Starr fellow is accurate, that's how he got into the mess he's in to begin with."

"Unfortunately for him, that's the way it appears. Then some radical group or individual with excellent computer hacking skills set out to make an example of him killing a bald eagle. The selling of the videotape to a national tabloid and having his picture plastered all over the country was simply a good beginning. I mentioned the DEA raid on his ranch. That's why I invited Alton McKenzie to come along with us. If this poison your agency is concerned about is there, as I'm fairly sure it will be, he can verify that it has been planted. Believe me, the DEA wouldn't have missed anything like a bottle of a banned substance."

Jefferson Tate added sugar and lemon to his tea and continued. "I believe the Compound ten-eighty was placed there to keep the media's attention. I'd like to handle this episode quietly as possible for two reasons; first, this rancher's had enough bad press already. Secondly, if nothing comes out about it in the news, whoever hacked this information into our computers might try again. This time we'll be ready for them. We'll have a trace within thirty seconds once they're inside our system."

Will chuckled with obvious satisfaction. "Now there's something I'd like to see, a spider caught up in its own web. Anyone who would use the harsh laws meant to control wanton polluters and criminals against the average person who can't afford to hire an entire law firm ruffles my feathers."

"I'm glad we can cooperate on this matter, Will. I appreciate your attitude."

"After what you've told me I wouldn't have it any other way. Still, I'd lay off popping any chicken hawks if I was you."

Jefferson Tate smiled broadly. "Around my place they'll be safe as a congressman's pension." He cast an eye toward the front door. "I can't understand what's holding up Alton. He's generally punctual as Greenwich when it comes to time."

"If he's flying in on the same airline I did, it's likely the pilot's still looking for some more bumps to hit."

The waitress approached their booth and extracted a pad from her print apron. "Are you gentlemen ready to order?"

"We're expecting someone else to join us," Jefferson said.

Will Jameson swallowed hard and stared longingly at the

Conestoga wagon burdened with temptation. "Perhaps we could hit up the salad bar while we're waiting. I'm planning on having one of your steaks, but right now my belly's rubbing on my backbone."

"Certainly sir," the waitress answered with a professional air. "I'll bring out another place setting." Then she spun with the precision of a soldier and marched off.

"Cheerful lady," Will quipped. "She makes my mother-in-law seem like a barrel of laughs. And she's been dead for years."

"As I mentioned earlier, folks hereabouts have had more government officials poking around than they care for. This Caleb Starr incident has brought a lot of unwanted attention to Lone Wolf, Texas, and polarized peoples' attitudes. Most will simply be glad when we all go away and leave them alone."

Will Jameson started to answer when he noticed the FBI agent focus towards the door and give a nod of recognition.

"Well, up jumps the devil," Jefferson said with a sly grin as Alton McKenzie approached and slid into the booth alongside him.

"Sorry I'm late," Alton said in his usual flat voice. "I drove up from Laredo, and there was some unexpected road construction that held me up." He raked his dark eyes over Will as if he were comparing him with a wanted flier. "You must be Jameson with the EPA. Let's eat lunch and get on with business. I have to be back in Laredo tonight. We have a surveillance underway on a marijuana smuggling operation there. I only spent the time to drive up here because Agent Tate asked me to."

Will Jameson quickly decided he didn't care for the DEA man. There was no arguing about getting on with lunch, however.

Jefferson poured a glass of iced tea from the pitcher on the table and set it in front of McKenzie. "Alton's not all business. He just acts that way most of the time."

McKenzie chewed on his lower lip and mustered a slight smile of contrition. He stuck his hand across the table to Will. "I'm sorry. Sometimes I forget my manners. Glad to meet you, Mister Jameson."

"Just call me Will. I agree with you on lunch. Let's get to it."

After heaping plates of salad and steaming bowls of black bean soup had been devoured, there was time for more talk.

"When we conducted the drug raid on Starr's ranch I made an error in judgment," Alton announced.

Jefferson spoke up. "The information in your computer banks told you there were drugs hidden there. It wasn't your fault the report was false."

Alton shrugged his shoulders dismissively. "I'm not referring to that. Generally it's routine to do a citizenship check on everyone involved. I was so upset as to how things turned out I neglected to follow procedure with the old Mexican who lives there. He has no criminal record, but he's in this country illegally. When I discovered my error, I sent an e-mail to Immigration and Naturalization in San Angelo. They'll take care of the old wetback."

Will Jameson noticed the shocked expression on Jefferson's face and decided to chase a chunk of blue cheese around his plate with a cracker and keep silent.

"I wish you hadn't done that," Jefferson Tate said with resignation. "That old guy's lived there for a lot of years. It's the only home he has."

Alton leaned back and laced his fingers. "My job, and yours, is to enforce the law. That's what we get paid to do. There's legal ways to enter this country, and anyone, I don't care who they are or how old, chooses to not follow the rules, they can live with the consequences."

Jefferson sighed and rotated his glass of iced tea. In his mind's eye he visualized the frail Jesus Santiago with building sadness.

Pandora's box had already been opened. There was nothing to be done to rectify the situation. Alton had been correct when he said it was his duty to uphold the law. Only long ago a wise man had once written *there is the letter of the law and then there is the spirit of the law.* His instincts were right. It *was* time to retire.

The strait-laced waitress slid a platter-sized, sizzling T-bone steak cooked blood rare, just as he liked it, in front of him. Jefferson Tate found the steak was nowhere near as tasty as he remembered.

An all-too-familiar knot of anger and apprehension formed tight in Caleb Starr's gut when he stepped out on the porch and saw a black Suburban with white government plates heading toward his barn kicking up a billowing cloud of white dust.

The events of earlier this morning struck him like a high powered rifle bullet. *How did they know about that poisoned goat and all of the dead wildlife I just burned and buried?*

Then the rancher remembered reading about how military spy satellites were so efficient they could make out a newspaper headline. *Surely no, I'm not that big of a target. All I did was cover up a problem someone else set me up for. I've done nothing wrong, at least not lately anyway.*

Caleb twisted up the corner of his mouth in exasperation and headed to see what reason they had for being here this time. Briefly he wondered why there was only one black vehicle. In his experience government agencies descended in packs, like coyotes or wolves.

The Suburban skidded to a stop in front of the open barn door. A mixture of fear and hatred coursed through Caleb Starr's veins like acid when he recognized the driver through a fog of caliche dust. It was Alton McKenzie, the DEA agent who had slammed a rifle butt into his gut while he was handcuffed and ordered his home torn apart.

Caleb held kinder memories of the huge, silver-haired black man who climbed out of the passenger side door. The man's name was Tate, and, if memory served, he was with the FBI. It was hard to keep all of the alphabet soup agencies straight in his mind. Who the rotund, bald man was that departed from the back seat, Caleb hadn't a clue. At least the fat man and Tate were both able to smile. That seemed to be a rare trait among federal employees.

There were myriad chores yet to be done and Caleb wanted to be finished and cleaned up and have a meal ready for Hope this evening. The sooner he found out what these people wanted and got them out of his hair, the sooner he could get back to work.

"What can I help you men with today?" Caleb asked as he strode up wearing a forced expression of friendliness.

Jefferson Tate met Caleb with his hand held out in greeting. "Please don't be alarmed, Mister Starr. Our visit may help us discover who has planted a lot of bad information about you and possibly save you from a lot of further grief in the process."

Caleb returned the big man's handshake with a feeling of trepidation. "What, exactly, do you mean about 'further grief'? I'm already likely to lose my ranch and go to jail for protecting my chickens. Now what under God's green earth is wrong?"

Tate nodded to the bald man who now stood by his side. "This is Will Jameson with the EPA in Dallas."

Great, another agency out to get me, Caleb thought. *This IS about that poisoned goat.*

"Good to meet you, Mister Starr," Jameson said with an unexpected tone of courtesy. He also greeted the rancher with a handshake.

Caleb noticed Alton McKenzie stayed by the Suburban, his hands thrust deep into his pockets. He coldly surveyed the barn where old Jesus sat in his cane rocker just out of the sun, whittling.

"If you men don't mind," Caleb said, "I'd like to get on with why you're here. I've got a lot of work to do."

Taking turns speaking, Jameson and Tate quickly explained how information had been planted into the EPA's computer system that the rancher had been using a long banned poison to kill eagles and that a bottle of the substance was in his barn. Tate quickly added, Alton McKenzie had come along solely to verify the poison was not here during the DEA raid, and they did not believe he had any knowledge of its presence on his ranch.

Don't volunteer anything or they'll twist it and use it against you. Quentin Miller's words burned into Caleb's thoughts. He shrugged his shoulders in resignation and sighed. "Let's go see what you can find."

Jefferson Tate hesitated. "Then we do have your permission to conduct a search on your private property?"

Caleb snorted, "There's nothing in there that hasn't already been pawed through or ripped apart by your buddy or one of his storm troopers." Try as he might, the rancher couldn't contain his contempt for Alton McKenzie or his actions.

Tate and Jameson made no reply, only nods of understanding.

After a few brief minutes inside the sprawling barn, Will Jameson slid a bale of hay from the weathered plank wall. "Come and take a look at this, men."

Caleb was closest to the EPA agent. He stepped over and squinted at the brown pint-sized bottle wrapped in shadows. It looked to him like an old-time medicine container. "I honestly don't know what that is. I've never seen it before."

Alton McKenzie plunged forward, brushing Caleb aside. He extended his arms to keep others at bay and glared at the bottle for a long moment. "That was not here before," he growled. "None of my men would have missed anything that obvious without having it tested."

"I'd venture it's your Compound ten-eighty," Tate said turning to look at Jameson. "What are the rules of handling it?"

Jameson chuckled. "More than you'd care to know—if that *is* ten-eighty. I'm guessing until we get it back to the lab, we won't know what is inside it. Perhaps the FBI could simply take it into evidence? Whoever planted it there simply carried it in. I don't see why it can't leave here the same way. It would be embarrassing to call out the Hazmat trucks over a half-full bottle of horse liniment."

Jefferson Tate stretched a pair of thin rubber gloves over his huge hands with a look of satisfaction on his face. He extracted a plastic evidence bag from his pocket then stepped around the DEA agent, knelt and picked up the brown bottle.

"This is not following correct procedure," Alton said simply.

Tate grabbed the bottle. "Now Alton, you honestly don't believe this stuff is an illegal drug cache?"

"No, of course not."

"Well then, it's none of the DEA's concern. The FBI will take full responsibility."

Alton McKenzie spun and stalked out of the barn. He hesitated to glower briefly at Jesus who simply kept at his whittling, then climbed back into the Suburban that had been left running to allow the air conditioner to continue in operation.

"We're going to try and keep this under wraps," Tate said to Caleb as they turned to leave the barn. "Doing that might cause who planted this to tip their hand."

Will Jameson interjected, "I'll have this taken to the lab tonight. By tomorrow we'll know the results and what we're dealing with. Believe me, I'm really glad not to know right now."

Caleb Starr was shocked by how the situation was being

handled. He knew full well if the two men by his side weren't stretching a bunch of rules, his ranch would be overrun with Feds mighty shortly. "You'll let me know?"

Tate nodded. "I'll give you a call when I hear from the EPA. I need your word to keep this quiet," his voice grew firm. "I mean *totally* quiet about what happened here."

"You've got it," Caleb answered. He held no doubts as to what the contents of the brown bottle were. Those dead coyotes hadn't made it ten feet after taking a bite from the goat carcass. There was no poison he knew of except possibly cyanide that killed so fast.

Once the black vehicle had spun and roared off, Jesus came shuffling from the barn. "I was right, *señor. El Diablo* has come to Lone Wolf."

Caleb felt unbelievably lucky the way things had gone. His mood was buoyed by the knowledge that Hope would be here again tonight. "Maybe he won't hang around much longer, Jesus."

The old man focused on the departing Suburban glinting in the bright summer sun. "*Si señor,* I wish the same, but *El Diablo* comes in many forms. I fear he does also not give up easily."

"Reckon it'd put a bunch of preachers out of a job if he did," Caleb said with a sly grin as he spun to head off. His thoughts were focused now on sweet smelling perfume and sparkling emerald eyes.

Chapter 30

Marsh Wheelan cast an anxious glance at the pacing, caged grizzlies as the rhythmic beating of the huge Sikorsky sky crane helicopter's blades faded over the verdant mountain to the west. Being this close to the grunting, hulking beasts made him nervous, even though he'd been repeatedly assured they were gentle as pet dogs.

"You leave them locked up in that cage until I give the okay and we're ready to film," Marsh barked to Sam McSwain, the burly guide with a wooly white beard whom he had hired to assist and protect him. He wasn't enough of a fool to place himself in the slightest jeopardy unnecessarily. Any animal as big as a grizzly bear was most certainly a very real danger, no matter what the idiots he'd bought them from had told him. The forty-four magnum pistols loaded with hollow-point bullets both men wore on their belts were not there for show.

Ah, but the money and fame this could bring him.

He remembered the words his stern father had repeated to him many times. *There are no substantial rewards for anyone who hasn't the courage to take real risks.*

This didn't mean a person needed to be foolish about the risk part however.

Sam McSwain ambled over and peered through the iron bars of the massive cage. "They look plenty shook after that 'copter ride. Once they get settled down a mite, I'll get them some food and water."

Marsh looked at the snorting grizzlies but ventured no closer. "Those bears will be just fine until morning. By then they'll be ready to drink whatever we put in their cage. I want to add a special treat I brought along to keep the brutes under control. I'll trust those beasts a lot more once they've had a good, heavy dose of tranquilizer."

The guide studied the bears for a moment and shook his head sadly. "The critters seem to be gentle as a lamb. From what I've been told, they're used to being around people and have been in a lot of movies and television shows. They also look mighty thirsty. Are you sure we shouldn't let them have some water?"

"Right now we're going to set up camp," Marsh declared. "I don't want a cold rain shower to come along and drench me or my equipment."

Sam's bushy beard masked his expression of annoyance at his employer's arrogant attitude. Many of the people he guided these days were of his ilk. That's why he'd grown the thing in the first place. Marsh Wheelan was an insufferable punk. While this type of client was all too common, this jerk would undoubtedly win grand prize in an asshole contest. He was glad he'd charged three hundred dollars a day for his services. Normally his fee was half that. Considering Wheelan's haughty disposition, he still felt underpaid.

The guide clenched his teeth to remind himself to keep his mouth shut, then set about unloading two large fiberglass containers that had been flown in earlier. As he had expected, Marsh Wheelan watched with a stern eye while keeping his arms folded across his chest. Physical labor of any type was obviously beneath his stature in life.

Sam extracted two tents; one was large enough to hold a dance in. He held no doubts who the tiny pup tent was for. This lightened his spirits. At least he wouldn't have to share living quarters with his hoity-toity employer.

The tents were to be expected. The seasoned guide's eyes widened in amazement at what else had been transported in. There was a gasoline powered generator—totally illegal in a wilderness area—along with several gallons of gasoline to keep it running. Wheelan had even flown in a portable refrigerator along with crates of exotic foodstuffs and several bottles of wine already iced down in coolers. To top off the extravagance, Sam took out a huge stereo system and portable color television set along with a small satellite dish to insure good reception. There was no doubt about it now in Sam's mind; he was working far too cheaply.

Two hours of hard work later, Sam had the camp set up according to Marsh's precise instructions. After a prolonged inspection that would have done justice to a Marine Corps drill instructor, Sam actually thought he could detect a faint smile cross Marsh Wheelan's pinched face. This came as a disappointment; he had grown certain his employer was incapable of any degree of pleasantry.

"Once you have fueled and started the generator," Marsh said while filling a single long-stemmed wine glass with a delicate Chablis, "you may go and erect your own shelter. Inside the box marked 'guide' you will find sandwich meat and bread along with some bottled water. I wish you to shut down the generator for me at precisely eleven o'clock. Tomorrow will be quite a busy one for us both."

Sam McSwain doubted the veracity of the word "both," but went about his assigned task.

Once the muffled whirring of the generator engine began echoing off the towering pine and tamarack trees, Marsh went inside his huge tent, slipped a Kiss CD into the stereo and cranked the volume up to the highest decimal.

The guide placed an open hand to his forehead and decided

to pack his tent a good half mile up wind. Once shadows began filling the valley he would sneak in and feed and water those poor bears, even if he did get fired for his actions. It would be downright cruel to subject the grizzlies to that racket on an empty stomach.

Marsh Wheelan filled his crystal glass with the last of his second bottle of excellent wine. He took extraordinary care that none of the annoying sediment entered his glass. The wine, he acknowledged, was adequate even though it came across slightly tart for his discriminating palate.

He took a sip and strode outside to admire the canopy of stars that twinkled against the blackness like jewels in a king's crown. Marsh basked in the satisfaction of his remarkable ability to manipulate people and situations.

Soon, very soon, he would run for a political office. That was where all *real* power lie. Perhaps, using his flourishing good name as an environmental activist, he could inveigle a slot in the next election in his native state of California. It came as a disappointment he would be forced to limit himself to state politics for awhile.

Ah, but Washington would be easy to springboard to once he'd polished more contacts there as he had so successfully done in California.

Movie stars and recording artists, all of them filthy rich, called the Golden State home. Many of the thirty plus million people who lived there idolized a staunch environmentalist as much as any actor or singer. In a short span of time his name would be revered as a savior of the wilderness. Marsh Wheelan felt immensely proud of himself. His intuition and goals were right on target, and *so* obtainable.

The harsh ringing of his cell phone jerked him from his delightful reverie. Marsh went inside his tent and, wearing a frown, clicked off the stereo that was playing one of his favorite Led Zeppelin CDs. It was an annoyance to be bothered in such a pristine area. Once he held a seat of power, one of his first acts would be to outlaw cellular phones on public, forest land.

His scowl melted when he identified the twangy, nasal voice on the other end. It was Hale Cross's trademark and had garnered him millions of dollars and admiring fans. The shit-kicker announced that he had chartered a helicopter and would be on hand tomorrow to watch the bears frolic in their new mountain home. He mumbled on about how much he needed to get a "feel" for the area. Marsh choked out his fawning acceptance and felt a wave of relief when the meddling fool said his goodbye and closed the connection.

"Shit," Marsh cursed aloud as he slammed the phone onto the folding table. Magnum pistols and groggy, tranquilized bears would stand out like a boil on a call girl's face. If that obtrusive, caterwauling idiot had only stayed in Los Angeles, he could film those blasted grizzlies with absolutely no risk to his person.

Then it dawned on him that the simpleton guide he'd hired and he could hide the guns under their belts at the back and keep them covered by their jackets. As usual, Marsh's sharp intellect had found a way to reduce his own peril. Still, not being able to slip those bears a soothing narcotic Mickey Finn was a real pisser.

The secret of being a winner is the ability to turn defeat into victory.

His stern father's words boomed inside his head like a clap of thunder. *There are no great rewards for those not willing to take great risks.*

Marsh downed the last of his wine and popped the cork on a fresh bottle using his ornate silver-handled opener. He was so upset from the phone call he neglected to check the vintage or appraise the aroma of the cork before filling his glass.

He clicked the stereo back on and found the music soothing. A quick glance at his watch told him he needed to place his filet mignon on the glowing charcoal grill and have dinner out of the way before that bearded stumblebum shut off the generator.

The bacon surrounding his prime steak was sizzling to perfection when he downed the last of the wine and prepared for his evening repast. A delightful burgundy would be a wonderful accompaniment with the filet and fresh asparagus. A loaf of hot, fresh baked bread smothered with creamy butter would be wonderful, but he was in a wilderness area. A man must make do.

After one or possibly two more nights stuck out here in the middle of nowhere, he would be able to return to more civilized surroundings. Marsh needed to put on the facade of watching after those mangy bears before abandoning them to their fate. Image, in this world, is everything.

Tomorrow, he decided, would be an excellent opportunity to press Hale Cross to help grease the wheels of getting him into public office. Things always worked out well for a man of his superior intellect. Marsh sliced into his blood-rare steak with a smile of satisfaction.

Before his father's bum ticker gives out on him, the old fart would finally be proud of his son.

Chapter 31

Tip Conroy wolfed down a mouthful of chocolate chip cookie and cleared his throat with a gulp of cola as Monica Blandon strode into the sheriff's office. A quick glance at the blank blotter and open paperback novel on her assistant's cluttered desk told her nothing of consequence had occurred in Lone Wolf during her visit to San Angelo.

The pudgy deputy leaned back in his chair, an expression of smugness showing in his eyes. "You won't guess what I found out when I dropped by the bakery this morning: John Trotter's closing his hardware store. Just as soon as he can sell out, his wife's going to quit her job and they're planning to move to Las Vegas, Nevada. He's telling folks with the price of oil being so low they simply can't make a living here. Everyone knows better. After losing Hector's account and the way he spouted off to Caleb, nobody'll trade with him. Shucks, your husband has more customers these days than Trotter gets." Tip's lips curled in a devilish smirk, "Of course ol' Bones has had people dying to do business with him for years."

Monica groaned and took off her gray sheriff's hat, hung it on a wall peg and shook her hair loose. "Tip, that joke is older than dirt, but this must be a day for revelations," she said in a straightforward manner that erased all traces of humor from the deputy's cherubic face, "because I just found out who it was that hacked all of the damning and false information about Caleb into the Fed's computers."

The deputy bolted upright, his mouth open in obvious astonishment. "Well, let's go arrest the slimeball son of a bitch."

A thin look of disbelief crossed the sheriff's face at her deputy's cursing. Tip Conroy was a hard-shell Southern Baptist and a deacon in the church. This was the first expletive she had ever heard him utter and underscored just how disconcerted he was over her brother's problems and what it had done to the town of Lone Wolf.

"There's more to it than that—a lot more," Monica said on her way to grab a soda from the refrigerator. "First off, his crime was a federal one, so the FBI will have jurisdiction."

"And they're welcome to that piece of butt wipe, but I'd really like to be the first one to slap a set of cuffs on 'im. Who is the culprit anyway?"

Monica took a moment to savor the frigid air that drifted from the open refrigerator. The ancient air conditioner rattling away in the front window seemed to lose more ground in its battle against the heat every summer. She extracted a sweaty can of orange pop and flipped open the tab.

"The bastard is Marsh Wheelan," she spat his name as if the words themselves were bitter. "He works, or rather did before they fired him, for the Run Free Organization. He holds a doctorate in biology and was here to help with the eagle release program of theirs. Dianne Petrov is the district supervisor and the person I went to see. The poor lady is so shook by everything that's happened she's a wreck. Tristan's getting nearly beaten to death was the straw that broke the camel's back, so to speak. Dianne even went to the hospital and donated blood for him."

"If she knew what this Wheelan was up to, why'd she wait so blasted long to come out with it?"

"It's not that simple, Tip. For one thing there's no way to prove any of it. All we know for certain is he sold the videotape of Caleb holding that dead eagle to *The Weekly World Probe*. Run

Free fired him for that, then when they decided to file a suit for damages, he disappeared."

Tip Conroy shook his head in dismay. "Well, go on."

Monica sighed. "She said he was an absolute genius with a computer. Dianne Petrov described him as a little weasel with delusions of grandeur and totally devoid of any morals. Wheelan told her he planned to start his own environmental group. She's certain he believes making an example of an eagle killer will win him a lot of support. The sad part of it is, he's likely correct. There's a lot of radicals out there looking for a cause."

"But he's torn both Caleb and this town apart."

"For a man like she described Marsh Wheelan as being, people are only used as stepping stones. All we can do is get this information to that FBI fellow, Jefferson Tate. He's a good man, and I believe he'll pull out all stops to catch this Wheelan and possibly help Caleb in the process."

Tip motioned toward the door with his hand. "Tate spent last night over at the inn."

The sheriff's brows drew together in puzzlement. "What in the world is the FBI doing back here in Lone Wolf?"

"Why don't you go ask him?" Tip said. "That government car of his was still there less than an hour ago when I went to buy these cookies. I'll—"

Monica Blandon slammed her soda on the desk and was out the door before the deputy could finish his sentence.

Jefferson Tate surveyed the sheriff from across a scarred wooden booth in the restaurant at the Lone Wolf Inn wondering why she had come rushing in to see him. It was obvious she was worked up over something. He supposed it was about the bottle of banned poison. A twinge of anger poked at him that Caleb Starr hadn't kept quiet about the matter as he'd promised. Then he reminded himself she *was* his sister.

He still didn't have the results from Will Jameson concerning the contents of the bottle. Likely the EPA laboratory in Dallas hadn't gotten around to analyzing it yet.

The government is always prompt no matter how long it takes, he thought.

Aside from waiting on the EPA, there were other reasons he had decided to stay for awhile. It felt good to be out of the impersonal, always busy office he inhabited in the federal building in Austin. With the cell phone tucked away in his pocket and a laptop computer plugged into a phone line in his room for e-mail, there was little he couldn't do from here anyway.

Fatigue from a fitful night spent tossing and turning in his bed was a reminder of the real reason he had stayed in Lone Wolf. That had been caused by Alton McKenzie's brutal and uncalled for action of reporting the old Mexican, Jesus Santiago, to the Border Patrol. Into the wee hours of morning Jefferson's irritation had welled inside him like bile. He had been in the bureaucratic loop far too long, however, to believe there was much he could do.

John Dowd, the local agent in charge of the San Angelo area, had been surprisingly cordial and helpful when he had talked with him on the phone earlier. They had agreed to meet later in the day to discuss the situation. Throwing an old man out of his home for no reason other than his being a Mexican smacked of racism and had dredged up bitter memories that still festered. Anything he could do to help the old fellow would be better than looking the other way.

First, he needed to soothe the distraught sheriff. He shot a furtive glance around the restaurant and was relieved to find their booth was distant enough from other diners for their conversation to remain private.

Blast Caleb Starr for not keeping his mouth shut like he promised.

The less tongue wagging there was about that Compound

ten-eighty stuff the more likely the chances of finding out who had hacked into their computers.

"Good to see you again, Sheriff Blandon," Jefferson said. "Let's order you something cold to drink, and you can join me for lunch, my treat."

"Thank you, sir. I'll take you up on a glass of iced tea, but I have a feeling once we've talked you may want to put off lunch for awhile. I'm just happy to catch you here in Lone Wolf. I hope your being in town doesn't mean more trouble for Caleb."

Jefferson was taken aback. *Perhaps the rancher had kept his word and not mentioned anything to his sister about our visit yesterday. If he had, I'd doubt she'd be glad to see me. But if this isn't about the poison, then what?*

The FBI agent swirled the spoon in his glass of iced tea. "Well, sheriff, why don't you come out and tell me what you came to see me about and just how I may be of assistance?"

Monica Blandon did just that.

Jefferson Tate didn't attempt to mask his surprise and outright delight of having the first solid lead on the hacking crime. This was one perp he would enjoy nabbing for several reasons. "You're right about us postponing lunch, ma'am. I need to get to my computer, make some calls and do a background on this Wheelan. If he looks like our man, I'll order him put under surveillance at the very least. Hackers are like drug addicts: they keep right on doing it until they get caught. I'll drop by your office later and fill you in on what I come up with."

"Please do," Monica said. "I have a real interest in this case."

"I know," Jefferson said.

It took less than an hour of punching keys on his laptop before Tate became convinced Marsh Earlson Wheelan was their man. He chuckled to himself when he thought back to his college days when the connotation of names had been a hobby of his.

Earlson, from old English, meant "nobleman's son" or "rich man's son." In Wheelan's case this fit like a hand into a glove.

Hollis Wheelan, Marsh's father, was indeed a very wealthy man. There had been many investigations by both federal and state agencies into questionable stock trading and real estate deals by Hollis, but no convictions or even an indictment.

Marsh Wheelan's background, while somewhat enigmatic, fit the FBI's profile for a computer hacker, or worse.

While he held a doctorate degree in biology from a prestigious university, there were many warning signs, some of which were obvious contradictions that most likely had been caused by computer tampering.

The State of California showed he had a perfect driving record. By using the FBI computer system and retrieving older files, he found four speeding tickets and one conviction for DWI.

Marsh Wheelan was a man who knew how to bury his trash quite well.

Of most concern to Jefferson were some early reports from Marsh's grade school teachers of cruelty to animals. One teacher had given him a bad grade only to later find her pet cat burned to death and stuffed into her desk drawer at school. Again, nothing could be proven, but the teacher had been certain enough it was him to make a note in his records.

Most disturbing of all was the fact that his current whereabouts were unknown. Jefferson punched in orders for a thorough background check and an order to pick him up for "questioning" when and if he could be located. He had nothing to charge Marsh with. This situation would likely change very soon.

"Computers can bite both ways, Mister Wheelan," Jefferson Tate mumbled as he put out orders that would send dozens of FBI agents into action. It might take a few days to obtain a clear picture of this man. There was little doubt in his mind that when the reports were in he would have plenty of evidence to make an arrest.

His cell phone jangled. He answered it before it rang again. "Special Agent Tate speaking."

"Hello, Jeff," Will Jameson's friendly voice drawled into his ear. "Sorry to be so long getting back to you. I don't think you'll mind the delay, however. It took me awhile to do a little of that detective work you wanted."

"What did you find out? That *was* Compound ten-eighty, I'm betting."

"Sure enough was. Deadly as hell and twice as dangerous as cyanide. An amount the size of a pinhead would kill a coyote or a man in seconds. But I haven't gotten to the good part yet. The Mexican government has a tracer element put in each batch so they have some control over its use. They're not so backward down there as you'd think. There are also laws that it has to be signed for when someone buys it."

"You're yanking my chain."

"Nope. That's what took the extra time. We were able to trace the compound back to the manufacturer. Then, using the tag element we found what batch it was from and who had bought it."

"If you tell me a man by the name of Marsh Wheelan purchased and signed for some of that stuff, I'll kiss you full on the lips."

After a long moment of silence Will spoke, "I hope I never get the FBI on my back. You guys are so good it's hair-raising. That's the man. He bought a full pint bottle. I'd really like to know how you found that out."

"Just good police work," Jefferson chuckled.

"Can I ask you just one more thing?" Will's voice was pleading.

"Name it."

"Could you forget about that kiss? My wife's a tad on the jealous side."

"Just this once," Tate glanced at his watch. "Will, I've got to go. Thanks and we'll be in touch."

The FBI agent sighed. He needed to be in San Angelo to meet with the Border Patrol in less than an hour. Then he needed to decide just how much to divulge to the local sheriff.

On his way out the door his stomach grumbled. Jefferson Tate wished briefly he'd ordered room service for lunch. The way this day was shaping up, it was going to be a long one.

Chapter 32

Rosemary Page looked up from the electric typewriter where she was working on a form document and adjusted her gold-rimmed glasses to focus on Caleb Starr. A rare, thin smile crossed her lips. "Tell me, how is Mister Santiago getting along? I really should find time to visit with him." Her usual scowl returned. "Too few men have any appreciation for the works of William Shakespeare."

"I never met this Shakespeare person myself, so I have nothing against the man," Caleb drolled just to irritate her. There was something about the prim secretary that invited it. "But if he's a friend of Jesus, he's likely a nice enough feller."

"*Mister* Miller is in his office," she retorted tartly and returned to her typing, banging harder on the keys than before.

Caleb strolled through the open door and closed it behind him. Quentin Miller sat leaning back in his high-backed leather chair with his fingers laced behind his silver-haired head studying John Wesley Hardin's law degree. He didn't look around to see who was there.

"You know something, Caleb?" The attorney spoke in a voice that seemed to come from a long way off. "There are days when I wish I had lived back in my great-grandfather's time. Things were a lot simpler and easier to understand then. Nowadays even those of us who are supposed to be experts in the field of law have a difficult time telling what's right from what's wrong."

Caleb stepped up the massive desk, but remained standing

and joined Quentin in studying his collection of Hardin memorabilia as the attorney continued. "Have you ever heard of a Gordian knot?"

Quentin didn't wait for a reply. "King Gordius of Phrygia tied a wagon to the temple using this knot. The legend was that whoever was able to untie it would rule all of Asia. Many tried, but none succeeded. Then along came Alexander the Great. He sized up that knot, then simply took out his sword, chopped the darn rope and took the wagon. It worked too because he did wind up ruling all of Asia. Ever since I heard that story, I've been a great admirer of using the simple approach to a problem."

Quentin Miller swiveled around to face Caleb with a granite-like expression. "These days there are too many Gordian knots and not enough people with swords."

Caleb dropped down into a chair and ran a worried finger along his check. "I'd guess this is about me."

The lawyer acknowledged with a slight nod. "I've been on the phone and shooting off e-mail all day. Run Free wants to let the eagle matter drop. So do most of the other agencies and law enforcement personnel I've been in contact with."

"The word 'most' bothers me."

"Randall Whitehead and the Federal Wildlife Service are determined to prosecute. *Save the Planet* and a few other wacko organizations are threatening civil suits against you if this matter doesn't go to court. There has just been too much publicity given the incident. The knot has been tied, but darn it, I haven't been able to find a sword."

"Then I'm going to prison," Caleb's voice was like an echo from an empty tomb.

Quentin unlaced his fingers and held out his palms while showing a humorless smile. "Now don't go getting into the doldrums just yet. This rodeo ain't over. I've still got some strings to yank. There's a fair to middlin' chance we can plead this thing down to a fine. That way the Feds will have won the conviction they're after. A misdemeanor won't damage your record badly, and a few months of probation is something you can live with. At least it would be a way to put the matter behind you."

"I can't pay a big fine, Quentin. You know that."

"But you can. I've received over thirty thousand dollars in donations for your defense. That amount of money might settle the matter."

Caleb's eyebrows shot up in surprise. "That much money has been sent to help me. Who all would do a thing like that?"

"Like I've mentioned before, this incident has polarized some extremist groups on both sides. There are those who believe a person should be able to shoot or kill whatever they like. They're the ones that sent in the money. Others want laws passed and enforced to protect every animal, bird, fish, bug and plant on the face of the earth. Common sense lies somewhere in the middle of this chaos. It's simply too bad you got caught up in it the way you did."

"But it happened, and my dad always said there was no use crying over spilt milk. What bothers me is taking money from those radicals. Quentin, I would never have shot that eagle if I'd known what the blame thing was. Hell, I thought it was a chicken hawk."

"You know that, and I know that. Right now we're going to hope that federal judge in Lubbock will settle for a fine, regardless of where the money comes from."

"And if he doesn't?"

Quentin Miller's granite expression returned. "Let me worry about that," he quickly decided to change the subject. "Isn't Tristan getting out of the hospital soon?"

"The boy's made a quick recovery, thank God. Those

bastards could have killed him. I'm going to pick him up in the morning."

"That's great news. Remember, all storms blow over eventually. In a year or two this will all be forgotten."

Caleb sighed as he stood to leave. "It's the next few months that have me worried."

Tristan Starr winced as he eased himself onto the couch. He hurriedly masked his pain with a forced smile. "It sure feels good to be home. Those hospitals are chock-full of nothing but sick people. The food they serve there's guaranteed to keep them that way, too."

Caleb nodded in agreement and tried to muster a grin. Every time he went to the hospital it dredged up painful memories. "We're going to fix that problem. If you feel up to it, Jesus said he'd cook up a mess of burritos and tamales for dinner tonight."

"Anything with some flavor to it sounds great," Tristan said. "The food there sucks canal water big time. They even act like salt is a banned substance."

Jesus gave the boy a sardonic look. "Oh *si,* the dinner will be *muy sabroso.* I always add some jalapeños to make things interesting. This night I will use more than usual. In Mexico, *curanderos* believe the hot peppers can cure many ills and speed healing."

"Now don't go and put him back in the hospital," Caleb said facetiously to Jesus. "We just got him out."

The old man clucked his tongue and shook his head firmly. "I will do him no damage, but he must have *mucho* jalapeños to get well."

"That's okay, Dad," Tristan interjected, "if I hadn't been toughened up from eating Jesus's cooking, I'd likely still be in the hospital."

Those bastards nearly killed my son. Caleb's thoughts came crashing down like a rockslide. *And only for simply having a father who couldn't tell a chicken hawk from an eagle.*

At least Tristan's spirits were up enough to join in on poking fun at Jesus. Teasing the old man about his cooking had become a ritual. Ever since Laura had taken ill, the elderly patriarch had taken over the kitchen several days a week. He was an excellent chef, though on occasion he would prepare a dish that was fiery enough to cause beads of sweat to pop out on even his own swarthy forehead.

"Reckon you're right there, son," Caleb's voice was serious. "Anyone who can live through his Mexican food could survive most anything."

Jesus muttered something about *gringos* then shuffled through the doorway and headed off toward his garden, leaving the two alone.

Caleb shot a quick glance at his boy's new haircut. For some reason he hadn't explained, he'd had someone in the hospital trim his shoulder length mane to downright acceptable shortness.

For two years the rancher had been harping at Tristan to get a haircut, and now he'd done it on his own. This puzzled Caleb, but he was determined not to bring the subject up. For some reason, ever since the trouble over the eagle started the boy had done a lot of growing up.

Tristan cocked an eye at his father. "You haven't said a word about it."

"What?"

"Oh, Dad, you've been after me to get a haircut forever. Do you like it?"

Caleb simply nodded. Sometimes anything he said would send the boy into a rage. He didn't want that, especially now with him only being home for a short while. Silence seemed a safer approach to the subject.

"I do. It feels a lot better. Dad, I've been giving a lot of thought to things lately. If you think it's a good idea too, I'd like to buckle down and finish school. Then see if I can join some branch of the military. I'm going to need a college education, and I know," he hesitated, "it might, well, be easier, if we let the government pay for it."

Caleb felt dumbfounded. His first response was to wonder if they hadn't made a switch in San Angelo and sent him home with the wrong boy. This was the first time since his mother died that Tristan had mentioned having any plans for the future.

Staying on at the ranch, while Caleb had quietly wished for this, would have been a bad choice.

Hell, there might not even be a ranch for him to operate. Not by the time this mess is over with, he thought bleakly.

He adjusted his new pair of glasses Hope had cajoled him into getting—the blamed things never seemed to fit right—and measured his response carefully. "Son," Caleb said after a long while, "I think you've gone and grown up on me. If that's what you want to do, I'm all for it."

A broad smile washed across Tristan's face. "I'm glad. Dad, I know you need me here on the ranch, but I'll be earning money. I can send you a check every month to help out."

That familiar burning lump returned to its home in the rancher's throat. "You don't worry none about us. We'll get out of this problem and do just fine."

"I'm happy you're using the word 'us', Dad. That other toothbrush in the bathroom and bottle of perfume are Hope's aren't they?"

Caleb froze at his son's cognizance.

"Hey, it's okay. She's a sweet lady, and I like her a lot. I'm only sorry that I've acted like such a butthead lately." He held out his hand. "I love you Dad, and I want us to be friends.

There's enough trouble in this old world without having more at home."

Caleb stifled a sob as he stepped up and grasped Tristan's hand. He wanted to give him a hug, but realized that might undo the young doctor's stitching efforts.

"Friends," was all he was able to cough out as tears welled in his eyes.

The glaring orb of a west Texas sun was at its zenith, shooting down searing rays to further bake the already thirsty earth, when Caleb noticed a car approaching. The vehicle left a heavy cloud of powdery caliche dust hanging in its wake.

Tristan was napping with Useless on the couch in front of a rattling swamp cooler that only slightly kept the oppressive heat at bay. The rancher took a sip from the glass of water he'd come to the sink to get and wondered who had come to visit. His joy of having his son safely home was shattered when he made out the all too familiar white government license plate and red and blue lights on the roof rack.

Why can't they just leave me alone for a little while, he thought bitterly. *If I was out on bail for shooting a politician I wouldn't get this much harassment. When in this crazy world did we ever reach a point where some endangered species could cause a person this much grief without them going out of their way to instigate the matter?*

Caleb set down his glass and quietly slipped outside to meet whoever it was. Tristan needed his rest, and the boy certainly didn't deserve to be upset.

When the car pulled to a dusty stop, the rancher was taken aback to find the white Chevrolet sedan with a heavy black grill guard had a green stripe down its side and the words "Border Patrol" lettered on the rear panel. He couldn't fathom a reason for anyone from this agency to come calling.

A single uniformed officer climbed from the driver's side

door. The man removed his hat as he walked toward Caleb, revealing a silver-cropped head of hair. He held out his hand and gave a disarming smile.

"You must be Mister Caleb Starr?" he questioned in a pleasant tone.

"Yes sir," Caleb answered warily, shaking the preferred hand. "What can I do for you?"

"My name is John Dowd. I'm with the Department of Justice, Border Patrol. There's a matter that has come to our attention we need to discuss." He nodded towards Caleb's house. "Maybe it would be more comfortable if we went inside out of the sun."

Caleb sighed. "My boy, Tristan just got home from the hospital today. He's sleeping, and I'd rather not bother him."

John Dowd grimaced. "I heard about him getting beaten up. I'm terribly sorry about that. The paper said this morning he would make a complete recovery, which is great news. I'll keep this brief and be on my way."

"Okay," Caleb said. "Let's get on with it."

"It's about this man you have hired," he nodded toward the small house next to the windmill. "I'm afraid Jesus Santiago is an illegal alien."

Caleb Starr felt his backbone turn to rubber. He couldn't keep from casting a sorrowful glance toward the crude headstone underneath the huge sheltering Live Oak tree that marked Ernesta Santiago's final resting place.

"God help us," was the only reply he could muster.

Chapter 33

In Marsh Wheelan's vivid imagination, it was easy to picture the voluptuous blonde stripped naked and handcuffed to a king-size brass bed. He could almost feel the cold leather of a bull-whip handle in his sweaty palm, taste a coppery drop of her blood on his tongue.

Marsh was also quite certain he had seen the girl perform some rather amazing feats in one of his vast collection of porno movies. He made a mental note to check this out at his earliest opportunity. She had told him her name was Roxy Dawn, but he doubted her truthfulness. All sluts lie like a rug.

It was just that the blonde's presence was so distracting and tempting, like a full bottle of Scotch whiskey on an alcoholic's night stand. Marsh decided that some lucky plastic surgeon in Los Angeles probably paid cash for a shiny new Porsche convertible after Hale Cross wrote a check for those gigantic silicone jigglers that filled her overly tight sweater to absolute perfection.

The country warbler had brought his girlfriend along to watch those mangy caged grizzlies being freed back into the wild, accompanied by his nasal caterwauling, of course. He carried around his guitar and unfortunately insisted on playing the thing. Aside from the fact Hale Cross's singing reminded Marsh of the sounds a cat makes when it's in heat, the day had progressed wonderfully.

Hale Cross's blue-and-white jet helicopter had set down at

precisely eight-thirty this morning. Perfect timing to film before the usual afternoon clouds blocked the sun.

The landing of any aircraft inside a wilderness area was forbidden by law. There were exceptions, however. The government made allowances for extreme circumstances such as vital scientific research, interests of national security and, occasionally, humanitarian reasons. Marsh had chosen one from column "A", punched it into his powerful laptop that was linked to the Internet by a small satellite dish. The crooner's landing had been legal as a Fourth of July parade in some jerkwater town in Arkansas.

Ah, the power of a computer.

The sensuous blonde with captivating blue bedroom eyes who had accompanied the singer for the monumental event turned out to be simply sweet icing on Marsh's cake.

Hale Cross had shown great interest in Marsh's plans to save the environment by going into politics where he could be an effective instrument of change.

Then he pointed out to the shit-kicker and his bouncy girlfriend a finger of barren gray rock on a distant cliff.

"There were a nest of eagles there when we arrived," Marsh said solemnly. "Yesterday, the parents left in search of food for their young and failed to return. I can only assume the worst. If I were elected to office, one of my first moves will be to extend a large buffer zone around our wilderness areas to protect our precious wildlife. These areas will be set aside for only nondestructive and peaceful uses such as cross-country skiing, nature trails, and bird watching. Guns of any kind would, of course, be outlawed. We have to make a stand quickly." He cast a sad eye toward the distant cliff. "While there's still time."

"Oh, the poor starving babies," Roxy Dawn sobbed. "We must do something to save them."

"I'm afraid that isn't possible," Marsh said quickly. He didn't even know if there was a nest there, let alone one built by eagles. "If a human scent is detected, the parents won't return—even if they're able to. No, unfortunately nature must take its cruel course." He hesitated for effect, "*This* time."

Hale Cross wiped a tear from his eye, picked up his worn six-string guitar, strummed a few bars and began playing with verses for a new song that would undoubtedly become a national hit. Hale said he would title it, *"Should an Eagle Fall."*

> *"Soaring high,*
> *Soaring so high,*
> *Majestic wings spread against an endless sky.*
> *Freedom lies high,*
> *Freedom lies so high."*

Roxy Dawn began bawling like a baby. The entire scene was so sickeningly poignant Marsh Wheelan felt like upchucking on his L.L.Bean hiking boots. It was worth it, however. Now there was no doubt Hale Cross would fund his future to the tune of millions of tax-deductible dollars.

Ah, the power he wielded over people.

Hale Cross continued strumming his six-string.

> *"Dwell on your high mountain wall,*
> *And sail on, above us all.*
> *For man alone will make you fall*
> *Cry one, cry all, should an eagle fall."*

"We need to get on with the bear release, sir," Marsh said loudly, "while the light is just right for filming."

Actually Marsh had been wanting to put this off as long as possible, but having a pair of grizzly bears running around loose seemed preferable to listening to any more of this insipid whining. Led Zeppelin was far more suited to his tastes.

Sam McSwain stood patiently by the door of the steel-barred cage. Marsh noted to his displeasure the simpleton had filled both water and food pans for the grunting bears. While he hadn't been able to slip the grizzlies a healthy dose of tranquilizer, he'd hoped the sound of distant running water would lure them quickly from his presence. Now, thanks to an idiot, that wouldn't be the case.

Marsh slipped a hand under his jacket and felt the reassuring coldness of the forty-four magnum pistol tucked under his belt. He fervently hoped McSwain had done the same. Those bears looked bigger and meaner every time he glanced at them.

Hale Cross handed his guitar to the still weepy bimbo and held out his hand. "I want to wait until my cameraman gets into position," he said motioning to a long-haired young man packing a black case. Marsh had been so busy focusing on Cross and the blonde he hadn't paid the man any mind.

"I think my best angle would be from atop the cage," the cameraman said, causing Marsh to believe the young man wasn't as dumb as he appeared.

After a few minutes of preparation all was in readiness. Marsh made certain both his video camera and magnum pistol were at the ready.

Hale Cross had also brought along his own camcorder. "We can't afford to miss any of this stunning event," he announced. "Of course I'll do the music recording in my studio. Without some great video to accompany me, it just wouldn't work."

At least that's something to be thankful for, Marsh thought, suppressing his delight at having the singer keep quiet.

"Anytime you folks are ready," Sam McSwain said.

The cameraman made a final check of his equipment. "Let's roll."

Marsh was aghast when the guide slid open the bolt, swung the doors wide and just stood there, grinning. Having the moron mauled by a bear in front of his supporter would be a disaster of the first order. His heart skipped a beat, and he nearly pulled the gun from under his belt when a grizzly snorted and pushed its snout against McSwain's jeans.

The guide smiled and rubbed his hand on the bears ears. With a grunt, the second grizzly emerged. Marsh relaxed his grip on the pistol when it swatted a playful paw at its companion and both bears ran several feet down the hill and began romping then rolling happily on the verdant grass alongside the gurgling brook.

Hale Cross kept his eye glued to the video camera. He couldn't conceal his emotions. "Oh, this is *wonderful.* I've never experienced anything like this before. Mister Wheelan, you're a genius. I hope you're getting some of this."

Marsh jerked his hand from the pistol's grip and lifted the camcorder. "Yes sir, I must say I'm simply overwhelmed myself."

Sam McSwain sighed and leaned against the now empty cage to study the blonde while everyone else was engrossed with watching pet bears frolic. He had been guiding city slickers into the mountains for many years, but this trip had shaped up to be one for the record books.

Roxy Dawn was ecstatic, jumping up and down with "oohs" and "ahs" that caused a twinkle in the guide's eyes.

After about twenty minutes, the grizzlies simply sat on their haunches, side by side and began eyeing the people filming them.

"We need more action," the unnamed cameraman shouted.

Hale Cross lowered his camcorder and looked at Marsh. "Can't you do anything? My man is right. We need to see them do something besides just sit there."

"What do you think, Sam?" Marsh said, causing the guide to tear his gaze from the still bouncing blonde.

"Likely they're a tad worried. They've never been let loose

like this before."

"Oh, the poor things," Roxy Dawn intoned.

"The guide's correct," Marsh said with authority. "We must give them time to adjust to their new surroundings. It's nothing to worry about. Their instincts will take over soon. For now, we should leave them be."

Hale Cross nodded sadly. "Yes, of course. They're frightened by their newfound freedom. I'm only glad to have been a part of this." He looked up at the cameraman. "Mel, did you get enough footage?"

The young fellow patted the camera. "Yes, sir. I'd like just a couple of minutes to film some more of the area. Then, with some computer imaging we'll have a video that will sell in the millions. This was just so outstanding. It's hard to believe."

"My feelings exactly," Hale Cross said with misty eyes. He strode over and placed a hand on Marsh's shoulder. "You've given me more than I could have hoped for."

Now give me what I really want, Marsh thought, but said, "It was done for a cause, sir. One which I believe in with all of my heart and soul."

"I can see that," Hale Cross said. "I only wish I could spend more time in this pristine area." His lower lip quivered as he surveyed the bears. "But I have many demands on my time and must be leaving."

Roxy Dawn came over, black streaks where tears had streamed mascara down her rouged cheeks glistened in the sunlight. "Hale, baby, couldn't we stay just a little longer?" She cast a pained glance toward the grizzlies. "They just look so pathetic sitting there like that."

"They need less human contact, not more," Marsh spoke up. "Those bears are creatures of the wild. We should let them return to their natural habitat as soon as possible."

"Mel, be quick about finishing up your filming," Hale said to the man atop the cage. "Then we'll leave these poor animals in the capable hands of Marsh Wheelan." He wrapped an arm around the blonde's slim waist. "Come along, hon, we've done all we can here."

Hale turned to Marsh. "I'll be getting in touch with you shortly."

Marsh had a difficult time keeping a straight face as he accompanied the singer and his still sniveling girlfriend up the hill.

Several minutes later the two grizzlies turned their snouts in unison to follow the departing helicopter as it made it's way toward the rocky cliff to the east. It circled the craggy finger of rock twice, then disappeared over the horizon.

When the echo of beating rotor blades had faded and silence reclaimed the mountain valley, Marsh Wheelan marched over to face Sam McSwain. His earlier rage at the bearded simpleton had diminished somewhat due to obvious success with Hale Cross's money supply. However, he couldn't allow any of his orders to be disobeyed; it would be bad for his image to ever appear weak.

"I specifically instructed you not to feed or water those beasts," Marsh growled.

"That would have been cruel. I'm not gonna abuse any helpless critter for you or anyone else."

Marsh stiffened. "When you are in *my* employ, Mister McSwain, I expect you to do what I say and leave the thinking to me. Now I want you to run those stupid bears off into the woods. I don't care how you do it, just get them away from here."

Sam turned his head and watched as the bears playfully swatted water from the small creek at each other. "I ain't gonna be party to that. Those grizzlies are nothing but pets. They're old and won't last a week without someone to look after them."

Marsh's face grew livid, his fists knotted in rage. "You *will* do as I order," he screamed.

The guide simply chuckled. "For your information, I quit working for the likes of you yesterday. I've had a bellyful of self-important punks from the city. All of you have a cash register where your heart oughta be."

"I'll have you know I hold a PhD," Marsh spat. "I'm an expert on wildlife behavior."

"Stands for piled high and deep to me," Sam snorted. "I'd reckon you ain't got enough common sense to pour piss out of a boot. I'm telling you straight out, you little puke, paid or not, I'm going to stick around the area for awhile. Should something happen to those bears, I'll make sure the right people find out who was responsible."

A curtain of red fury unveiled itself in Marsh Wheelan's mind when the insolent hireling turned and began sauntering away. He reached behind his jacket and felt the cold steel of the magnum pistol.

He hesitated and took a deep breath. Better. A rash move now could upset his future plans.

The secret of being a winner is the ability to turn defeat into victory.

His father was right. He just needed to calm down and give the matter some thought. A cold bottle of Chablis and a croissant sandwich made with shaved ham and Swiss cheese would be helpful.

Marsh Wheelan kept his hand on the pistol and gave the romping grizzlies a wide berth as he headed to his tent to figure a way out of his dilemma.

Chapter 34

"Gotcha, you slippery son of a bitch," Jefferson Tate gloated aloud to the flickering computer screen, his face twisted into a satisfied smile. He punched a number on his speed-dialer, glad to be back in the Austin office where he had quick access to all of the agency's high tech toys.

A young woman's voice answered on the speaker phone, "Yes sir, this is Technical Specialist Greerson, how may I assist you?"

It took Jefferson a brief moment to adjust to the stilted speech that had been ingrained into every FBI employee since J. Edgar Hoover's time. After spending a few days in the field, the colder and more impersonal this formality seemed.

"Uh yes, Ms. Greerson, this is Special Agent Tate," he said, careful to emphasize the "Ms." Jefferson wasn't familiar with this person and didn't want to risk unintentionally offending her. "I've recorded a cell phone message that was bounced off Satellite G-12 at Oh-Six-Four-One hours. I'm showing it has a frequency trace signature that is in our Omega Shadow File database. Can you confirm this?"

The clicking of computer keys echoed from the black speaker. "Yes sir, Agent Tate, I have a definite bogie at that time for Omega Shadow Case number Twelve Twenty-Seven, and we have recorded both sender and receiver signatures."

Jefferson Tate's grin widened. "Can you confirm the sender's name?"

More clicking. "Yes sir, the phone is registered to one Marsh

Earlson Wheelan." A few seconds later she added, "And the receivers were Forest Service offices in Pendleton, La Grande and Baker City in the state of Oregon along with a copy to Whitman Air Force Base in Walla Walla, Washington. The message was of computer origin and gave special clearance from the Department of Interior for a helicopter landing inside of a wilderness area for special scientific research in the interests of national security."

"Please download the data for this intercept with Shadow File number Twelve Twenty-Seven to my base computer and send a copy to GPS and the assistant director's office." He added happily, "And thank you, Ms. Greerson."

Tate leaned back in his chair, took a sip of tepid coffee and sighed, *What people don't know* can *hurt them these days,* he thought.

A few years ago, in an effort to thwart drug dealers, organized crime and illegal financial transactions, the government had covertly ordered every manufacturer of cellular communications equipment to add a signature device to all transmitters. The resulting variation in wave frequency was slight and unnoticeable, but distinctive as fingerprints. It had been code named "Shadow File."

This tool had resulted in hundreds of arrests. Once the purchaser of a cell phone signed on with a carrier, it was a simple matter to program their specific wave code into the FBI computer banks. After that, every call made from the phone was automatically monitored and recorded. In FBI jargon "Omega" meant an active file, "Delta" was either closed or no longer being pursued.

Of course, Jefferson reflected, this was done only on a very selective basis and an elect few were even aware of the existence of Shadow File. Yet, he felt unsettled every time he used its benefits. It was simply too much like Big Brother for comfort.

Sometimes, to catch the bad guys you have to be just like them, he thought bleakly. *Or maybe a little worse.*

Jefferson punched in another number. This one was for GPS, or Ground Positioning Services. In a matter of moments, once they had processed the downloaded file information and computed latitude and longitude, he would know within a couple of feet where Marsh Wheelan had stood when he used his cell phone. Somehow it all seemed too easy.

Assistant Director Robert W. Prescott spun around in his chair, a thick manila folder grasped in his hands. He nodded for Jefferson Tate to take a seat.

"I see we've got our computer hacker located," the AD said, his expression a mask of stone. "The file mentions he is also wanted by the EPA for importing a banned substance across international borders. That gives us a multiple felony case."

"Yes sir," Tate said.

"You are aware we have a problem here?"

"Yes sir," Jefferson repeated. "But as you will note from some earlier transmissions that we've just recovered, the subject is most likely still in the area. He is conducting an illegal release of grizzly bears back into the wild." Tate hesitated then added, "Hale Cross, the country singer, of all people, is apparently financing the venture."

"Mister Cross should be more careful of the company he keeps."

"I'm sure he'll get the message loud and clear, sir, but I'm certain Mister Wheelan has done a very good job of appearing to be a legitimate environmental specialist. Now, about making an arrest of our subject. Have we been successful in getting clearance for a helicopter landing?"

"No, Agent Tate, there hasn't been and there won't be without an order from Congress. We are dealing with a wilderness area here. If you are going to take Marsh Wheelan into custody where he is, you'll either hike in or ride a horse. Unlike our subject, we are bound by laws on this matter."

A wry smile washed across Jefferson's swarthy features. "Then sir, with your permission, I'll contact the Pendleton field office and make arrangements. I've always been a great admirer of western movies. Leading a posse into the mountains after a fugitive is something not many agents get a crack at these days."

The assistant director remained stoic. "I fail to see any levity in the matter, Agent Tate. Mister Wheelan, however, seems to believe laws are made to be scoffed at. You have my authority to proceed with an arrest using any means at your disposal."

"Thank you, sir," Jefferson Tate said sincerely, bolting up to get on with the task. "I'll proceed at once."

"And Agent Tate," Prescott added with a slight hint of humor, "try to remember that you're with the FBI and not some cowboy in the Texas Rangers."

"Yes sir," Jefferson said over his shoulder.

It had been a long while since he'd felt so alive. The FBI agent strode down the concrete corridor with long steps, wearing a broad smile. He was looking forward to Oregon and most of all, slapping a pair of handcuffs on a man who had caused terrible grief to a lot of good innocent people.

CHAPTER 35

"But, but Jesus has been living here forever," the distraught Caleb Starr stammered to the border patrol officer. "No one has ever given any thought to him being an illegal alien." He shook his head sadly. "His wife's buried up there on that hill. He's just a harmless old man with no place else to go." Caleb looked down and worried a small rock with his boot. "I reckon my shooting that blasted eagle started this, too."

John Dowd put his cap back on to shield his head from the blazing sun and failed at an attempt to muster even a slight smile. "I'm afraid that's the facts of the matter. Alton McKenzie of the Drug Enforcement Administration officially notified us of the situation, and now the law must take its course." He quickly added, "It may not be as bad as you think. An FBI agent by the name of Tate came by to see me and said he had verified Mister Santiago has no criminal record and that he would vouch for him at a hearing. This will be of real benefit when we petition for lawful permanent residence."

A glimmer of hope caused Caleb to face the immigration officer. "Then you're not going to arrest him?"

Dowd shook his head decisively. "Nope, I'm just here to issue him a written notice to appear before a hearing officer in San Antonio. If you can furnish some witnesses and supporting documents to attest he's been in the country since before January of 1972 and the FBI vouches for him, that should be enough to do the trick." He hesitated. "Mister Starr, I hate to come out here and cause you any more problems. I feel bad enough for what you and Mister Santiago have been through, but—"

"Señores," Jesus said, shuffling toward them from his small home. "I do not wish to interfere." His dark rheumy eyes focused on the border patrol car. "But I fear this might concern me."

Caleb stepped around the officer and placed a hand on the old man's shoulder. It felt woefully frail. "There's just been a—a slight formality come up about your citizenship that we're dealing with. It's nothing to worry over."

"Madre de Dios," Jesus mumbled as he began shaking like a leaf in a windstorm. "*El Diablo* has come for me!"

"Calma," John Dowd said in perfect Spanish. "I'm not the devil, and I'm not here to do more than ask you to go before a judge in San Antonio. After that is done you can remain here legally, *mi amigo.*"

"Like I told you," Caleb said soothingly, "there's nothing to get all worked up about here. I'll get hold of Quentin Miller, and we'll get this taken care of *muy pronto.*"

The officer's face echoed sadness as he handed an envelope to the trembling old man. "This is a formal order to appear. Please follow the instructions, and all will go well. If you don't read English, I'll be happy to translate it for you."

A tear trickled down Jesus's dusky cheek as he surveyed the document. "I can read English quite well. But I still fear *El Diablo,* and San Antonio is a big and strange city. I am at home here where my garden and Ernesta are."

"We'll take care of getting you there," Caleb said. "It'll likely only be for a day at the most." He shot a questioning gaze at John Dowd.

"That's all it'll take," the officer said with an affirming nod. "Then this matter will be closed."

Jesus kept shivering as he turned to stare silently at his growing garden.

"I reckon you'll be leaving now," Caleb said.

"Ah," Dowd looked uneasy, "there's one more thing I have to take care of." He worried his lower lip as he took another white envelope from his shirt pocket and handed it to Caleb.

"What is it?" the rancher questioned cautiously.

"I'm truly sorry about this, believe me," the Border Patrol Agent said, "but the law is the law and I have no choice but to issue you a citation for hiring an illegal alien. Your court appearance date and your options are spelled out for you in the summons. Unfortunately, the penalty for this offence is usually a fine of two thousand dollars."

"See *señor?*" Jesus sobbed through quavering lips. "It is as I have said. *El Diablo* has come to Lone Wolf, and I fear he will not go away anytime soon."

Tristan Starr made a slight grimace when he reached out to refill his plate with a second helping of green chili burritos. "You went and outdid yourself this time, Jesus. These are so good I'll bet I could smuggle some into the hospital and sell 'em for ten dollars each. It's great having something to eat that tastes good again."

The old man continued poking listlessly at his food. He had yet to do more than sample a few small bites of his cooking. "I am glad you like my dinner. There is plenty, so eat hearty and build up your strength."

Hope Rexton daubed a napkin to her watery emerald eyes then gulped a huge swallow of iced tea. "If this stuff was any hotter I'd have to call out the fire department." She brushed away a wild strand of red hair with the back of her hand and winked slyly at Caleb who sat across the table from her. "Thanks for asking me over. It's good we can all be together." She grinned wickedly at Jesus. "Even if these burritos would peel chrome off a bumper, they are mighty tasty."

Jesus nodded morosely and continued forking at his food.

From the moment Hope arrived, she had realized something was wrong. Only Tristan was in genuine good spirits. Even though Caleb had greeted her with a hug and pecked a kiss on her check, he was plainly subdued and worried over something. More puzzling was Jesus. The old fellow leaned heavily on his cane, and his hands trembled more than usual as he went about preparing dinner.

Her instincts told her the two men were holding something back to keep from upsetting the boy who was striving to recover from surgery and a beating.

Perhaps she and Caleb could take a moonlit walk later on. That would be wonderful. Caleb Starr had found a place in her heart. There was no problem so great it couldn't be solved so long as they were together.

Some government agency has been around causing trouble again, Hope thought, forcing a smile to remain on her face. *If only they would leave him be, we could build a life together. The only reason Caleb hasn't said he loves me is because he doesn't want to involve me in his problems. Well, I love that man, and it's high time he found out just how enduring a woman's love can be.*

"Please do not think me rude," Jesus said, grabbing heavily onto his cane to stand. "I am very tired and wish to go to my house and read a book." He focused on Tristan. "And remember to take the medicines you brought home from the hospital. *Curanderos* and hot peppers may help, but I think a real doctor may work better, *quien sabe?*"

"I will," Tristan said. "Right after I finish these burritos. Those big white pills would put an elephant to sleep, but I'll take one anyway."

Caleb realized his son had made that last statement for his

benefit, in case Hope should stay for most of the night. Tristan had not only become a man, but an insightful one to boot. Of course, sleeping with a woman he was not married to in the same home with his son would set a bad example and could never be allowed to happen, no matter how much he yearned for Hope's sweet embrace.

"Are you feeling all right?" Hope questioned Jesus. "You didn't eat any of your dinner."

"I am fine, *señorita,*" he replied with a low smile. "The book I am reading is a very good one, and I wish to return to it. This afternoon while I fixed the dinner, I must have eaten more than I should have, for now I am not hungry. *Buenas noches mi amigos.*"

They watched as the old man shuffled off into the night.

"Great food. Jesus is the best cook north of the Equator," Tristan said loud enough for the departing patriarch to hear. "Those burritos were just right."

"If you're trying to get rid of a set of tonsils they were," Caleb blurted out. If he let Jesus leave without getting in a verbal jab, the boy would suspect something was wrong.

A short while later Tristan had retired to his room after making sure everyone watched when he swallowed his medicine.

"He's a different boy since he came home from the hospital," Caleb remarked in a hushed voice.

"I'm glad," Hope said, "after what he—all of you—has been through. Tristan could have gone the other way. Instead he's done some fast growing up, in the right direction."

Caleb grinned. "How about a nice long walk outside under the stars, little lady?"

"You big sweet talker, I thought you'd never ask."

Crickets chirped their nightly mating call and an owl hooted its greeting when Hope slid her arm around Caleb's waist. Together they ambled slowly along underneath a jeweled canopy of blackness.

After a lingering kiss, Caleb told her about the border patrol officer's visit.

"Now I know why the poor old fellow's so upset," she said sadly. "But things sound like they'll work out all right. If you can't find the time, I'll take a day off work to drive Jesus to San Antonio."

"You're sweet to offer but I doubt it'll be necessary. I'd reckon half the folks in Lone Wolf will offer to do the same. Everyone likes that old fellow."

"It was good of you and Jesus to keep this matter from upsetting Tristan."

"Jesus said the boy had been through worse than his problems."

"He's such a sweet man."

"That he is. Hope, there's more to what happened today."

She looked up into his eyes and placed her soft hands on his cheeks. Caleb thought they felt like the finest velvet.

"Lay it on me, big guy," Hope said jauntily. "We'll solve the problem together then get on to some heavy kissing."

He told her about having to pay a fine for employing an illegal alien and having another court appearance. Thanks to Hope and her happy demeanor, the matter that earlier had been so devastating now seemed to be a mere trifle.

"We'll handle it. Hold your head high and never, never, never give up, Caleb. All of this will blow over eventually. Even the worst of storms always do. The people who truly care about you will forever stick by you through thick and thin. Like I keep reminding you, no matter what, you'll always have hope. And look on the bright side of this evening."

Caleb was puzzled. "What do you mean?"

"The phone never rang once."

He gathered her into his arms, and the long gentle kisses that followed transported both of them to a place where only love flourished.

Chapter 36

Caleb Starr wondered why it was still dark outside when he came into the kitchen the next morning. He plugged in the coffee pot to start its usual sputtering and gurgling when he noticed rain drops on the window over the sink.

An unexpected gathering of low, black clouds giving life to a thirsty earth brought a satisfied smile to his stubble-bearded cheeks. The lingering aroma of Hope's sweet perfume completed a feeling that all was right with the world.

He sat in his usual chair at the table and watched the welcome rain streak downward. All too often what little moisture that falls in west Texas comes in the form of brief, violent thunderstorms. These were of slight benefit to the stunted grass that always seemed to be in danger of losing its tenuous presence. A slow ground soaker like the one in progress was a rare event. If it continued for even a few hours the countryside would quickly transform into a lush paradise. Then his cattle and goats would grow sleek and fat without him having to haul them expensive store bought feed.

"What's going on out there?" Tristan said as he came in and joined his father at the table. "Is that rain? It's been so long since I've seen any of the stuff I'm not sure if I remember what it looks like."

Caleb noticed his son had walked straight and now sat in the chair without hunching over as he had done last night. The boy was making a rapid recovery. A gnawing pain in his lower back reminded the rancher how good it was to be young.

"I wish it would keep this up all day," Caleb said. "We need every drop of it."

"I know we do, Dad. It's time for God to smile."

Caleb cocked his head and kept silent. He was still trying to adjust to Tristan's newfound attitude.

"Dad," Tristan stared straight into his father's eyes from across the table, "I know I'm just a kid with a lot to learn about life, but there is something I can say for certain."

The coffee pot shuddered and gave out a loud gurgle. Caleb got up, went over and filled two cups. He sat one in front of his son. "What might that be?"

"Hope loves you, and I believe you feel the same way about her."

Caleb was taken aback. He hadn't expected such direct talk from his own son.

"How would you know about a thing like that?"

Tristan's simple answer built a familiar fiery lump in his throat. "Because you look at her like you used to look at mom when she was still alive."

Monica Blandon gave out a sigh when the telephone on her cluttered desk rang. She was exhausted and haggard from the terrible traffic accident that had kept her up all night.

An older model pickup truck had blown a tire while traveling at a high rate of speed. The wreck had occurred on the main highway just inside the county line. This was nearly fifty miles from Lone Wolf.

The driver and two passengers, all young men, were from the border town of Del Rio. None had been wearing a seat belt and all were thrown from the truck when it had plowed into a bar ditch and rolled several times. Only one of the bloody victims had a shallow pulse when she arrived on the scene. A building storm kept the Med-Evac helicopter in San Angelo grounded. Before an ambulance arrived, the still living survivor had slipped this mortal coil. A profusion of empty beer cans strewn for hundreds of feet along the black highway told a sad story of youthful indiscretion.

It had taken her husband two trips to haul the three bodies into his mortuary. The ambulance attendants and Bones only had two rubber body bags between them. There was no way to transport all of the mangled remains without a third, necessitating the extra trip.

Monica knew what the blood alcohol tests she had ordered on the corpses would show. Trying to decide what to tell grieving relatives was the hardest job in law enforcement. Earlier she had faxed the Del Rio Sheriff's office, giving them the young men's names and driver's license numbers. She assumed the call was from them. Then would begin the sad job of notifying the next of kin. To spare their feelings, for awhile anyway, Monica would mention only that a blown out tire had caused the tragedy and all three had died instantly. The rain and black clouds outside the office only added the bleakness of her mood.

"Lone Wolf Sheriff's Department," she said lethargically into the receiver. "This is Sheriff Blandon."

"Well good morning, Sheriff," a happy sounding voice boomed in her ear taking her aback. "This is Special Agent Jefferson Tate with the FBI."

Monica felt as if a heavy weight had been lifted from her shoulders. Even a brief reprieve from the task facing her was welcome.

"And a good morning to you, Mister Tate. Are you here in town?"

"No, I'm two time zones west of you, in Pendleton, Oregon. The sun hasn't peeked over the horizon up here yet."

"What's going on in Oregon that concerns me?" Monica

blurted before she realized just how callous her words had come out. "I didn't mean to be so brusque, sir," she added quickly. "We've had a triple fatality traffic accident here. I've been working it all night."

"I'm terribly sorry to hear that." Tate sounded sincere. "Those must be awful. Informing the family is the worst part of all. God knows I've had to do it a few times in my career."

"Thank you for saying that, sir. It's one of those things that comes with wearing a badge we'd rather not think about too often. Now what may I do for you?"

"Actually, Sheriff," Tate's pleasant tone had returned, "I'm keeping you informed of what we're doing for you." He hesitated, "And your brother, Caleb."

Monica straightened. The FBI Agent had her full attention. "Yes, sir."

"We have located the computer hacker who caused you all of those problems. I'm up here to effect an arrest."

"He's in Pendleton?"

"Uh, no, unfortunately it's not a simple matter. Mister Wheelan is at a camp in John Day Wilderness Area. The only legal way we can get to him is on horseback. I'm working on that now. If I have any decent luck building a fire under some lazy civil servants, a few other law enforcement personnel and I will be headed up there by this afternoon. I expect to reach his position by tomorrow morning."

"Can't you just take a helicopter?" Monica questioned.

"No ma'am," Tate's voice betrayed his exasperation. "Nothing with an engine is allowed into those places. It's against the law. We'll get him just the same, though."

Monica sighed. "There's not much these days that *isn't* against some law it seems."

After a long moment of heavy silence, Jefferson Tate said, "I'll phone you once Marsh Wheelan is in custody."

"Thanks for keeping me informed."

The Sheriff of Lone Wolf County placed the phone back in its cradle. She laced her fingers behind her head, swiveled the chair around and stared out the window at the gentle rain, steeling herself for another phone call she knew would be coming soon.

Caleb was both surprised and pleased when Tristan came out of his room, after eating a hearty breakfast, wearing blue jeans and a western shirt. Since his son had gotten a short haircut he had only seen him dressed in a bathrobe. Now, a clean-cut, smiling young gentleman had replaced the surly teenager who had caused him so much heartache and consternation.

Aside from some lingering, angry purple bruises on his face, Tristan appeared to be almost recovered from his near fatal ordeal. Caleb's main concern was that the boy was going out of his way to shelter him from further worry. The doctor in San Angelo had made it plain Tristan needed several days of complete rest before leaving the house. Only Caleb's promise this would happen had insured the young man's early release from the hospital.

"Good to see you up and about," Caleb said. "I thought I might run into town and rent some movies. Why don't you tell me which ones you'd like to watch and I'll get them? I'd really like to see you put your feet up and take it easy for a spell."

"Thanks, Dad, but I've got enough homework to do to keep me plenty entertained. I'm determined to get that diploma quick as I can. If I need a break later on, I'll go borrow one of Jesus's books and read it. He's got more of them than the library."

"Just so long as you stay in the house and take it easy. That doc was plenty clear he didn't want to have to sew you back together if you went and did something dumb."

Tristan chuckled. "We can't have that. He's so ornery, he'd

likely use cat gut and no anesthetic." He shot a wicked grin at Useless who was curled up in a chair. "And there's the likeliest source of the cat to supply the gut. I'd reckon I'll do Useless a favor and do like the doc said."

The tomcat ignored him and began contentedly licking a paw.

Caleb thought his son's admirable attitude and humor were welcome as the rain that continued pattering against the windows. There had been far too little happiness inside this old house for a long while.

"About Jesus," Tristan shot a questioning glance at the vacant kitchen table. "I wonder what's keeping him. It's not like him to miss out on his morning coffee."

"He probably just don't want to come out in the rain."

"I don't know, Dad. He didn't act like he felt good last night. Maybe I oughta grab the coffee pot and run over to his place and check on him. I'll put on a slicker so I don't get wet."

"You go and work on your homework," Caleb said. "I'll take him some coffee, and it'll give me a chance to check the rain gauge." He smiled. "If I can only remember where I put the blame thing."

Minutes later, peering from underneath his sweat-stained Stetson hat, Caleb stood on the front porch of Jesus's small house. Through the front window, he could see the old fellow sitting in his easy chair. As usual, an open book was in his lap, and the lamp on the table beside him was glowing. He simply hadn't wanted to come outside into the rain.

Caleb stomped the mud from his boots and hollered loudly, "Hey Jesus, I've brought you some coffee."

Stone silence was his only answer. The handle of the metal pot was growing uncomfortably hot to hold. Caleb gave a snort of impatience and opened the door with his free hand. When he stepped inside the old fellow remained unmoving.

He's gone to sleep in his chair again.

Caleb set the steaming pot on the counter top beside the sink, reached up and grabbed a cup from the shelf. "Been morning for hours now. It's time to wake up and enjoy the rain. We might not get a chance to witness a sight like this again in a month of Sundays."

"Jesus," Caleb turned and observed his friend with growing concern. "Are you all right?"

In the glow of the reading light, Caleb's stomach knotted with dread when he noticed glazed, unseeing eyes staring at the open book. He froze in the black silence as a sharp pang of realization stabbed at his heart.

"Oh God, *no!*"

He took a deep breath and closed his eyes against building tears. There was no reason to hurry. Caleb placed the coffee cup that he held in his hands like a chalice gently down on the counter. Then, forcing himself to move on feet of lead, he went to where Jesus sat and placed a hand against the old man's neck hoping in vain to find a pulse. Life had long since fled the cold body. There was nothing he could do. Nothing at all.

Except mumble a prayer through quivering lips and fight stinging tears. Minutes passed like hours before the rancher could compose himself. Telling Tristan and Hope was a task he had to do. He couldn't allow himself to break down. No matter how terrible his heart was hurting, he had to be strong for their sake. There was no one else to do what had to be done.

Caleb's hand trembled when he reached out and closed unseeing eyes for all eternity. Lovingly, he bent over, picked up the book from Jesus's lap and folded it closed. He noticed it was the old sheepherder's most treasured possession, the dog-eared autographed copy of *The Time It Never Rained.*

Caleb clasped the book to his chest, stared out the window at the gentle rain and sobbed loudly. Now he did not try to hold back the tears. He was alone. There is a time to be strong.

And a time to cry.

Chapter 37

"Damn piece of Jap crap!" Marsh Wheelan snarled. He drew the recalcitrant cell phone over his head to dash it onto the floor of his tent, then hesitated.

While seeing the worthless piece of shit smashed into smithereens would be salve for his troubled soul, it might only worsen his dire situation. That damnable black phone could be his only link to the civilized world. Ever since the stumblebum guide had left, for some inexplicable reason, all he could receive was a recorded message from some snooty bitch telling him, "All circuits are busy. Please try again."

Even more perplexing and ominous was his very powerful laptop computer. "Carrier not detected" was the only thing the blasted machine would show on its screen.

It was obvious the batteries were well charged. The small generator, while he knew it to be nearly out of fuel, whirred away in back of his tent. Marsh had run the power plant all night hoping to build up the batteries, although there was no reason to believe that was the problem. He had plugged the laptop directly into the AC power output with the same maddening, "Carrier not detected" showing up.

He *had* to get out. There was no delaying the matter. And a helicopter was the only alternative to walking cross-country for nearly fifty miles. This was something he had no intention of doing.

Marsh Wheelan took a deep breath and exhaled slowly. Better. He gently laid the cell phone alongside a half empty bottle of very poor quality burgundy on his folding metal table.

The sight of the wine angered him further. Once he was out of this temporary plight there would be a purveyor of spirits in Sacramento, California, given a piece of his mind and educated on the pitfalls of misrepresenting his products. There were only three bottles left of what turned out to be an absolutely dreadful vintage. He needed its soothing benefits to see him through his jam. Then, he planned to pursue the wine peddler with vigor. He detested being taken advantage of.

The secret of being a winner is the ability to turn defeat into victory.

His father's familiar words boomed inside his head like a thunderclap. The old fart had wisdom, if nothing more, to recommend him.

Every puzzle, no matter how perplexing, always had an answer. Throughout his life, Marsh had prided himself on having the keenest intellect. He just needed to think on the situation.

He poured a water glass full of that inferior burgundy and downed it, dregs and all, with three gulps.

A feeling of comfort and power coursed through his veins. He stepped over to the boom box and inserted a Lynyrd Skynyrd CD into the player and cranked up the volume to its highest setting. The music had a tinny quality to it which displeased him. It would be wonderful when he could once again have a stereo system worthy of his discriminating ear. In a wilderness area, however, one must make do.

The beat of the music helped to focus his thoughts. There had to be a simple explanation as to why his communications devices were no longer functioning.

He was a trained scientist. The approach to solving any problem is to calmly and deliberately begin removing the obvious. He held no doubt the batteries were up to capacity. The phone and computer had the necessary power to operate. Secondly, it was imperative a signal be beamed from the proper satellite.

Why that devious son of a bitch.

Sam McSwain had obviously altered the setting of his portable satellite dish. Marsh snorted with grudging admiration at the simpleton's understanding. The guide had given the impression that operating a light switch was high tech.

It would be a simple matter to realign the dish. Then, with any decent luck, he could spend the night in a luxury hotel.

Promising a huge bonus to the helicopter company would undoubtedly do the trick. Money spoke of power. And most of all, Marsh Wheelan understood power.

He stuck the forty-four magnum pistol under his belt and fidgeted through a plastic box until he found his compass. Those blasted grizzlies hadn't been poking around his camp, but he had seen them romping along the stream. After witnessing the guide rub their ears, Marsh doubted the bears were actually much of a danger to him. Nevertheless, if they came close, he planned to shoot them where they stood.

Better safe than sorry.

Fluffy white clouds floated lazily in a livid blue sky. A gentle breeze rustled the pine and tamarack trees. In the distance birds twittered their greeting. Marsh noticed nor heard any of this. His attention was focused on the satellite dish and the stereo blared from his tent.

Marsh cast a quick scan for the bears and saw nothing. He walked up the slight hill to the dish and unfolded his compass. A quick reading showed the Azimuth setting to be absolutely correct for the location. This was puzzling. The tent pegs driven into the ground to firmly hold the receiver also showed no evidence of tampering. When a check of the vertical showed perfect, Marsh's legs felt rubbery.

There must be a defect in the coaxial cable.

Carefully and methodically, he got down on his hands and knees and began scrutinizing the rubber-coated lifeline to the outside world. Then, to his building horror, the generator began sputtering. After a moment of jerking and coughing, the little machine grew silent. Inside the tent, Lynyrd Skynyrd faded into the sounds of the forest.

The generator is out of gasoline, and there is no more. Damn that guide to hell for not stocking an adequate supply.

Forcing himself to calm down and concentrate on the task at hand, Marsh continued checking out every foot of the cable. He noticed his hand trembled as he ran a testing finger along its black covering. After tracing the line into his tent, he conceded there was absolutely nothing wrong with either the dish or the cable.

He emptied the bottle of that dreadful wine into his glass and hurled the empty through the open tent flap. There was a satisfying crash when the bottle shattered on a nearby rock.

Marsh chugged the putrid liquid and began surveying his meager supplies. The wonderful shaved ham and Swiss cheese was gone, as were the filet mignon steaks. There were only a few strips of bacon along with some disgustingly stale bread left in his storehouse. That and the remaining bottles of repulsive wine would be his dinner.

What will I eat tomorrow? And the next day?

Then his father's stern voice echoed inside his troubled mind once again. *You're nothing but a pantywaist, boy. At least act like you are my son. Stand straight and try to imitate a man for once.*

"You arrogant old fart," Marsh shouted to no one. "I'll be glad when you're dead, and I have your money."

The day was still young, but Marsh fished another bottle of wine from the cooler. When he did so, it struck him that in a few hours both of his small refrigerators would lose their ability to keep his food or wine cool. This was a real pisser and an added incentive to renew his efforts.

He grabbed up the cell phone and punched the buttons with a shaky finger. The same bitch with a nerve-wracking voice droned in his ear, "All circuits are busy. Please try again."

"You slut!" he screamed. "Get me an operator."

The voice repeated coldly, "All circuits are busy—"

Marsh slammed the phone closed and laid it on the table. He forced a deep breath and went to the boom box. At least it held a fresh pack of alkaline batteries. He flipped the switch from AC to DC power. In less than a second his delightful, soothing music had returned.

Using his ornate silver opener, he extracted the cork from another bottle. To his pleasant surprise the cork gave a delightful aroma. Marsh rinsed the glass with distilled water and filled it with burgundy. He rolled the glass carefully and observed the wine left a film clinging to the sides, as a good vintage always should. A sip told him he had at least one decent bottle left in his meager storehouse to enjoy.

With a newborn feeling of confidence, he sat down and switched on his laptop.

Ah, the power of a computer.

The screen flickered to life and the icons became crystal clear. He moved the mouse to connect with the Internet.

"Carrier not detected," flashed onto the screen.

Marsh Wheelan tried once again.

"Carrier not detected."

Icy pinpricks of fear began working down his spine. He was miles from even a jerkwater town. He was nearly out of food and wine.

And he was all alone.

Desperately Marsh tapped the mouse pad.

"Carrier not detected."

For the first time in his life, Marsh Earlson Wheelan was beginning to understand what real fear was all about.

Chapter 38

Bones Blandon reached out and placed the back of his hand against Jesus Santiago's neck. He shook his head sadly and turned to his teary-eyed wife who stood by his side. "The poor old fellow's heart just quit beating. From the temperature of the body and lividity apparent in his arms, I'd say he passed away sometime early last night."

Monica Blandon nervously adjusted her thick leather gun belt. It seemed heavier and more uncomfortable than she could ever remember. She swallowed hard and tried to cast off the maelstrom of anguish that wrapped around her like a cocoon.

"At least he went peaceful," Monica said softly, remembering the nightmarish vestige of a young man who only hours ago had died choking on his own blood while she watched helplessly. "That's something we can be thankful for."

Tip Conroy cast an eye at Caleb who stood near the open door with a sheltering arm wrapped around Tristan's shoulder.

"If it's all right with you, Mister Blandon," the deputy said, "I reckon we oughta move Jesus over to your place."

In the county of Lone Wolf, it falls on an elected Justice of the Peace to pronounce someone dead and order the disposition of the body. Only in rare instances where foul play is suspected are autopsies ordered performed. This entails taking the corpse all the way to San Antonio, the nearest city with forensic specialists, an expensive task for a cash-starved county like Lone Wolf.

Lane Blandon had held the title of Justice of the Peace for fifteen years. The fact that he was an undertaker and also levied fines on people his wife had issued tickets to made for many jokes, but no substantial complaints. He had been known to bury people for no charge when their families, if any, were too poor to pay. Most locals were given a light fine or warning for minor violations of the law. Only out of state drivers who attempted to speed through the county were given the task of supporting the Lone Wolf legal system. Bones was a well liked and trusted man.

The undertaker gave a solemn nod. "I think that's what we need to do." He looked at Tristan's sad face. "I'm going out to the hearse and get a gurney. Caleb, I believe you ought to get the boy back to the house. He's taking a lot of medication, and it won't do for him to catch a cold."

Caleb gave a look of understanding and turned to his son. "Let's go, Tristan. These men have a job to do, and we're just in the way."

Bones gave a sigh of relief as he watched Caleb and Tristan fade away into the mist. The rain had mostly stopped now. Only patches of heavy black clouds like the one overhead gave out any moisture. On the hill behind Jesus's little house, a ray of sun shot earthward signaling the life giving rain was coming to an end. They never seemed to last long enough.

He looked toward the frail remains sitting in the chair and thought, *rain and good people share one thing in common: neither seem to stick around long enough.*

It was nearly noon when Caleb came out on his porch again. Only a few clouds lingered on the eastern horizon and a fiery sun had begun drying the earth. He was relieved to be finished with all the phone calls that had to be made.

The rancher chewed nervously at his lower lip when he thought back on how badly Hope's heart had broken when he told her the sad news. He desperately wanted to wrap her in his arms and make the hurt go away. If only he could. If only *anyone* could.

Tristan had finally dropped off to sleep with Useless curled up by his side. His son had been so distraught any words of comfort had failed. When the boy's incision began to cause him pain from sobbing, Caleb had insisted he take a pain pill and go to bed. Those big white tablets did their job once again.

He was alone now. For a long while Caleb studied the muddy gashes left in the earth where Bones's hearse had backed up to the door where Jesus had lived for so many years. Then he focused on the old man's growing garden and thought how happy Jesus would be if he could see how much it had already grown from the rain.

He put off looking at Ernesta's grave for as long as he could. The burning lump that seemed to have found a permanent home in his throat built up steam. There was no doubt that soon there would be another headstone to gaze upon.

Caleb strode down the steps and onto the caliche road that squished under his weight. He walked until he came to the top of the small hill behind the ranch houses. For a long while he stood surveying the countryside.

Then, from the hip pocket of his faded blue jeans, he extracted the summons Jesus had been issued to appear before some judge in far off San Antonio. It had been on the night stand beside the old man when Caleb had found him that morning.

Paper can kill surely as a bullet, he thought.

Caleb Starr took the white envelope and ripped it in two. He folded it and tore it again. The last thing he did before leaving was throw the pieces down and grind them into the muddy earth with the heel of his boot.

Jefferson Tate fished inside his jacket, trying to grab the ringing cell phone. He had not ridden a horse for several years, and the constant jogging complicated the task. Making certain he had a good grip on the thing, he pulled it out and flipped open the mouthpiece.

"This is Special Agent Tate."

A woman's voice answered in measured, precise words, "Yes sir, Agent Tate, this is Tech Specialist Greerson with the Austin Field Office. Are we clear to communicate?"

Jefferson could barely contain a chuckle at the uncalled-for formality of her speech. He was riding a horse alongside a roaring creek inside a wilderness area accompanied by nearly a dozen fellow officers of the law. Shadow File information was, however, only transmitted over a secure frequency. Ms. Greerson had simply followed the rules by asking if he was clear, meaning no one else could overhear their conversation.

"Yes, Ms. Greerson, I'm clear. Please proceed."

The specialist's words were so deliberate they seemed computer generated. "Target number twelve twenty-seven is still showing activity. An unusual amount to be exact, sir. Every minute or so the target is attempting to activate the frequency."

The FBI agent grinned. *March Wheelan is actually panicking. Those little high tech toys of his he used to destroy people's lives with aren't working anymore.*

"Thank you for the update, Ms. Greerson. Keep the block on his signal. I anticipate we will be at the target's position by tomorrow morning. Tate out."

He snapped the phone closed and returned it to its leather case. The fact that Marsh Wheelan was desperately and futilely attempting to summon help only added to his enjoyment of the magnificent country he was traversing.

Rugged mountains shrouded with verdant trees stabbed at an azure sky. Billowy clouds floated lazily among their lofty peaks. Crystal clear water from melting snow tumbled and gushed around boulders in the canyon alongside the trail. If God ever decided to take up residence on this earth, Jefferson decided, here is where He would dwell.

Four armed Forest Service personnel, nattily dressed in immaculate green uniforms led the way. They were obviously familiar with this country, never once consulting a map or compass.

An assortment of lawmen who were fortunate enough to garner horses brought up the rear. Surveying the majestic country, Jefferson understood why only a lack of mounts had kept the numbers as low as they were. Taking Marsh Wheelan into custody for computer fraud could certainly have been accomplished with far fewer men.

Aside from the Forest Service officers, the Oregon State Police, Federal Fish and Wildlife, along with the local county sheriff's department were all represented.

Jefferson found it a matter of great satisfaction that he was the sole FBI man. It turned out none of the other FBI agents knew how to ride a horse. All told there were eleven men, including himself, and fifteen horses, three of the animals were used to pack along needed supplies. The one riderless saddled horse was intended transportation for Mister Marsh Wheelan to use on the return trip.

Jefferson Tate inhaled the pine scented air and basked in the glorious mountain scenery. At the rapid pace they were maintaining, he wouldn't be here nearly long enough.

Prairie Dog Pete filled a metal tray with sweaty, long-neck bottles of beer and waddled over to the table. A somber quiet filled The Slip Up Saloon while he passed them around. At Hector Lemmons request the jukebox had been unplugged. Music should be reserved for happier times.

Quentin Miller was first to break the respectful hush. He held out his brown bottle of Lone Star Beer. "Here's to Jesus Santiago, may he live forever in our memories."

Rosemary Page, who sat by his side, tapped her bottle to his. "He was a good man, and he knew his Shakespeare."

Staring out a window, Rollie Turner said, "We're all gonna miss that old fellow. I can't remember back to when he wasn't around. He was one of those people that I expected would live forever."

"Yeah," Hector Lemmons said with a snort, "he might've done it, too, except for the damn government harassing Caleb an' him over that blasted bird."

Quentin Miller ignored the old rancher's statement. "Tristan is the one I feel sorry for most of all. He just got home from the hospital after being nearly beaten to death, and now he has to suffer through this. Jesus was like a grandfather to that boy."

Prairie Dog bent over, picked up a twenty dollar bill that was in front of the lawyer and thumbed to make change. "I agree with Hector. Jesus wouldn't have had that heart attack if the government had left him alone."

Bones Blandon shook his head. The undertaker's eyes were bloodshot from stress and lack of sleep. "There's no way anyone can say that for certain. He was well onto eighty years old. There's two rules a man in my profession learns to live with. The first one is good people die. The second one is you can't change rule one."

After a moment of stony silence, Rosemary spoke, "It is my understanding, that Father Juan Ibarra of Saint Augustine's Catholic Church will hold a Rosary for Jesus the day after tomorrow at seven P.M."

Bones nodded. "You're right about the Rosary, and the funeral will be held in the church the day after at ten in the morning. The old fellow never, to my recollection, ever set foot in the church after his wife died. But I heard he did send them money once and awhile to help out. I suppose we'll bury him out at Caleb's place, next to his wife." He shot a glance at Quentin Miller. "I'm sure that's what Jesus requested."

Earlier, the lawyer had mentioned Jesus left a will and that he had been appointed executor.

Quentin Miller nodded. "That's exactly what his wishes were. Even the part about a Catholic funeral. I'll put together the necessary paperwork to do the burial at the ranch."

Prairie Dog looked dumbstruck. "You need a permit to bury someone?"

"It's just a formality," Bones replied, keeping his eyes fixed on Quentin. "We're taking care of the matter."

The pudgy bartender sighed, then trundled away sipping on a beer as he went.

Hector Lemmons said, "The way things are goin', fairly soon a person's goin' to need a permit from some agency just to die."

"The foundation of civilization is built on law," Quentin Miller said. "Without rules we would be governed by anarchy."

Prairie Dog realized he had made the incorrect change. He came over, laid a five dollar bill in front of the lawyer and gave him a puzzled look. "In my book, this 'Anarky' guy couldn't be much worse than the president we got now."

Rosemary Page groaned.

Bones Blandon, Rollie and Hector gave in to laughter.

Quentin Miller chuckled and took a swallow of beer. "You know something, my friends? I believe with all my heart that Jesus wouldn't want us moping around. The old fellow always did enjoy happy times." He smiled at Prairie Dog. "Thank you for bringing this to our attention. Bring us another round, and we'll remember the good times." The lawyer's grin turned sardonic. "And put this one on Hector's tab, with a good tip added for your trouble."

Prairie Dog Pete turned and shuffled off to fill the order. The pudgy bartender had no idea what he had said that buoyed everyone's spirits, but the sound of laughter breaking the black mood made him proud of himself. Perhaps, he wondered, it might be all right now to plug the jukebox back in.

Chapter 39

In a smoke filled barroom on the side of San Angelo where respectable ladies do not visit, Dianne Petrov sat alone on a wobbly stool and downed her sixth martini. She tapped a cigarette loose from the crumpled pack and lit it.

"Hey, how about another over here?" she said to the unsmiling man behind the bar. There weren't many customers. Dianne doubted there ever were.

But the drinks are cheap, which is helpful. Ever since being fired from her job at Run Free, alcohol had been her constant companion. An anesthetic served up in a glass.

Not so very long ago her life had been so simple and straightforward. How long ago was it? She can't remember for certain, only that it was before Marsh Wheelan.

The bastard.

Even thinking of his name caused bile to rise. He visited her in the bitter hours of darkness whenever she slept.

Dianne Petrov awoke screaming every night now, the nightmare always the same.

A majestic bald eagle glides peacefully about a lush meadow winging its way along a meandering stream. Suddenly the blast of a gunshot rips the pastoral scene. The eagle explodes into a cloud of feathers and blood, it plunges earthward, crashing into the tall grass.

She runs toward the fallen creature, hoping desperately there is something she can do to help. Only the bloody remains she finds are not those of an eagle. The battered body of young Tristan Starr lies crumpled in the field. He stares at her with pain-glazed eyes.

Then a gloating and smiling Marsh Wheelan is by her side holding a smoking shotgun.

"This is grand fun," he says, handing her the gun. "You can shoot the next one."

For some reason that can only be explained by who or what orchestrates the adumbral world of dreams, she takes the weapon.

A shadow crosses the shimmering sun. She raises the lead-heavy gun and fires. A form begins tumbling down from above, growing larger as it approaches.

The thing falls with a sickening thud alongside the beautiful creek. She walks over to inspect her handiwork.

A jolt of anguish strikes her like lightning.

Again she sees a bloodied Tristan Starr crumpled into ruin, his life fluid leaking crimson onto the shiny green grass. His head turns toward her, his eyes are pleading.

"Why?" the boy asks, *"why?"*

Marsh Wheelan chortles, "I told you this was fun, didn't I. We can keep doing this forever. Can't we *Dianne?*"

Her own shrill screams awaken her.

Now she faced another night, another nightmare.

"Get me my drink," she slurred to the stoic barman.

"Comin' lady," he answered dully and set the long-stemmed glass of comfort on the battered bar in front of her.

The clock on the wall showed it was not yet seven in the evening.

Time flows like cold syrup.

"Buy you that drink, li'l lady?" a burly unkempt man in need of a shave said.

She didn't remember him coming to her side. He smelled of

body odor, but she smiled sweetly at him. "Yes, I'd like some company."

At least he would keep her mind off nightmares. For a while anyway.

Some strive to remember.

Dianne Petrov strove to forget.

CHAPTER 40

The yellow orb of a full moon encompassed by infinite stars that sparkled like diamonds against the night sky floated high above the rugged mountains of eastern Oregon. The haunting calls of an owl perched high in a tamarack tree echoed eerily from rocky cliffs.

In a gentle valley surrounded by craggy peaks that jutted like shadowy medieval castles, Marsh Earlson Wheelan sat staring numbly at a blank computer screen. The sprawling tent served to amplify the nocturnal sounds of nature in this remote area, adding to his discomfiture. The low hissing of a gasoline lantern dangling from an overhead metal rod was his only reminder of the trappings of civilization.

The secret of being a winner is the ability to turn defeat into victory.

His father's haranguing voice was inside his head again, the arrogant self-righteous old skinflint.

You're nothing but a pantywaist, boy.

Marsh needed to think on his dilemma. He *had* to think on it. And also drive the old fart's rasping voice into some dark corner of the netherworld where it belonged.

He placed a Megadeth CD into the player of his boom box. Then he made certain the volume dial was turned to maximum before he flipped on the power switch.

Ah, the calming beat of good music.

To celebrate he grabbed the bottle of wine off the table and took a swig, then grimaced at his gauche act. Marsh Wheelan chided himself for his lapse of mien and, with an expression of contrition, refilled the crystal glass that sat alongside the computer. No person of such fine breeding as his should ever allow himself to become so distraught as to do such a thing.

The simple fact of the matter was that he would have to walk back to civilization. While this was certainly a real pisser, it was nothing to get so worked up over as to drink wine straight from the bottle.

Following a compass and map would be a childlike task for a man of his keen intellect. While the nearest petty town was fifty miles distant, a check of the topographic map he had brought along showed a paved road to be about ten miles due north.

A piece of cake for a man in prime physical condition like he was.

The close spaced lines on the map indicated his short cut to civilization could be somewhat steep in places, but he held no doubts of his ability to traverse the distance with ease.

Once he got to the road someone would undoubtedly offer him a ride. Then he would make his way to Portland, reclaim his Bronco, and get the hell back to California where there were decent restaurants, money and tender young girls.

The die had been cast when the last vestige of electrical power had fled the batteries in his potent laptop computer and cell phone.

Natural phenomenon! Marsh bolted upright with sudden cognition. *Sunspots! Why of course, how could I have been so naive?*

Any trained scientist knew that a flare-up of sunspots would blank out satellite signals. Likely they were over now. And there was a slight chance the batteries might have recovered some of their power. This would be a rare occurrence, but he sincerely deserved it to happen.

Marsh sat down at his wonderfully powerful computer and

clicked on the switch with an anxious finger. He gazed at the screen as a person might keep watch over a beloved pet that had passed away, hoping by some miracle it still contained a spark of life and return to the living.

This miracle was not to be. Not even a pinprick of light crossed the screen. The computer's batteries were dead as Abraham Lincoln and going to stay that way without an influx of electrical current. This was another pisser now that he knew the problem had been sunspots all along.

If he could run the generator for even a short while, he would be able to ride out of here tomorrow in the comfort of a helicopter.

But there was no gasoline left. Not even a drop. Thanks to an idiot.

A tumult of red rage flooded his being.

All of this is that imbecilic guide's fault. He abandoned me here in this Godforsaken place. I hired him to look after my welfare, and he ran out on me. I'll ruin that bastard Sam McSwain if it takes years to accomplish. I'm a powerful man. No one treats me like this and gets away with it. I'll have his guide's license revoked. Then I'll sue him for every nickel he has or ever will have. The arrogant fool will wind up living underneath a bridge begging for food when I'm finished with him.

Marsh felt better now that he had even another stimulus to hike out of here and get on with things that really mattered in life. Suing someone would be a fun diversion while he built his political base.

A grumble crossed Marsh's lean belly. He realized he hadn't eaten for hours and stress had thrown his stomach into an upset.

Shortly, the sweet smell of sizzling bacon filled the tent. Much to his distress there were only eight slices. This meant he would have to do without breakfast in the morning. At least it was only ten miles to that paved highway.

A taste of hardship might be an experience he could turn to his advantage. He could tell supporters of his budding career about his firsthand knowledge of the wilderness he had sworn to protect.

Temporary defeat turned into long term victory, Marsh thought with welling pride.

That ought to hold his father's voice at bay for awhile.

You're still nothing but a pantywaist and a disappointment to me, boy.

The voice grated worse than ever. The more he tried to push the old man's vociferations out of his head the more often he came to visit.

You'll never amount to anything because it takes a backbone to be a winner. And you weren't born with one of those, boy.

"I'll show you," Marsh hissed through clenched teeth. "When I become a senator or congressman you'll be proud of me." An evil smirk crossed his face. "And then I'll ruin you."

The bacon started to burn. He took a fork, turned it and finished his glass of wine. Only one bottle remained, a meager offering. While the sizzling bacon finished cooking, he removed the cork in it with his ornate silver handled opener. The aroma was gratifying. Apparently only one of the bottles of burgundy had been of poor vintage. Nevertheless, he intended to complain to the store that had sold him the wine. A real man would never let himself be taken advantage of.

Marsh eyeballed the bacon and decided it was done. A turn of the dial shut off the propane to the stove and extinguished the flame.

He then turned his attention to the few slices of bread that remained. Even by the inadequate light he made out some specks of mold.

A dishonest supermarket chain had sold him an inferior product that should have been pulled from the shelf long ago.

This repulsed and outraged him immeasurably. No man of his stature should have to endure eating stale bread, let alone some that actually had mold growing on it. The foul product would certainly upset his delicate digestive system more so than it already was.

Marsh consumed two glasses of wine while he contemplated the disgusting fare. He really had no choice but to eat it. At least he had found an unopened jar of chutney sauce which would most likely disguise the taste of moldy bread admirably.

Using a silver butter knife, part of a treasured set he hated to part with, Marsh scraped away as much of the greenish mold as possible, washed the knife then spread a heavy layer of chutney on two slices of bread. Grabbing a fork he reached toward the bacon. At least it appeared fresh and would undoubtedly be tasty.

You're an idiot, boy. Hiking across ten miles of steep mountains requires energy. You'd best save some food for morning.

Marsh winced at his stuffy father's grating voice of wisdom. This time the old fart had made sense. He thought back on the narrowly spaced relief lines on the topographic map and realized it could take nearly a full day to traverse those steep and rugged miles.

With a sigh of grudging understanding, Marsh forked half of the bacon from the skillet onto the chutney covered bread. He had underestimated the state of his hunger and wolfed down the inferior sandwich with huge bites. Then he stared greedily at the strips of golden brown bacon that remained.

Go ahead and eat it all. Prove I'm right about your being a lamebrain, boy.

Damn, that old fart just wouldn't leave his head. He forced his eyes from the bacon and drank some wine. There might be enough to do the trick. He desperately hoped so anyway. Normally it took four or five bottles to make the voice go away.

Ah, but the dreams of times to come.

As he worked his way toward the bottom of the bottle, Marsh Wheelan contemplated what his future life would be like.

In his sprawling, twelve-thousand square foot mansion set in the middle of hundreds of lush California acres, a huge wine cellar would be lined with hundreds of rare and expensive bottles. The image of rows of rare vintages was so vivid he felt as if he could almost reach out and grab one.

He relished the plans of grand parties that he would hold beneath swaying palm trees beside his crystal clear, Olympic-sized, heated swimming pool. Powerful politicians and the giants of finance and industry would come from around the world to attend. They would land their private jets on his own runway.

Ah, the sweet joys of success so richly deserved.

Thinking of another room below ground brought a grin of pure satisfaction to his face. In his mind's eye, the vision focused to crystal clarity. This was to be his own private playground where he could indulge his desires to the fullest without the slightest hurry. In the center, bolted tightly to the concrete floor was a king-size bed with shiny red satin sheets. An overhead mirror gave wondrous views of the proceedings. Chrome steel handcuffs and leg irons attached to brass bedposts glistened in flickering candlelight.

Of course, the ceiling and walls were totally soundproofed so as not to disturb his guests.

Ah, the wonderful serenade of a girl screaming while he whipped her creamy flesh bloody.

Along the back wall he planned to reconstruct a rude tailgate to a wagon. He was *so* anxious to try his hand with a bullwhip. He had read where a knout with steel spikes on the leather tips cut through to expose white bone with a single heavy blow. It would be most interesting to find if this were true.

Marsh was jolted from his delightful reverie by a slowing beat of the music. The batteries in his boom box were running out of power. He cursed his luck and switched the stereo off. The delightful tunes of Megadeth faded into the sounds of nature. Even more of a pisser, he was hungrier now than ever. That pathetic sandwich had only served to whet his appetite.

You disgust me, son. You've always been a loser and you'll stay one all your life.

"Get out of my head, you miserable old son of a bitch!" Marsh yelled.

He poured the last of his wine into the glass and chugged it. Now there was no music or wine to silence his father's yammer.

But he did hold other aces up his sleeve. He was no fool.

Marsh slipped a gold case from his jacket pocket. He extracted two yellow Narcol capsules, popped the powerful sleeping pills into his mouth and washed them down with a glass of tepid distilled water. He *would* sleep tonight.

His father's voice be damned.

While he waited for the narcotic to take effect, he surveyed the glass vial of white powder and little straw that would assure his escape tomorrow. After inhaling two lines of nose candy those rugged miles he faced would be like a walk in the park. A man could go for days without food using the wonderful effects of cocaine. The few slices of bacon between moldy bread would serve merely to keep his delicate digestive system in order.

Marsh Wheelan was a winner.

He stripped down to his undershorts then walked over to the cot and wrapped up in the soft, goose down sleeping bag. Even the hooting of that blasted owl couldn't keep him from the arms of Morpheus now.

The last thought that crossed his mind before he drifted off was that he would make his father proud of him yet. No matter what it took. Then, the old fart's voice might leave his head forever.

Cryptic fingers of ocher light from a lowering moon hiding behind jagged mountain peaks played hide and seek with shadows along the valley floor. Marsh Wheelan lay sleeping inside his tent enjoying the sweetest of dreams when something—a movement or noise—he wasn't certain which, jolted him awake.

The Narcol capsules had done their job well. A veil of fog shrouded his consciousness. Being taken from much needed sleep was irritating enough. But he had been dreaming of his recent wonderful experience with the Mexican whore. This made the return to reality a real pisser. He had only begun whipping her. The best had yet to come.

A guttural snort from the open tent flap lifted the drug induced fog from his mind with a blast of adrenaline.

Marsh unzipped his down filled sleeping bag, tossed it aside, spun around and sat up. Though he wore only a pair of black briefs Marsh did not notice the chill air.

A pair of wide-set, glowing animal eyes only scant feet away captured his full attention. Outside of the tent, through the open flaps he plainly made out the bulky, undulating mass of what could only be a bear. The beast's head was poking inside, testing the air with loud sniffs that were as chilling to Marsh as a snake's hiss.

You're in deep shit now, aren't you, boy? His father's voice gloated.

Marsh forced his old man's presence aside and tried to focus his still bleary eyes on where he had left the magnum pistol.

Damn!

He had unfortunately left it underneath his crumpled clothes. Less than two feet from the snorting animal. The weapon would be of no use. The beast was nearly on top of it.

Calm down, he thought, as keenness returned to his drugged mind. *It's just one of those pet grizzlies. They're harmless. Even Sam McSwain who is an idiot can handle them. And here I am a trained biologist and scientist.*

Marsh also began to realize leaving a dead member of an endangered species behind shot full of holes might cause him embarrassment at some later date.

In this world, image is everything, he thought.

The bear gave out a deep grunt and stepped closer. In the shadowy light Marsh could see it was heading toward the skillet that held the few slices of bacon destined to be his own breakfast. He couldn't allow some flea infested, toothless old animal to get away with upsetting his plans and eat the food he needed.

Marsh's bare foot brushed against an empty wine bottle. A perfect weapon to teach an unruly bear a much needed lesson. He bent over and wrapped a firm hand around the cold glass neck of the bottle.

You've got no backbone, boy. You've always been nothing but a sniveling pantywaist.

"I'll show you!" Marsh yelled at his father.

The bear turned toward him as Marsh swung the wine bottle with all his might and smashed it over the beast's snout.

"Shoo bear!" he shouted angrily. "Go away. Get out of here!"

A shaft of moonlight shot through the opening of the tent.

Marsh's blood turned to ice water as he realized his mistake.

This was not one of the pet grizzly bears he had flown in. It was smaller and its sleek black coat of hair glistened in the wan light.

This bear was wild.

And it held no deep ingrained fear of man.

None whatsoever.

And it was probably *really* pissed off at him.

The beast shook its head and roared with unbridled primal fury.

Let's see you turn this *situation into a victory, boy,* Hollis Wheelan chortled.

A scream born of unadulterated fear escaped Marsh's lips.

Long white fangs sharper than knives lined the red maw that came charging for him with the force of an oncoming train.

Marsh Earlson Wheelan, a man who cherished power above all, was scant seconds away from finding out what *real* power was all about.

CHAPTER 41

Jefferson Tate returned his cell phone to its leather case on his belt after checking in with the Austin office as protocol demanded. Furtive, questioning glances from other lawmen showed their wonderment, yet none came out and questioned the FBI agent as to why his phone worked here in the middle of nowhere.

He could not have answered them truthfully if they had. There were many classified secrets in government work that required a stony silence to stay that way. Nowadays criminals were, for the most part, far more sophisticated than when Jefferson had joined the bureau.

The use of high technology had spread like a cancer among the ranks of professional lawbreakers. They had found computers and the Internet to be far more efficient tools of the trade than a gun or mask ever were. It took a concentrated and covert effort on the government's part to stay one step ahead of today's shrewd criminals.

Those millions of taxpayer dollars supposedly squandered on six hundred dollar hammers and thousand dollar toilet seats hadn't been wasted. One of the benefits were some neat devices fixed to orbiting satellites that gave a few select federal officials and the military the ability to communicate instantly, no matter where on the planet they happened to be.

Gordon Lusk, of the Federal Wildlife Service, rode alongside Tate as the group began their early morning trek up the beautiful tree-lined valley. Jefferson had grown to like the man. The officer was about his age and close to retirement. Gordon sported a bushy, soup-strainer moustache that drooped down alongside his cheeks, and long gray hair spilled from beneath his hat.

To the FBI agent, Gordon Lusk was the spitting image of every picture he had seen of the famous frontier lawman, Wyatt Earp. This only served to enhance the feeling he was part of an old time posse chasing down the bad guys.

The area they were traversing was lined on both sides of the canyon by towering gray peaks that shot into a cloudless sky to heights well above where any tree could survive.

"This is magnificent country," Jefferson said. "You're a lucky man to live in such a scenic state as Oregon."

Gordon spat a wad of snuff and said dryly, "If you don't count the seven months of winter where the snow's ass deep to a tall Indian, I'll agree with you."

Jefferson grinned. "I'm from the south myself. I've never seen snow piled *that* high before."

"Come back in six months and I'll be happy to introduce you to some."

"I'll hopefully be retired by then. The wife and I have bought a place in Mississippi. I'll settle for a picture."

Gordon chuckled. "Smart man. I can see why the FBI hired you." He motioned with his head to the mountain range on their left. "Hard to believe there's a highway on the other side of those peaks, isn't it?"

Jefferson Tate squinted at the jutting spires. "I would have supposed we were a lot farther from civilization."

"Might as well be," Gordon said, returning his gaze to the trail. "God builds some mighty fine fences. They're so steep a mountain goat would break its stupid neck trying to cross them. This makes for an easy job checking who goes in and out of here. If they don't come back down the way we're headed in, they're likely still there. The place where Wheelan has his camp is basically in what you would describe as a box canyon."

Jefferson felt a wave of satisfaction. "So our suspect has to be there because he's got no other way out unless he gets a helicopter?"

The game warden spat another wad of tobacco. "That's the size of it. He might as well hold out his hands for the cuffs because we *are* gonna bring him in."

Jefferson started to speak when one of the lead horses, ridden by a Forest Service man, nickered loudly then wheeled, nearly throwing the officer to the ground.

Gordon Lusk's eyes widened with amazement when he gaped up the trail and saw what had caused the ruckus. "Will you look at *that?* For Pete's sake!"

The four Forest Service men rapidly backed their panicked horses deep into the trees away from the trail, giving a wide berth to the burly man with a bushy white beard who was leading two huge grizzly bears with ropes tied around their necks.

Jefferson Tate was aghast. "I have heard of Grizzly Adams but sure never thought I'd actually run across him."

Gordon patted his shivering horse. "We'd better get down and go visit. These animals will panic if we get any closer."

Jefferson stared at the huge beasts. "You're worrying about the *horses* being shook."

"Nah," Gordon said nonchalantly as if encountering a man leading a pair of bears was a common occurrence. "If those critters were gonna hurt anyone they'd have done it by now."

Jefferson followed the Federal Wildlife officer in dismounting. He decided if he actually lived through this he'd have a tale to tell not many would believe.

A wide-eyed young sheriff's deputy slid a rifle from his saddle scabbard.

"Put that away you blasted idiot," Gordon fumed. "If you're so scared of bears sonny boy, stay home with your mommy the next time."

The deputy's face flushed red as he returned the weapon to its scabbard.

Gordon Lusk grinned broadly at Jefferson and motioned with his hand. "Well, let's go get acquainted with Grizzly Adams."

As the duo approached, the bears sat down on their haunches and began batting each other playfully. Their good-natured behavior did little to alleviate Jefferson Tate's feeling of foreboding. Outside of a zoo, he had never been so close to what he knew to be ferocious beasts. This time however, there were no steel bars to protect him.

"Howdy gents," the man holding the ropes said. "Sam McSwain's the name. I'm a registered guide out of John Day. Don't fret the bears any, they're gentle and used to being around people. They were in movies and TV shows for years. They're just big pets."

REALLY big pets, Jefferson thought, and he certainly wasn't convinced about the gentle part.

"How did you come by them?" Gordon questioned as he shook McSwain's free hand.

"Oh, some damn fool who hired me to help him film a supposed release of grizzlies back into the wild had 'em flown in by a big helicopter. He claimed to have gotten all the necessary permits, but I doubt he really did. The whole shebang was staged just to shoot some stupid music video. Now I'm taking the poor critters out of here. They're too old and used to folks caring for them to make it on their own for long."

"This person who hired you," Jefferson said, still keeping a respectful distance. "His name wouldn't be Marsh Wheelan by any chance?"

"Yup," McSwain said with a nod. "That *was* the damn fool's name."

"What do you mean *was?*" Jefferson asked. "He is still there isn't he? I'm an FBI agent and have a warrant for his arrest."

"Now why doesn't that surprise me?" Sam said. "I figger he broke durn near every law there is for a wilderness area. Had a generator to run his refrigerator and computer. Then the flaming fool had a 'copter fly in that popular country singer, Hale Cross and his girlfriend. Boy, was she ever a piece of work.

"After they finished their filming and Cross took off, Wheelan and me had a parting of the ways. I quit him when he told me to run these poor bears off into the woods to die. I just can't abide arrogant educated idiots."

"But he *is* still there?" Jefferson questioned again.

"Oh yeah," Sam McSwain said with a wag of his silver beard. "You'll find most of him inside what's left of that circus tent of his. It'll take a spell to piece *all* of him back together."

"Marsh Wheelan is dead?" Gordon asked, incredulous. "What in the world happened to him?"

"Got bear bit terrible bad last night." McSwain stepped back defensively against the playing grizzlies. "Now it wasn't *these* pets. They were with me when it happened. From what I could figure out when I found him this morning, a wild bear, most likely a big black, got to poking around inside his tent. Now them black bears have got an attitude like a mother-in-law, but Wheelan was too educated to know that.

"From all of the broken glass, I'd guess Wheelan didn't take kindly to the bear and smashed a wine bottle over its snout."

His beard twisted into a smile. "If you want to rile a wild bear, he couldn't have done a better job of it. That black went and shredded him like a dog will tear up a rag doll." He clucked his tongue, "Couldn't have happened to a nicer guy."

"Well, son of a bitch," Jefferson said.

"Leastwise he won't make a fuss when we cart him back," Gordon Lusk said in his deadpan voice. "And the taxpayers will save a bundle on a speedy trial. I'm glad I thought ahead and brought along a body bag. Looks like the thing will come in handy after all."

From over in the trees, a Forest Service official shouted to McSwain, "You have a permit for those bears?"

Sam McSwain held out the rope. "They ain't *my* bears. Go ahead and take 'em if you've a mind to."

The Forest Service man's mouth dropped open, a look of horror plastered on his face. "No, that—that's all right, you go ahead and keep them."

"I thought you'd see things my way," Sam said. He turned to Jefferson and Gordon. "Gentlemen, it's been a pleasure, but I need to get to moving. I've got a far piece to travel, and I'd like to make it out of here before dark."

Down the canyon, every law officer moved his jittery horse well into the trees, clearing a wide path for the man and his bears.

"I'll need your address and phone number," Jefferson said. "There will be an inquiry."

Sam dug into his pocket and extracted a business card. "Reckon this oughta work. Keep it in case you'd like to come back and spend some time here without all the excitement. When you take away the assholes, this is pretty fine country." He chuckled. "Of course I guess you could say the same for most any place."

Jefferson and Gordon stood aside as the guide prodded the grizzlies to their feet and began leading them down the trail.

After several moments the lawmen and their still spooked horses reassembled.

"When I get back and file my report," Jefferson Tate said, "I'll likely get sent for a visit with a shrink. I'm not even sure I believe what just happened myself."

Gordon Lusk placed a fist under his chin and thought for a moment. "The FBI agent has a point," he said looking around at the other lawmen. "It might be a lot less trouble for all of us if we simply say we ran across a guide who told us our suspect was deceased. Sure would cut down on the paperwork and questions from reporters."

"Well, *I* never saw any grizzly bears," a Forest Service man said quickly. "They've been extinct here for years."

A deputy sheriff spoke up. "What bears is he talking about?"

"Someone see a bear?" a state trooper asked. "I must've missed it."

Gordon spat another wad of tobacco juice. "Now that we all agree on what we *didn't* see, let's get on with it. The suspect's camp isn't two miles ahead."

The horses, nervous from the scent of blood mixed with bear drifting in the air, forced the lawmen to tie the mounts a short distance from Marsh Wheelan's camp and proceed on foot.

Gordon Lusk, packing a black body bag under an arm, was the first to approach the shredded tent. He poked his head through the open flaps. "I reckon we don't need to check for a pulse."

Jefferson Tate and the young sheriff's deputy who had earlier pulled his rifle, joined Gordon in gazing at the mangled remains that lay on the blood soaked floor.

Marsh Wheelan's abdomen had been ripped open, his intestines looped across his body like limp ropes. Black flies buzzed thickly around the corpse and crawled in and out of gaping wounds.

"Oh my God," the ashen-faced deputy said.

"Wonder where his head wound up?" Gordon asked in his usual monotone. "Oh well, I reckon he never had much *good* use to put it to, anyway." He handed the rubber body bag to the wide-eyed deputy. "Bag him, Dano."

The young officer gagged, placed his hand over his mouth and ran to lose his breakfast.

Jefferson Tate couldn't suppress a slight grin at the Federal Wildlife officer. After many years of working with stern-faced, humorless federal agents, having someone like Gordon Lusk around was a welcome change. "The boy has a lot to learn about being an officer of the law."

"Yep," Gordon replied. "And I'm helping him to learn it."

Underneath a collapsed and broken folding table Jefferson found what he wanted: Marsh Wheelan's laptop computer. From the hard drive he hoped to be able to recover much, if not all, of the data that had been hacked into the federal computer systems. While he no longer needed it as evidence to convict Wheelan, it might be useful to help Caleb Starr.

A pang of guilt stabbed at him. Jefferson had been enjoying the trip so much, he had given no thought to the plight of Jesus Santiago. Alton McKenzie's uncalled for reporting of the old man to the Justice Department galled him. The least he could do would be to appear as a character witness at the hearing. Now that his presence was no longer required here, he needed to get back to Texas.

"Gordon, you fellows can handle this without me looking over your shoulder," Tate said. "Just get plenty of pictures; I'll need them for my report. I'm going down by the horses and make some phone calls."

A short while later, an Oregon State Trooper approached Gordon Lusk, who stood writing in a note pad. "I thought I'd seen it all today, but this is one for the books."

"What's that?" Gordon asked idly.

"That FBI man. I always thought they were all chiseled out of granite."

"Well?"

"He's down by the creek leaning against a dead tree, sobbing like a baby."

"Let him be and don't tell anyone else. Whatever could hurt a man like him so bad isn't to be taken lightly."

"No sir," the somber trooper said with a nod. "I'm certain it isn't."

Chapter 42

"These dad-blasted things would have been enough of a puzzle to cause Einstein to go on a three-day drunk," Caleb Starr fumed as he made another attempt to knot his necktie. He checked his handiwork in the mirror and sighed, the wrong end hung three inches too long. "And I doubt if he ever figured out how to do it. Building an atomic bomb would definitely be easier."

Hope Rexton stepped over, smiling at his ranting. With a few easy motions she had the tie knotted perfectly. "You're right, big guy. It's a real brain strainer."

Caleb muttered, "Well, I never have call to wear one very often."

Thank the Good Lord, he thought.

The last time he had been forced to wear a suit and tie was for Laura's funeral. Every time he saw the thing hanging in the closet, painful memories came crashing down on him like an avalanche. Now he was forced to add to the weight of his future reminiscing by having to wear it to Jesus Santiago's funeral.

It's all my fault the old guy's gone, he thought bitterly. *If I hadn't shot that eagle he would still be tending his garden and reading books. The summons he was handed turned out to be as deadly as the poison that killed those coyotes and buzzards.*

Tristan jerked Caleb from his sad reverie when he held his own tie out to Hope.

"Ma'am," he said respectfully, "could you please fix mine,

too? Dad's right about these things being an aggravation. I sure never want to suffer with a job where I have to dress like a politician or banker all the time."

Hope kept her beaming smile, quickly knotted the tie and drew it close. It made her feel good to be needed. Times like these made her wonder deeply why she had wasted years of her life with a man who returned her love and caring with browbeating or worse.

She felt an added kinship with Tristan. Both had their spleens removed because of blind hatred and rage. From her nurse's training and own experience, she knew his immune system had been compromised. Tristan would be susceptible to infections for the rest of his life. The young man had mentioned several times of late that he planned to join the Marine Corps once he received his high school diploma.

Hope knew this was an impossible dream, and the realization stabbed at her heart like a red hot knife. Tristan would never pass the physical. She did not know what to tell him. Whatever it was to be, now was certainly not the time.

"I've never understood what men have against getting dressed up," Hope said. She stepped back and gave an admiring glance. "Both of you look like perfect gentlemen."

Caleb cocked an eyebrow. "I'd venture you might be right about the gentleman part."

Hope Rexton's perpetual smile fled like morning dew beneath a fiery Texas sun. There could be no more postponing what had to be done. She brushed nervously at her knee-length black dress, then looked at Caleb. "I suppose we should be going now."

Caleb gave a nod of agreement and strode toward the door of his ranch house with Tristan by his side. Hope followed with quiet understanding. She doubted herself if she could speak now without sobbing.

When they stepped onto the porch, they focused their attention toward a yellow backhoe parked alongside a fresh mound of dirt under a spreading live oak tree. Points of sunlight shooting through rustling leaves danced on the dark earth like tiny fallen stars.

Hope pulled her gaze from the gravesite, walked over and slid behind the wheel of her Mustang. Tristan followed and winced slightly as he climbed into the back seat. Caleb put on a pair of sunglasses and sat alongside the stoic redhead.

It took her a moment to insert the key with a trembling hand. Then without a word, she put the car into gear and they headed for the church in Lone Wolf, leaving a cloud of white dust hanging in the still air.

The funeral for Jesus Santiago was held at ten o'clock on a muggy, cloudless Saturday morning. The huge number of cars that lined the road in front of Saint Augustine's Catholic Church bore mute testimony to the great number of friends the old man had made during his many years.

Hope Rexton pulled to a stop in Blandon's driveway. Monica, who also wore a black dress, and the undertaker came outside to meet them. They walked together the short distance to the church.

Tip Conroy sat in the sheriff's cruiser that was parked in front of Bone's hearse eating a cinnamon roll. He gave a nod of recognition as they passed.

Father Juan Iberra met them at the door and escorted the party to a reserved pew on the front row of the little church.

Before the burnished altar, surrounded by garlands and bouquets of colorful flowers, was the open white casket that held the mortal remains of Jesus.

The service was conducted in both English and Spanish. All too quickly, it seemed, Father Iberra's ceremony had been completed. The rites and sacraments of the Catholic faith were fulfilled. While organ music played softly, Quentin Miller stood up and asked the sad-eyed priest if he could say a few words.

Father Iberra gave a solemn nod.

Quentin, who for the first time in anyone's memory wore a somber suit, went to stand in front of the casket.

He turned to face the assemblage. The famed courtroom orator seemed to be having difficulty finding his voice. After a long while he cleared his throat and began.

"We are not gathered here today to say our farewells to a mere man. Instead, we bid goodbye to our friend, Jesus Santiago, and the way of life he so enjoyed.

"I will never pass by the river without remembering seeing the old fellow there on the bank, holding a fishing pole. The simple pleasures he loved should be a lesson to us all, for life is fleeting.

"In these troubled times we will miss the guidance and wisdom such as Jesus was blessed with. He saw the world through clear eyes of understanding, tempered by the passage of years.

"We are all richer for having known him, for he was schooled by nature who is the greatest of teachers.

"Jesus was a friend to all, and hate found no quarter in his soul. While we must commit his mortal remains to the earth, we shall not remove his memory from our midst.

"On my journey through this valley of tears, I have learned many things. I have come to know the writings and teachings of brilliant scholars and observers of the human condition. All agree that two of the most noble and powerful words ever uttered by man are love and friendship.

"Of Jesus Santiago I can only say this: he was my friend and I loved him."

Rosemary Page sobbed aloud. Hope Rexton and many others

daubed a tissue at damp eyes.

Grizzled ranchers with leathery faces, wrinkled from years of toil under a blazing sun, choked back tears. Caleb Starr and his son Tristan made no such attempt to hide theirs.

The words had been said.

It was time to take their friend to his eternal resting place.

"I'll bring out his headstone and set it in a day or two," Bones said to Caleb. "He'd bought it a few years ago, imported white marble of the best quality money could buy. He had me engrave both his and Ernesta's names on it. All I have to do is carve in the date he—left us."

Rosemary Page gazed with misty eyes at the open grave that now held the casket. "I wish I'd gotten to know him better. There are too few men who know the works of Shakespeare."

"Reckon we could all say the same," Hector Lemmons said. "We don't seem to appreciate folks until they pass away."

On long tables with white coverings beneath sheltering oak trees, women began placing bowls and trays burdened with food. Caleb guessed the assemblage that had come to bid their final farewell to Jesus likely numbered at least two hundred.

Hope Rexton wrapped an arm around Caleb's waist. "He got a good send off," she said softly.

Caleb adjusted his sunglasses. "He did get that all right. The old fellow sure had a passel of friends."

A vaguely familiar voice spoke from behind Caleb, "Mister Starr, I would like to give you my condolences." Caleb turned and immediately recognized the burly FBI agent, Jefferson Tate.

"I didn't expect to see you here," Caleb said somewhat brusquely. He then remembered Tate's earlier kindness and tempered his remark. "I didn't mean to come across gruff, sir. It's been a trying day. Monica told me that you had called her. I'm glad you took the time to come."

"No apology necessary, Mister Starr," Jefferson Tate said. "After all you have had to endure, I wouldn't blame you if you asked me to leave."

Caleb motioned with his head to the row of tables. "I'd feel honored if you'd stay and join us."

Jefferson nodded. "I thank you sir, but my time here is limited. When I found out Jesus Santiago had died of a heart attack, I felt I had to come to his funeral. Both of us realize what caused his passing. The law can be ruthless at times."

Caleb said nothing.

The FBI agent continued. "You probably know by now we found the man who hacked in all of the false computer information that caused much of your trouble. His name was Marsh Wheelan, and he was dead when we got to him. The agency is doing everything in its power to set the records straight as to your background."

Caleb looked sadly at the grave. "I'm just sorry it took too long."

A tear leaked from Jefferson Tate's eye.

"So am I, sir," he said. "So am I."

Chapter 43

A phlegmatic Rosemary Page ushered Caleb Starr into Quentin Miller's office. The rancher glanced for a moment at the massive "cannonball" safe with its door draping open on one hinge. Then he took a deep breath and slumped into a familiar chair in front of the lawyer's desk.

Quentin leaned back in his leather swivel chair and adjusted his turquoise bola tie.

"Would you like a cup of coffee?" the secretary asked.

"I reckon I'll pass," Caleb said. "There's a mile of fence that needs tightening, and I'd best get to it shortly."

"That will be all, Miss Page," Quentin said with a dismissive wave.

This caused a ripple of concern to course through Caleb. Whatever it was that possessed the lawyer to be nice to his secretary had to be serious.

A fleeting shadow of sadness crossed Rosemary's face before she turned and left the room, shutting the door in her wake.

"We might as well get to it," Caleb said. "I don't suppose you asked me to come by to play dominoes."

Quentin cleared his throat and began drumming his fingers on the oak desk. "There are some things we need to discuss. The first is the will Jesus left."

"The old fellow's been gone for a week now, yet every morning I look out the kitchen window expecting to see him working in his garden or heading over for a cup of coffee."

"Time is the only cure for some wounds. By the way, how is Tristan doing?"

"His body seems to be knitted up in fine shape. He's thrown himself into schoolwork to keep his mind off of what all's happened. I'll feel better when he can smile again."

Quentin Miller pressed his lips together and began thumbing through a stack of papers on his cluttered desk. "Jesus Santiago was a far more astute man than most would suspect. He started putting money in the stock market back in the nineteen fifties. The wily old fellow didn't have much to invest, but he stuck every dollar he could spare into buying Blue Chip stocks. He had his account set up so dividends bought more shares. Add in some stock splits and the fact he let it build, in today's market, it amounts to a respectable sum."

Caleb cocked his head in amazement. "I'm sorry he didn't have some family to leave it to."

The lawyer found the folder he was looking for and opened it. "Jesus had me change his will into a trust not so very long ago. He appointed me as trustee. Like I said, he was a very astute man, and he did have family he cared for very deeply—you and Tristan."

"Oh," Caleb muttered softly. The burning in his throat restricted any further comment, so he simply nodded.

Quentin swallowed hard then continued. "When your legal and financial problems intensified over the, ah, difficulties arising from the shooting of that eagle, Jesus became rightfully concerned. There was a very real possibility any inheritance could be taken from you by the courts."

Caleb wagged his head in gloomy agreement.

"I have already been served, as your attorney in fact, with two lawsuits filed by radical groups claiming they have been damaged by 'loss of enjoyment of wildlife' through your actions. I may be able to get these thrown out as frivolous, but I can't say this for certain. It was reasons such as these that prompted Jesus to leave his estate solely to Tristan."

"What good will that do?" Caleb blurted out. "He's my son."

Quentin leaned back and fixed his piercing eyes on the rancher. "Tristan is not party to any of your—difficulties. The entire one hundred and twelve thousand dollars went into a trust fund until he reaches the age of twenty-one. There's not a thing anyone can do to get their hands on that money."

Caleb couldn't contain a gasp of astonishment. "Why, I wouldn't have guessed for a second that old fellow had so much money."

"Jesus was a man of simple pleasures. Books and smoking tobacco were his biggest expenses outside of food. He made it plain when he told me you had provided him with the ability to live as he wanted. His last wish was to be able to do the same for your son."

"My God, Quentin, I just don't know what to say."

"Just accept this is what Jesus wanted."

Caleb shuffled his boots on the floor and worried his tongue against his lips while staring at the slowly turning overhead fan.

Quentin Miller spun his chair around and studied John Wesley Hardin's framed law degree while he waited patently for the distraught rancher to reclaim his composure. There was nothing but bad news remaining. He was certainly in no hurry to burden Caleb with more problems. As his lawyer, however, he had to do what must be done.

After the passing of a few slow minutes, Caleb spoke, "You mentioned there were other matters. I suppose those lawsuits you mentioned were just for starters."

Quentin tore his gaze from the diploma and turned to face Caleb. He was surprised and pleased by the firmness in his voice. The rancher would need all the resolve he could muster.

"There is no way I can sugarcoat what's going on over your

shooting of the eagle," the lawyer said. "I have called in every marker I have with politicians, and it has all came to naught. They are afraid of how they would appear to the voters if they came out with any support. When that blasted picture of you holding a dead eagle got plastered on the front page of a tabloid and the news media began their feeding frenzy, the issue became a political hot potato."

Caleb said," I can't say this comes as any surprise to me. It seems every day the mail brings new death threats or letters with checks in them. No one believes it was an accident I shot that eagle. One side wants to crucify me, and the other wants to make me into a champion for their cause.

"Quentin, I just want this mess to go away, but I know it won't. And now I'm getting the sick feeling you're about to tell me the worst is yet to come."

The rotund attorney began drumming his fingers on the desk again. "There haven't been any decent prophets around since the Bible got written, or I would consult one. I really wish I could tell you how all of this will turn out, but I can't."

Quentin Miller's brows drew downward in a thoughtful frown as he continued. "Randall Whitehead of the Federal Wildlife Service is pursuing the matter with vigor. The most troubling of all is the federal judge who will hear the case and decide the penalty—there will be no jury to play to.

"Kurt Gerhard is a man of high political ambitions. He's a young man in his early forties and is openly soliciting funds to make a run for the United States Senate. I suppose I don't need to explain to you where much of his funding is coming from."

"No," Caleb said with resignation. "I reckon you don't. Its just that I always thought judges were supposed to be impartial."

"For the most part they are. This is why I have done everything in my power to get another judge to hear your case."

Caleb Starr felt his heart beating heavily in his chest. The faces of Tristan, Hope and old Jesus flashed past his mind's eye. "The government is going to make a public example out of me, aren't they? The FBI agent, Jefferson Tate, told me my record has been set straight, and they know the only thing I've ever done wrong was shoot that eagle."

His eyes turned pleading. "Doesn't what happened to Jesus and Tristan and the drug raid on my ranch matter at all? They put us through hell. Quentin, has it all boiled down to the fact that I'm just being used as a pawn in a game to garner votes and power for some damn federal lackeys to use as a stepping stone?"

Quentin Miller sighed deeply and leaned back in his chair. He felt as if he were delivering another sad eulogy. "The world we live in today is far from perfect. The very concept of right and wrong, what is black and what is white, has been fogged into shades of gray. Our legal system has become so complex that nearly anyone can be convicted of *something* if the government sets out to do such a thing. Anyone who watches the news on television or reads a newspaper knows what a special prosecutor can do to innocent people.

"Morals no longer enter into the picture. What began as a government by the people, for the people has been corrupted into government by special interest groups that have money and influence to get whatever laws they wish passed and enforced.

"I wish this weren't the facts of the matter, Caleb, I surely do. But hiding our heads in the sand and wishing won't accomplish anything."

A profound numbness filled Caleb's being. It had first descended over him with Laura's death. Lately, it had come to be his only solace in times such as these. "I suppose I'd better make arrangements to have someone watch after the ranch and Tristan."

The lawyer sat upright and spoke with purposeful defiance.

"Now don't go digging a hole to jump in just yet. We don't know for certain what's going to come. On the good side, we have over fifty thousand dollars stuck away to pay fines. I also did manage to get a postponement on your trial until the eighth of December. A lot can happen in that length of time. Judge Gerhard might get himself elected to office or run over by a truck. Either one would be fine by me."

Caleb stood and surveyed the lawyer with a stony expression. "Thanks for all you've done." He turned and walked away.

When he got to the door, he opened it and hesitated. "That fence still needs stretching," he said, keeping his back to Quentin Miller.

Then Caleb quietly shut the door behind him and left.

Chapter 44

It was the twenty-second day of December and a dreary, pewter sky lay heavy over Lone Wolf County, Texas. A bitter north wind howled relentlessly across a leafless landscape. The first day of winter was being ushered in with an icy breath.

The rhapsody of nature's fury echoed inside the house at the Lone Starr Ranch from rattling window panes and walls that creaked and groaned with each gust like aged bones.

Caleb tossed another mesquite log into the fireplace and watched until the flames grew. He stood and turned to Hope Rexton, a sly grin on his face. "I reckon any brass monkeys left outside tonight will be singing soprano come next summer."

She stepped close and ran a velvet hand along his cheek. "Poor things, no one ever remembers to bring them indoors until it's too late."

Hope basked in the humorous banter and small talk they had been enjoying. It served to postpone the discussion that had to come. She had come to love this big man with all of her essence. In spite of his many troubles, Caleb Starr always treated her with tender kindness and caused her to laugh when tears would have come easier.

After the trial in Lubbock had drawn to its fateful close and the sentence passed, Hope had given up her cottage in town and moved her few possessions into Caleb's home. That had been nearly two weeks ago.

In a small town like Lone Wolf, such an action would

normally have set tongues to wagging. Instead, after the news about Caleb Starr broke, everyone, it seemed, including hard-shell Baptists, went out of their way to wish them well.

Hope's heart still danced from when Caleb had told her that he loved her. She understood, as did most, that love would be all the rancher could offer for a long while. Laws written nearly two thousand miles away in distant Washington, D.C. and enforced by an unreasoning bureaucracy had descended upon her dear one with an iron fist.

Beginning tomorrow, Hope Rexton thought, *I'll have time for tears. Far too much time for them.*

Now was the time to be strong.

"Hey, how about we watch a movie, big guy?" she asked happily. "I've got a copy of every film Humphrey Bogart ever made. *The African Queen* with Katharine Hepburn is an absolutely great flick. What do you say I toss some popcorn in the microwave and start the tape?"

Caleb reached out and drew her into a sheltering embrace. "That sounds good. I like old Bogie movies, too. Will you sit by me on the couch to watch it? I want to be close to you for as long as I can."

Hope forced herself to imprison a sob. His simple request had pained her greater than any hurt she could remember. She stood on her tiptoes and brushed an answering kiss to his lips. Then she dashed away to the kitchen, knowing he understood.

Sometimes lovers are forced to communicate with messages spoken silently by the heart.

Useless lay stretched out on a throw rug in the front room where he was staring intently at the Christmas tree Hope had insisted they put up. The big tomcat had been tossed outside several times for climbing it and swatting at the colorful shiny balls and glistening tinfoil icicles that dangled temptingly from green branches. He weighed the amusement versus another trip into the cold, then curled into a ball and purred himself to sleep.

Hope busied herself with cleaning away the last remains of dinner. She scraped the nearly full plates into the trash and placed them in the dishwasher. Neither of them had done more than pick listlessly at their food.

Caleb had been standing beside her and staring out the kitchen window for some time now.

To her secret delight, his expression was not one of sadness. He had a firm set to his jaw and defiance shown in his eyes. This gladdened her spirits. Hope's training as a nurse had taught her that depression is anger focused inward toward oneself.

She allowed him several minutes, then washed her hands, wiped them dry on a towel and stepped closer to his side. Through the gathering darkness they could barely make out Jesus's lifeless house in the distance.

The wind had died, bringing on an oppressive silence after howling across the bleak countryside for the entire day. To Hope, the house felt quiet as the inside of an empty tomb so she went and clicked on the radio. A wailing country and western song about love gone wrong filled the air as she returned to Caleb's side.

"It'll be at least next August before I can look through this window again," he said keeping his gaze to the dimming twilight.

Hope squeezed his hand and said nothing. They had been through this many times before. Talking about one's troubles can often be the only salve for an overwrought soul.

Caleb continued, "Quentin said I should be home by then." He sighed. "A year in prison for trying to save a two-dollar chicken. Somehow, getting four months knocked off my sentence if I stay on 'good behavior' doesn't seem right. I still can't accept the fact that I've done anything to deserve this. All of us, especially Tristan, has had a season in hell because of Marsh Wheelan and some government agents. I was naive enough to believe that might count for something, but I was wrong."

"Quentin has said several times he would appeal to a higher court," Hope said.

"No," Caleb said stoically. "It has to come to an end. When I get through this, we can put the sorry mess behind us." He wrapped an arm around her waist. "Then we can start to make a life for ourselves. I feel like I've been sucker punched by a bully, but damn it to hell, they're not going to beat me!"

Hope melded herself to his side. "There you go, big guy. Let's count our blessings. Tristan received his high school diploma and made it into the Army despite his condition. Thanks to Jesus he has a good trust fund to see to his future, and he is determined to go on to college. We have every right to be proud of him. Quentin said all of your fines have been paid and the other lawsuits have either been dropped or thrown out."

"A hundred thousand dollars," Caleb said. "That judge would've hung me if the law had let him. What hurt me the most was when those people cheered when he gave me the maximum sentence he could."

Hope felt a tremble pass through his muscular body as he continued. "I don't believe Quentin about having had that much money sent in for my defense. I know in my heart Hector Lemmons and he paid a big chunk of it but won't own up to it. Now Hector's going to look after the ranch while I'm away." He hesitated. "And I'm still driving that pickup he loaned me."

"Those men are your friends, Caleb. Few people are blessed with friends like yours. If the situation were reversed, you would do the same from them. They know that."

He gave her a hug. "I have a lot to be thankful for. Just knowing you'll be here for me makes me feel like the luckiest man in the world. Darling, things will only get better. I'm actually looking forward to turning myself into the Federal Marshals in San Angelo tomorrow morning. The sooner I pay them eight months of my life, the sooner we can get on to living the rest of it—together."

Neither were able to contain a gasp of surprise when another song began playing on the radio. It was the new hit single by Hale Cross: *Should an Eagle Fall.*

Eagle, eagle flying so high,
Majestic wings spread against an endless sky.
Freedom is your maiden name,
Yet they slay you just the same.

"I'll turn it off," Hope said quickly.

"No," Caleb said firmly. "Let it be. This is how things are. That singer will make millions of dollars from an eagle, and I'll go to prison over one. The world has changed while we've been busy trying to make a living. No one can fix what's happened. All we can do is learn from it and keep moving on."

Fluffy flakes of snow began falling from a dark sky. A few splattered against the window pane to melt and trickle down the glass.

To Hope it was as if angels were weeping from above. Tears welled in her emerald eyes. "I love you, big guy."

He drew her close. "I know," he said softly.

Caleb and Hope stood together for a long while staring silently out the window at the gently falling snow.

A contented smile washed across their faces as unsaid words passed between them. They had good friends, family and a deep abiding love to build a future on.

No one could ask for more.

I know not whether laws be right,
Or whether laws be wrong;
All that we know who lie in gaol
Is that the wall is strong;
And that each day is like a year,
A year whose days are long.

Oscar Wilde—*The Ballad of Reading Gaol*

ABOUT THE AUTHOR

Born in the shadow of Pike's Peak, **Ken Hodgson** has enjoyed various and interesting careers. He has worked in a state mental hospital, been a gold and uranium miner, worked as a professional prospector and owned an air compressor business. He has written hundreds of short stories and articles along with over a dozen published novels in various genres.

Hodgson is an active member of Mystery Writers of America and International Thriller Writers.

He lives on a small ranch in Northern New Mexico with his wife and prime editor, Rita, along with two totally spoiled cats, Sasha and Ulysses.